WICKED LIES

M.V. KASI

Copyright © M.v. Kasi
All Rights Reserved.

In loving memory of my grandfather.

Thank you for instilling the reading and writing habit in me from a young age. And thank you for always being proud and supportive of me. I feel privileged to have been loved by a kind, wise and generous-hearted man like you. I will cherish our memories together forever.

And to all of us.

May we emerge stronger in our lives with hope and compassion.

Contents

Contents

Prologue

"This is so risky, Anya. If you don't return in thirty minutes, I'm calling the police."

It was dark outside the car and raining heavily. Anya wanted to call the police too, to warn them of the illegal activities going on inside an exclusive club. But instead, she and her friend sat in a car parked outside the club.

"I'll be back soon, Trupti," she promised. She tucked a small package into the inside pocket of her long overcoat.

Anya's friend continued to look worried. "Let me come with you," she insisted.

"No, Trupti. Wait for me here. I'll call you if I need help."

Anya had wanted to come alone, but her friend insisted on joining her.

Taking a deep breath, Anya twisted her hair into a knot and placed a small pink hairclip before pulling on the coat's hoodie. She then got out of the car and quickly shut the door before running towards the building's entrance.

Two guards stood in front of the main door. Their eyes swept over her long overcoat and hoodie with a small frown. "Sorry, madam," one of them said. "This club is for members only."

Anya pasted on a smile. "I'm an invited guest. I have the passcode."

The guards exchanged glances before one of them handed her a small keypad.

With slightly trembling fingers, Anya entered the passcode given to her. A small green light flashed, indicating it was approved. The guards then pushed open the heavy doors.

"Thank you," Anya murmured before stepping inside.

A blast of cold air hit her, making her shiver since she was wet even with her long overcoat. As soon as she took a few steps inside, the doors behind her shut closed.

She felt strangely trapped and alone in an unknown place. A few more steps revealed a dimly lit, large foyer with a reception desk. But no one was seated behind the desk. She mostly saw men and a couple of women standing in the corners and smoking.

Anya felt their curious eyes directed towards her. With giggles and slight swaying, they seemed drunk. Anya was thankful her hoodie and long overcoat hid her identity.

She passed by a woman wearing a short dress. The man standing next to the woman had his hand under the dress. Anya tried not to lower her eyes and kept walking.

"She doesn't seem to be the kind to gamble or entertain," a woman said aloud. "Unless she is hiding a surprise under that jacket."

There was drunken laughter.

Anya felt her cheeks heat, but she tried not to show any outward reaction.

I'm going to kill you, Sohan.

Anya cursed her brother for the hundredth time that night. Her brother was in trouble yet again. She had been about to go to bed after having spent a relaxed evening watching a movie with her friend when she received a call from her brother. He had sounded frantic.

"I need help, Anya. I'm in big trouble."

"Don't tell Papa or Ma. Just come with the documents."

The call was brief. After begging her to bring some documents from his apartment, he had given her instructions to enter the club he often visited.

Anya sucked in a deep breath. Despite her nervousness, her eyes took in the high-end interior of the club. As a professional architect, she could see that a lot of money was put into the décor and maintenance of the place.

To the outside world, it was an exclusive club. But it was where rich men got drunk and gambled in high stakes, most of them losing their family's wealth in the process. Her brother had gambled away one of his apartments and a car that night.

Anya knew her father was going to blast him when he found out.

Pushing away anger and worry, she continued to go inside. The crowd began to thicken, and she could barely see much or breathe well due to the heavy smoke.

Just as she was about to go towards the room her brother had directed her, a man blocked her way.

"Excuse me," she said.

The man was drunk. He was holding a glass of whiskey and swaying on his feet. "Are you naked under that long coat, darling?" he asked.

Disgusted, she tried to step around him, but there was no place to go as the room was filled with drunk men and scantily-clad women.

"I'll pay you generously," he slurred. He pulled out a thick bundle of notes and waved it in front of her.

The man thought she was a paid escort. He suddenly caught the front of her long jacket.

He was about to pull her close and stuff the money into her pocket when someone's arm held the drunkard's collar and shoved him away.

"Back off," a deep voice rumbled out a warning from behind her.

The drunken man frowned. But when he looked behind her, his frown melted and he smiled drunkenly. "Ah. I didn't know you paid for her already. No issues, mate." With that, he staggered away to another woman.

Anya was embarrassed to have been spoken of as a paid escort.

Before she could turn completely to speak to her rescuer, another drunken man bumped into her, causing her to fall onto her rescuer's chest.

Dammit!

Feeling even more embarrassed, she immediately pulled away, but her hair got stuck on her rescuer's shirt button. She tried to tug frantically, but apart from the pain of hair being pulled, she was still stuck.

"You're making it worse," her rescuer's deep voice stated. "Let me do it."

His warm hand enclosed around her upper arm, and he dragged her with him away from the crush of the crowd.

"Where are you taking me?" she asked, feeling alarmed.

He didn't say anything. Before she could go into panic mode, her rescuer stopped at a place that had slightly better lighting. It was also deserted. She couldn't see or hear anyone.

Her heart began to thud. She waited for a few tense moments. Even as she braced herself to fight off the stranger, she felt slight tugs on her hair as the man worked on releasing her from his shirt button.

Biting her lip, she waited.

The man was tall. Her eyes were at the level of his chest. Away from the smoke-filled room, she could smell the man's subtle yet expensive spicy cologne. And at the close proximity, she could also feel the heat of his skin through the single layer of cloth of his light blue shirt.

Her cheeks heated at the unexpected intimacy. A small pinging sound on the floor indicated that the man had to pull out the shirt button to release her entangled hair.

"All done," the man's deep voice said.

Anya immediately took a step back. She raised her head and was about to thank him, but her words died in her throat. Instead, she stared at the man.

He was tall. Very tall. And quite broad and muscular too. With wide shoulders and a broad chest, he looked like a professional athlete. The crisp light blue formal shirt he wore did not hide the solid muscles.

But it was his face that held her captivated. It was an intriguing mix of elegance and ruggedness. He had dark, piercing eyes with thick lashes, chiseled cheekbones and a strong jaw. His nose was slightly crooked and appeared as though it had been broken sometime ago and healed.

He looked striking yet imperfectly handsome. He looked stunning.

The man was watching her intently. The intensity of his stare both unnerved her and held her captivated. His eyes pierced through her as though he could discover things about her with just a gaze.

A strange sense of familiarity filled the air between them even though she knew she hadn't met or seen the man before.

"Are you here alone?" he asked.

His deep, commanding voice snapped her out of the daze. She blinked a couple of times, remembering why she was at the club.

"Yes." Her eyes fell on his shirt, where one of the buttons was missing. There was no brand logo on the shirt, but it looked quite expensive.

"Let me pay for your shirt," she offered. She tried to reach in her coat pocket when she realized that in her hurry, she had not carried her wallet or any money. "I-I... don't have money with me right now, but I can..." She trailed off at his look.

His mouth twisted slightly as he watched her. Slowly, his gaze swept over her face and lingered on her lips. She had a feeling he thought she was offering to make a different type of payment.

Oh God. Does he think I'm a paid escort?

She should feel offended, but her heart raced and her lips tingled with his intense stare.

"I—" Before she could say something, she heard a familiar voice.

"Anya!"

It was her brother. She turned to see her brother running towards her. The sound of his footsteps was loud on the polished floor.

"What the hell took you so long?" he demanded.

"I just came in a few minutes ago. I had to go to your apartment first for the documents."

Her brother looked slightly annoyed rather than grateful. "All right. Give me the documents quickly and leave."

Anya was angry. "I'm not leaving without you. Handover those documents and come home with me." She pulled the documents from the pocket inside her long coat.

Anya's brother looked like he wanted to argue. But seeing her angry determination, he relented. "Fine. I'll drop off the papers and come." He grabbed the documents and ran back along the corridor.

Feeling slightly relieved, Anya turned.

But the handsome stranger who had rescued her was gone. She hadn't even heard him leave.

Strange disappointment filled her. Pushing away the irrational feeling, she turned to hurry out of the club when she stepped on something. It was the fallen button. Impulsively, she slipped it into a pocket and continued to hurry out.

It was still raining heavily.

As soon as she got into the waiting car, her friend let out a sigh.

"Thank God, you are back. I was about to call the police before barging in." Trupti looked freaked out.

"I'm fine," Anya told her friend with a small smile. "I gave the documents to my brother. He's coming with us."

Trupti nodded before frowning. "Your hair is dripping."

Anya realized her hair was loose and got wet in the rain. Her hairclip was missing.

"It... it must have fallen somewhere in the club," she replied.

It must have fallen on the floor when the handsome stranger tried to release her hair from his shirt button. Her cheeks heated that she didn't look for her hair clip and instead picked up the stranger's shirt button.

She was embarrassed about the strange pull she felt towards a complete stranger, especially the one she met in a gambling club.

I hope our paths don't cross again.

***

He stood near the window on the top floor and watched her through the rain as she left the club and entered the car parked outside.

"Was that really her?"his brother's voice asked.

"Yes."

His brother let out a disbelieving scoff. "I can't believe that dumb fuck would call his sister to a place like this."

He hadn't expected it either. And neither did he expect to see or talk to her.

"Since she saw you, she might cause a problem, bro. Until things fall into place, you'll have to be careful not to let her see you again."

He didn't say anything.

Sukanya Kashyap wasn't a part of his plans. But after meeting her, he now knew she would be a major part of his game.

Very soon, their paths would cross again.

CHAPTER ONE

"The sculpture in the middle of the courtyard looks outstanding, Anya."

"Yes, Anya. Your ideas are quite unique. I simply love this entire décor!"

Anya smiled at the older couple whose house she had re-designed. "Thank you, Mr. and Mrs. Vora. I'm glad you both like it. It was a pleasure for my team and me to work with you."

The older couple loved traveling and had collected many items over the years. Anya highlighted those items and used their memories of the places they travelled to decorate their home.

The older woman smiled. "You are a pleasure to work with too. I'm going to tell your mother what an awesome job you have done."

Anya continued to smile, not saying anything. She knew her mother's reaction wouldn't be what her client was expecting.

"Thank you again, Mr. and Mrs. Vora. Enjoy your new home. I'll be leaving in a few minutes."

With a smile, she looked around and saw the guests the Voras had invited to show off their newly decorated home.

Anya was invited too and introduced to the guests. There were plenty of appreciative murmurs, and most of the guests had taken her company's visiting card, which she had readily available for the occasion.

"Anya, can I speak to you privately for a moment?"

Anya felt a trickle of annoyance. But pasting a polite smile, she turned to face the man who was her client's son. "Yes, Mr. Vora?"

Although she had only interacted with the older couple for a major part of the project, she did occasionally have to take inputs from their son. She didn't like the creepy vibes he put out.

"Don't be so formal, Anya," he said with a wide, toothy smile. "I told you many times to call me Ritwik. I know your brother quite well. We often hang out at the club together."

Which only meant that Ritwik Vora also gambled like her brother.

"Let's go and talk privately somewhere. I told my parents I'd finish the pending paperwork."

Anya wasn't expecting the clients to sign off on the project's final paperwork right then. They could mail it to her office anytime.

But the client's son seemed determined.

"Sure, Mr. Vora."

There was a creepy satisfied smile on the man's face as he stepped closer than what was needed and led her upstairs to the Voras' office area overlooking a beautiful garden.

As soon as they stepped in, there was a clicking sound of the office room door being locked.

Anya clenched her teeth as she went into the middle of the room and waited near the desk.

"Ah. Finally, some privacy," he said with a smirk.

The man was handsome by normal standards, but his presence left her cold. He was an entitled rich man who thought most women could be impressed with money and status.

She was hardly impressed.

Ignoring the creepy smile, she looked at him. "Even after you sign off on the project, my team and I would continue to assist in the near future if there are any issues."

He came closer until his expensive, yet cloying cologne filled her nose. "I'm glad we'll remain in touch," he whispered. "My parents will be busy for a while with their guests. How about I show how appreciative I am with your stellar job?" His finger slid on her arm suggestively.

The level of annoyance along with anger shot up inside her, and she took a step back. "I'm not interested in you, Mr. Vora," she said in a cold, clear voice.

"Why not?" he asked. His voice was a combination of whining and frustration. He held her arms. "I'm rich and eligible, and so are you. We can also get married soon."

She fisted her hands. "It takes more than just money for me to be interested. And I'm not rich. My parents are."

That didn't make him retreat. He came at her more aggressively. He had her more or less trapped against the office desk. "Oh, come on, Anya. Stop playing hard to get. I know you were panting for me right from the beginning of this project. I could sense it."

Anya's jaw clenched. "You are wrong. Move away from me," she gritted.

He didn't move away. He leaned in closer with a smirk. "Why the outrage?" he asked. "It's not like you are some blushing, innocent virgin. You have been married before, so you know enough about men and sex. Your ex-husband said you were a wild thing who had to be constantly satisfied. I know I can keep you satisfied." He thrust his hips against her suggestively, letting her feel his arousal.

Anya raised her knee and slammed it hard against his groin.

There was shock on his face before he collapsed on the office room floor.

"I had warned you to back off," she said to the man curled up in a fetal position, groaning in pain.

She stepped around him and walked out of the office room.

Just when she reached the ground floor, she came across her client. "Done with the paperwork already?" the older woman asked.

Anya forced out a smile. "Not yet, Mrs. Vora. I told your son there's no hurry. He is going through the documents more closely."

"Oh. That's good, dear."

"I'll get going, Mrs. Vora. Thank you once again for inviting me. Enjoy your new home."

Waving the older woman goodbye, Anya stepped out of the house.

She was still angry and annoyed as she got into her car and drove away. She hated men like Ritwik Vora and her ex-husband. They thought they were God's gift to women. They weren't.

Once you took away the bank balance, they were nothing. A person should be worthy enough in other ways for her wanting to spend the rest of her life with them. Unfortunately, she was surrounded by rich, entitled men—including her father and brother.

Barely a few minutes later, she received a call. It was from her brother.

"Dammit, Anya! Why the hell did you do that! Ritwik is my friend!"

Anya clenched her jaw. "Your friend didn't back off when I warned him off."

There was a momentary pause. "Still," her brother grumbled. "Ritwik said he proposed marriage to you, and you just attacked him. I was planning to start a business with him. Now, he might not be interested anymore because of how you've humiliated him."

Anya's anger grew, but she stopped herself from arguing with her brother. She knew it would be of no use. "I'll talk to you later," she said.

Before he could say anything, Anya ended the call.

Taking a deep breath, she dialed another number.

"So, how did it go?" her friend Trupti asked.

"We have six potential clients," Anya told Trupti who was also her business partner. "But I think we might have trouble getting the final sign-off on the Vora project."

"Oh, what happened?" There was concern in her friend's voice.

Anya sighed. "The asshole made a pass. The idiot somewhat proposed marriage too and thinks I should be grateful because he has money, which by the way, is his parents' money. He also called me horny because he heard that from my ex-husband."

Trupti let out an angry breath. "Bastard. What did you say?"

"I kneed him in his balls."

Trupti chuckled. "Oh God, Anya. I would have loved to see that scene."

Anya smiled. "It isn't pretty seeing a grown man mewling on the floor. Anyway, we already have the contracts signed and payments made through checks. I took the final pictures and video of the place."

"Yup. Let's hope the bastard doesn't create any trouble."

Anya knew he might. He had already complained to her brother. He would be too humiliated to tell his parents about what had happened in the office room, but he might cause trouble in other ways and say the house wasn't done well.

Luckily, she had dealt with men like him before and knew how to handle them.

"Are you on your way home?" Trupti asked.

"Yes." She was looking forward to having a relaxed Friday night.

"I'll be done soon with the penthouse showing since there are enough offers already. I'll pick up a bottle of wine and dinner and come by your place."

Anya smiled. "That sounds awesome."

Ending the call, Anya continued to drive home.

***

Thirty minutes later, she drove through her neighborhood.

She parked her car in front of a small single-level house that she called home. As soon as she got out of her car, one of her neighbors pushing a stroller waved at her.

"Hello, Anya."

Anya smiled. "Hi, Preethi. How are you? And how is little Akshay doing?"

The young mother looked exhausted, but her smile was happy. "Akshay and I are doing great. He started teething."

Anya smiled at her neighbor's excitement. "Done with your steps?"

The younger woman shook her head. "Not yet. I didn't go walking this morning, so I still need to finish my thousand steps."

Anya laughed. "All right then. Carry on."

She waved goodbye, letting her neighbor continue with her walk around the neighborhood.

Most of the houses were small or mid-sized, and most of the occupants were either retired couples or young families. Anya enjoyed living in the lively neighborhood where people often went for walks and children played outside. It was quite different from her childhood home and neighborhood where she and her brother had no one else to play with and barely saw anyone stepping out of their huge homes.

Letting out a deep sigh, she unlocked the door and stepped inside.

It was only seven o'clock, but the long working hours and the evening's events made her feel exhausted.

Just as she entered her living room, her phone began ringing. It was her mother.

Anya groaned softly. She wanted to ignore the call, but she knew her mother would not give up calling, so she answered the phone.

"Anya, where the hell have you been all day!"

"Working, Ma. Today is Friday."

There was a dismissive scoff. "I called you at least three times. I wanted to confirm that you are attending the charity auction next Saturday."

Anya had no plans to attend it, but she didn't have the patience to argue with her mother right then. "I'm still thinking about it, Ma."

"What do you mean by still thinking? You better attend it. I have a dress readied for the occasion. Drop by tomorrow to pick it up. By the way, Surya will be there too at the auction."

Her ex-husband's presence was why Anya had no intention of attending the social event.

"I'll talk to you later, Ma. I just got home."

Her mother scoffed but luckily ended the call.

Anya let out another sigh as her exhaustion grew. Taking a deep breath, she turned on the lights.

A smile covered her face seeing her small, cozy living room with the dining area and kitchen attached in a semi-open space.

Trupti often teased her saying that her house was far too simple for a successful interior architect who had renovated many high-end luxury homes.

Anya deliberately kept her home décor simple and functional. It soothed her mind. With neutral colors and furnishings made from reclaimed wood or bought from a renovation where antique pieces were replaced by modern ones, her home looked eclectic. She also kept things that reminded her of happy memories. Several indoor plants were highlighted by her vast stone collection, a lamp made from sticks collected during her childhood and a few framed pictures of her favorite childhood place were among the décor. They made her feel at home.

She pushed open the windows and the small patio door to the backyard, letting the cool breeze flow in. Since Trupti was bringing food, she didn't have to cook that night.

She took a quick shower and wore her comfortable night pants and t-shirt when the doorbell rang.

She answered the door and saw her grinning friend. "Let the party begin, girlfriend!"

Anya laughed and let her friend inside before shutting the door.

They spent the rest of the evening chatting and laughing while a movie played in the background.

"I can't have another glass of wine," Anya said with a laugh. "Remember, I have an appointment tomorrow morning."

Trupti frowned. "Oh yeah. A hotel tycoon client."

Anya sighed. "Yes. Although I still think you should go instead of me. Penthouses are your specialty." Anya preferred the traditional décor style over modern contemporary ones.

"But the client had asked specifically for you," Trupti reminded.

They had received an email with a vague mention of a client who was an international hotelier wanting renovation services from Soul Spaces. Anya was asked to meet the client at the penthouse.

Anya was going to follow the normal protocol and meet the client to see if the project was viable and worth taking on.

Trupti giggled. "Maybe the mystery hotel tycoon is hot."

Anya rolled her eyes. "Most hotel tycoons are middle-aged or old."

Trupti grinned. "Try not to knee the middle-aged, pot-bellied hotel tycoon in his balls."

Anya laughed. "I won't. But you might have to because I'm going to tell the client you would be taking up the penthouse renovation."

Trupti laughed.

They finished up dinner. Trupti helped her clear the dishes before preparing to leave.

"All right," she said. "I'll let you catch up with your beauty sleep. Meanwhile, I have a hot date with BOB tonight. I have to pick up some extra batteries on my way."

Anya laughed. "Have fun and say hi to BOB."

Waving her friend good night, Anya went into her bedroom. Even though she was physically tired, she wasn't sleepy. A strange restlessness filled her mind.

Maybe it was Trupti's comment about BOB that made her think of him.

Someone with dark, piercing eyes and a bold yet slightly crooked nose. Someone imperfectly perfect.

It was embarrassing that she didn't need a battery-operated boyfriend. All she needed was a shirt button. She went into her closet and drew out the white shirt button she kept safe for the last two months. Holding the button, she went and lay on her soft, comfortable bed.

Her breaths grew faster as she rubbed her finger gently against the smooth button. Her eyes fell shut, and the image of the darkly handsome stranger who rescued her at the club filled her mind.

Her path didn't cross with the stranger in real life, but he was often featured in her deepest fantasies.

"Are you here alone?" he asked.

The memory of his deep, rumbling voice made her skin break into goosebumps. Her breasts peaked in arousal.

"Let me pay for your shirt," she offered.

His sensual mouth twisted slightly as he looked at her. Slowly, his gaze swept over her face and lingered on her lips. She had a feeling he thought she was offering to make a different type of payment.

The scene at the club began playing out differently in her mind.

"Come with me," he said. His warm fingers wrapped around her upper arm once again as he dragged her somewhere.

"Where are you taking me?" she asked in a breathless tone.

This time, he took here where it was dark, and they were hidden under the shadows.

He began unbuttoning her long coat.

"What are you doing?" she asked as her breaths turned faster and rougher.

"Taking my payment," his deep voice whispered into her ear while big hands slipped under her long coat and went between her legs.

Barely, a few moments later, hot pleasure invaded her body. She reached the pinnacle with a soft cry and felt all the coiled tension flowing out from her body. She slipped into a deep, satisfying sleep while still clutching the white button in her fist.

CHAPTER TWO

"Hello, I'm Anya from Soul Spaces. I have an appointment at nine."

After sleeping like the dead the previous night, Anya had woken up early feeling quite refreshed. She got ready for her morning appointment and drove to the financial district where her potential client's penthouse was located.

She was greeted by a smiling young man waiting downstairs in the lobby of a tall building.

"Good morning, madam. I'm Ravi. I will be assisting you to the penthouse." The man led her into an elevator. "Sir is finishing up a meeting and will be with you shortly."

Anya felt annoyed. Yet another entitled, rich man who was going to waste her time, especially her weekend time by making her wait for him.

The elevator stopped on the topmost floor and opened up to a private lobby. The heavy main door was kept open, and they walked into a spacious penthouse.

Anya frowned, looking at the penthouse interior—a well-decorated, finished interior.

She had expected an unfurnished place. But the place was furnished in a minimalistic décor with beautiful accent rugs, paintings and sleek furniture.

The spacious living room overlooked the city from a massive balcony. She walked towards it and could see a swimming pool, a Jacuzzi and lounge chairs along with a full bar outside on the balcony.

"The penthouse appears lived-in," she said.

The dining area to the side of the living room was completely furnished too.

Ravi looked surprised. "Of course, madam. Sir has been living in the penthouse for two months."

Anya wasn't entirely surprised. She had come across a few clients who wanted to renovate to something different within a short period of time. But two months seemed extreme.

Since it was the client's money and he could spend it however he wished, Anya was only concerned about the scope of the project. Trupti would eventually be taking up the actual renovation.

"Please wait here, madam. I'll let sir know you have arrived."

Anya gave a brief nod. While she waited, she looked around to get a sense of the client's taste.

The man seemed to have excellent taste. Although the place had a minimalistic décor, the pieces chosen were unique. One particular painting caught her attention. It seemed somewhat familiar.

She went closer to look at it. It was a painting of two children playing in a river. She found it beautiful and moving, especially seeing the carefree faces. She recognized the painting. The original was destroyed in a fire.

"It's called *The River*," a deep voice stated.

Anya's heart jerked at the sudden interruption, and she turned around, only to gasp out in complete shock.

A tall man in a dark suit stood only a few feet away from her. With her heart thumping crazily, she stared at him. Her brain refused to rationalize who she was seeing.

"My God," she whispered. "It's you."

This can't be happening. I must still be dreaming.

But it was him. The dark, piercing eyes, the high cheekbones, hard jawline and the bold yet slightly crooked nose were all the same. In the clear light of the day, he was even more devastatingly and strikingly handsome. She blinked several times, but it was still the same sight in front of her.

He was the darkly handsome stranger who had rescued her in the club.

There were days and nights when she thought she had only imagined the strong pull she felt towards him that night. But right then, the familiar pull buzzed like live electricity around her.

Her face burned as she recalled the previous night when she had fantasized about him while holding his missing shirt button.

Oh God.

She had to control the urge to run away from him, so she didn't have to face him ever again.

Keep your calm. He doesn't know what you've been doing with his missing shirt button.

His dark eyes flashed as though he could read her mind. It unnerved her and shook her calm.

"I-I'm here for an appointment," she stammered out.

She wondered if he was her client's guest. Whoever he was, she badly hoped he was leaving.

His eyes continued to flash, and his mouth twisted into a small smile. "I'm Bhargav Varma," he said. "Your client."

She stared at him in shock. He was the hotel tycoon—her mystery client.

He wasn't a middle-aged man like she had expected. He appeared to be around her age, which mostly meant he inherited his wealth and hotel chains. No wonder he was at a club where rich playboys like him and her brother often frequented.

Even though the thought had crossed her mind over the last two months, she still felt let down that her darkly handsome rescuer was yet another entitled playboy.

She slowly began to get angry and outraged that he had deliberately set up this meeting to collect his payment.

How dare he do this even after knowing I'm not a paid escort.

Does he think all women can be bought?

He was watching her. His eyes scanned her clothes, taking in her dark formal suit with pants, her flat, sensible shoes and her slightly oversized handbag. She always dressed the same during her work because she often went to client sites that were still under construction, and she carried the basic tools in her handbag.

Taking a deep breath, she pulled herself together. Pasting a polite smile, she spoke to him in a firm businesslike tone. "Mr. Varma, thank you for choosing Soul Spaces to renovate your home. My business partner has more experience in penthouse interiors. I prefer houses. I'm going to ask her to get in touch with you right away."

There was no reaction on his face. "I want you," he stated bluntly.

Her heart leaped in shock. "What?" she asked.

"I want you to work on my project, Miss Kashyap."

Pushing away her irrational reaction to him, Anya focused on her anger at his assumption that she would agree to whatever he wanted.

"I'm sorry, Mr. Varma. Unfortunately, it's not a decision you can make." Anya knew she was being rude to a potential client. But her anger and disappointment drove her.

His expression still didn't change.

She raised her chin slightly. "If you are still interested, please contact Soul Spaces, and my business partner will help you. Goodbye, Mr. Varma."

She expected him to be pissed off, but a small smile appeared on his face.

Once again, her heart began racing at the slight twist of his beautifully shaped mouth. Feeling annoyed by her reaction, she turned to leave.

"The Vardhaman Estate."

She had taken a couple of steps when she froze at his words. Slowly, she turned to him in shock.

"What?" she asked.

His dark eyes pierced into her again. "The project is the Vardhaman Estate."

Her heart began to thud loudly. "But... but the estate is under the government's control."

He shrugged. "Very soon, it won't be."

Under normal circumstances, she would have thought it was an arrogant statement made by yet another rich, entitled man. But the cool confidence Bhargav Varma exerted made her believe him.

Or maybe she wanted to believe him.

"I want you to be a part of the team I'm putting together to restore the estate. And the reason I picked you specifically is because I found out you are one of the people familiar with the place."

Anya was familiar with the place. Her heart thudded as happy memories and nostalgia overwhelmed her. "I spent most of my childhood holidays there."

"Good," he said. "Then you should be happy to see the place again in a few hours."

Stunned, Anya stared at the man in front her. "What?"

"We are going to the estate right now." He pulled out a sleek phone from his pocket, called someone and gave them instructions. "We'll be leaving in ten minutes."

Meanwhile, Anya was too shocked to digest the sudden turn of events.

He ended the call and looked at her. "Let's go, Miss Kashyap."

Pushing her shock away, Anya gathered her outrage at his arrogant order and assumptions. "I haven't said yes to the project, Mr. Varma. I can't just accompany you on a day trip to the estate."

That is, if he was taking her to the estate in the first place. She knew nothing about him. She hadn't even known his name until a few minutes ago. All she knew was that he was a hotel tycoon who frequented high-end gambling clubs.

Bhargav Varma watched her. A shiver ran through her body while his intense gaze bore into hers. "Are you afraid of me, Miss Kashyap?" he asked, his deep, rumbling voice making her feel things she shouldn't be feeling.

Her cheeks were on fire as she was once again reminded of the previous night when she had fantasized about him and his deep voice.

"I'm not afraid," she replied even as her breath hitched slightly. She tried to control her heart from racing as well. "The estate is a three-hour ride from here, which means it would take us almost an entire day to return. I have some other important things to do later today."

She suddenly realized why the current appointment was made on a Saturday morning. Even before their meeting, Bhargav Varma was sure she would agree to the project and join him on the day trip.

The fact made her angrier.

His mouth twisted slightly, reading her thoughts easily. "I'm a businessman, Miss Kashyap. Time is always of essence to me. I always plan ahead. We should be back before lunch, and you can get on with your important things."

Anya frowned, not knowing how that was possible to be back so soon.

But she knew she couldn't say no. Seeing the Vardhaman Estate restored was her dream.

In fact, not even in her wildest dreams had she expected the chance of a lifetime. She knew that if she turned down the offer, many architects would jump at the chance to be a part of restoring one of the most beautiful estates in the country. And she badly wanted to see the place again.

She could read nothing on Bhargav Varma's darkly handsome face as he waited for her to reply.

Taking a deep breath, she ignored the strong warning and awareness she felt towards him and nodded. "All right. I'll join you, Mr. Varma."

His mouth twisted again into a small smile, but the smile was far from reassuring.

The warning bells inside her rang louder even while the strong awareness blasted back tenfold.

***

Anya's stomach kept fluttering hard, and it wasn't just because she was inside a helicopter. It was mostly because of the man seated next to her looking outside as they took off from the top of the penthouse building.

Bhargav Varma left her completely shaken.

Who is he?

Why did he buy the Vardhaman Estate?

She badly needed those answers. She wanted to ask him, but the sound of the helicopter was too loud. She had to wait until they reached their destination.

She also had to get control of how she reacted and felt around him. It was silly and immature of her.

Although there were a few inches gap between their seats, she still felt a strong buzzing awareness towards him. A familiar spicy and musky scent of his cologne filled her senses, and she felt her cheeks heat when her eyes fell on his long, thick masculine fingers tapping casually on the handrest area between their seats.

Dragging her eyes away from his fingers, she kept her eyes straight ahead.

Get a grip! He is your client!

She took deep breaths as she reminded herself of that fact repeatedly.

Thirty torturous minutes later, the helicopter began slowing down.

Bhargav Varma turned towards her. She couldn't see his eyes because he was wearing his sunglasses, but she knew he was watching her. "We are at the estate," he said.

Anya's heart began racing. But this time, it was in anticipation of being at the estate.

She couldn't see the Vardhaman mansion yet, but they had entered the estate area which was roughly around five hundred acres. A minute later, the mansion came into view.

Anya's breath caught in her throat, and she bit her bottom lip as nostalgia and other emotions overwhelmed her. It had been over fifteen years since she had been to the place. Although her parents had visited it a few times before the banks seized the estate and it ultimately went under government control, she wasn't allowed to accompany them.

The helicopter landed at a distance in front of the mansion.

Anya released the clasp of her seat belt and got up before following her client out of the helicopter. She shook her head no when he offered her a hand while getting down into the thickly weeded area.

His mouth twisted slightly as he stepped back and allowed her to step down on the ground herself. Luckily, her flat shoes allowed her to get down easily.

Anya stared at the sight in front of her, and her heart clenched seeing the mansion up close. The once stunningly majestic and beautiful mansion now appeared as a neglected structure covered in thick climbing weeds.

She followed her client once again while he walked through the thickly-weeded path that once used to be a well-paved stone driveway. They walked around the large marble water fountain covered with climbing weeds and dead leaves.

Climbing the marble steps carefully, she noticed that most of the outward structure was actually quite intact. The massive marble columns in front of the mansion were also in perfect condition.

The door was bolted shut to stop trespassers from entering. Disappointment filled her thinking the visit was limited to only the outside of the mansion. But Bhargav Varma waited next to the door while a man who appeared to be a security guard joined him and unlocked the door.

The guard pushed open the huge carved door. The wood was no longer shiny, but the door seemed to be in perfect condition.

The inside was dusty and filled with cobwebs. Most people would see just the dust, cobwebs and peeling paint with missing furniture and ceiling fixtures. But Anya slipped into her professional mode. She focused on the bare bones of the structure. Her eyes took in the impressive high ceilings, beautiful marble flooring with intricate designs and the two circular winding stairways that led to upstairs. The large formal living room was bare, but her mind conjured up memories of the stunningly beautiful chandeliers, paintings and artifacts that had once adorned the place, which must have been either sold by the banks or stolen.

"So what do you think, Miss Kashyap?" her client's deep voice asked.

Anya turned to see him watching her closely. He had taken off his sunglasses, and the intensity of his gaze once again felt as though he was looking deep inside her.

"The structure seems sturdy," she replied.

He gave a brief nod. "A team of engineers will be inspecting it next week to see what needs to be repaired or fixed."

Anya frowned. "But the sale is not completed. I'm not sure without the permissions that the structure can be inspected."

Bhargav Varma didn't seem bothered about it.

"Do you think you can restore the place?" he asked instead.

Anya wasn't too sure. "I have memories and pictures of the interiors which I can recreate. But I'm not sure it will be entirely accurate."

"It needn't be the same. I want it to be a fusion of the original décor with modern add-ons."

Anya stared at him.

He was a hotel tycoon who had purchased the large estate.

Suddenly, her heart jolted, and anger and outrage shot up inside her. "Mr. Varma, if you are thinking of knocking down several mansion walls and making this place into a hundred-room hotel, I suggest that you don't. The Vardhaman Estate used to be listed as one of the best royal estates. It is a heritage site and must be treated as such!"

He didn't react to her long and sudden passionate outburst. He watched her as she more or less glared at him.

"The restoration will be done without disturbing the original structure."

She was relieved by his statement, but she also felt embarrassed when his mouth twisted slightly. "You seem quite attached to this place, Miss Kashyap."

She was very attached. Even after fifteen years, she often thought of the place and the memories. "I am. The family who used to live here were my family's close friends."

"I see."

He didn't ask anything else. Anya was sure he must have heard about how the entire family had died tragically fifteen years ago.

"What about the outside?" she asked. "Will the restoration work continue outside as well?"

He nodded. "There are a few people in the nearby village who used to work for the family. Some of them remember the landscaping."

Anya was glad. One of the best features of the estate was the various orchards, vegetable patches and beautiful flowering bushes.

She looked around at the large formal living room. "I would like to take pictures and measure the rooms." She knew it was too premature, but she was too obsessed with the place and the memories not to begin working on recreating the designs. She was more or less desperate to see her past come alive in graphic designs and models.

A masculine brow rose at her request. "We can look at some of the rooms on the ground floor. The rest of the place might not be safe until inspection."

She knew he was right.

They walked along the large formal living room and went to the sunroom, library room, dining area and music room. She took several pictures and used her measuring beam to get the rooms' dimensions.

They were inside the nearly empty music room which only had a grand piano covered by a fading dust cloth. Anya was surprised that it hadn't been sold. Luckily, it was too big and heavy to be stolen.

Anya was pushing aside the dust cloth when something big flew out of it. She shrieked and turned to get away when she bumped into a hard chest.

"It was a bat," Bhargav Varma's deep voice murmured. "It flew away."

Feeling embarrassed by her reaction to a small bat, she tried to step back from him. But she couldn't.

Her hair got stuck into his shirt button.

Not again!

She tried to release her hair, but she didn't succeed. Her fingers tingled as they brushed against his shirt button, and she could feel the hard muscles of his chest.

Oh God.

"Let me do it," he instructed. His deep voice was gruff.

Her cheeks heated, but she stayed still. It took a few tugs, and then finally, her hair was released. This time, his shirt button remained intact.

Her cheeks grew hotter at the thought of his missing shirt button in her closet at home.

She raised her head to thank him, but her voice got stuck in her throat when she met his eyes. He was watching her with an intense look that made her heart race faster. She held her breath completely when he stepped closer.

She nearly jumped out of her skin when his fingers cupped her jaw, and the slightly roughened pad of his fingertip brushed against her cheek. He was most likely wiping away a smear of dust from her cheek.

His mouth twisted slightly at her reaction. "Are you always this jumpy, Miss Kashyap?" he asked. "Or is it just with me?"

She was embarrassed. It was just with him. She wouldn't normally allow her clients to come that close to her. But with him, the strong pull and awareness made her feel a false sense of intimacy.

Taking a deep breath, she stepped away. "I need to take a few more measurements and pictures," she murmured.

There was a knowing flash in his eyes as she evaded his question.

They continued to go from room to room while she took more pictures and noted the measurements. It was a huge mansion with nearly a hundred rooms. It would make a decent-sized luxury hotel or resort without having to disturb the original structure.

But a part of her heart ached that a place that had been home to a beautiful close-knit family with so many happy memories was going to be used commercially.

"Life is not black or white. Stop foolishly believing in dreams."
Anya was reminded of those harsh words yelled at her by her father.
"Don't go there," Bhargav Varma's deep voice cut in to her thoughts.
Blinking a few times, Anya paused. She was about to step out of the spacious sunroom.
"You can take pictures of the outside after the weeds have been cleared.
She nodded, knowing it wasn't safe as there might be snakes in the thick weeds.
"Let's head back," he said.
She thought it was too soon, but when she looked at her watch, she was stunned that they had been at the mansion for well over three hours. Time flew when it came to the place she loved.
He watched her with a twist of his mouth. "I believe you have important things to do later today."
Her cheeks heated at the lie she had told him earlier that morning. "I can reschedule," she murmured.
With a small smile, he led her out of the sun room. Once again, awareness grew stronger while she followed him out to the helicopter. They were seated next to each other, and he handed her a bottle of water.
A soft brush of fingers had her quickly snatching her hand away from him. His mouth twisted again knowingly. It was odd and embarrassing that she was overreacting to his presence. Considering she would have to work for him for a while, she knew she had to pull herself together and ignore the attraction.
The helicopter ride was silent, and they soon landed on top of the penthouse building. Her client led her into a private elevator.
At his close proximity in the private elevator, her cheeks heated while goosebumps peppered her skin. His spicy cologne filled her senses and was becoming addicting. It reminded her of the time in the club when they had met for the first time. She was also reminded of the times when she lay on her bed with the memory of his cologne, his deep voice and darkly handsome looks.
It was beyond mortifying that she thought of him that way.
He was watching her right then with a hooded look. "Join me for lunch," he said.
It sounded more like a command.
Anya's heart leaped. She shook her head. "I can't."
His mouth twisted slightly in amusement. "You can't have lunch?"

"I... I don't have lunches or dinner with my clients, Mr. Varma," she lied.

She had gone on several lunches and dinners with her clients, but they were mostly with couples. Occasionally she had gone out with single men and women clients as well to get a sense of their style and details, but she had always considered them business meetings.

A lunch meeting with Bhargav Varma would be a disaster and hardly qualify as a business meeting. Not when he watched her with his hooded eyes, and her heart raced with his nearness.

She had to maintain distance from him to be able to work for him.

"Have other teams visited the estate as well?" she asked, changing the topic.

She badly needed other people around to dim the intensity of inappropriate awareness she felt towards him.

The flash in his eyes indicated he knew she was changing the topic. "Not yet," he replied. "Although I've spoken to a few and had some initial talks."

The restoration would require a large team of architects and designers along with engineers and workers. Although she had the added advantage of being familiar with the mansion, when it came to experience, there would be many senior architects who would lead the effort.

She realized that the elevator didn't stop at the penthouse level. They had reached the parking garage. Her heart thudded as they stepped out together and he walked her to her car.

How does he know this is my car?

There were plenty of other cars parked in the underground parking. And she had parked in a visitor's spot.

"I'll see you on Monday at eight sharp," he said. "We'll go through the contract and timelines. Have a good weekend, Miss Kashyap."

Before she could say anything, he walked away towards the residents' parking area.

Anya stared until he disappeared. And then, slowly she moved and got into her car.

Who are you?

CHAPTER THREE

Anya wanted to go to her office right away, but she had to drop by her parents' place first.

She drove towards an upscale area where her parents had been living for the past fifteen years. Before that, they had been living in a modest home in a normal neighborhood. The sudden upturn of their family finances had changed their lifestyle drastically.

Anya had hated every minute of it.

She stopped her car in front of a huge three-story building with luxury cars parked outside on display. With a sigh, she got down and went to the door before ringing the bell.

A young, nervous-looking woman answered it. "Good afternoon, madam."

Anya smiled at the maid who was hired only a month ago.

"Good afternoon, Lata. Are my parents home?"

"Both sirs went out. Your mother is in the dining room having lunch."

"Thank you."

Anya had hoped to simply collect her dress and leave. But now that her mother was surprisingly home, she would have to stay a while longer.

She stepped into the house where she spent some of her childhood and most of her teenage years. But unlike most people, she didn't feel any nostalgia or comfort. The beautiful, high-end designs with some of the best antique pieces left her cold. All she felt was defensive.

She knew what was coming when it came to conversing with her mother. It was always an argument. Most of her teenage years were spent arguing with her parents. She had to beg them to enroll her in a good college, beg them to allow her to pursue her architecture degree and then beg them to allow her to wait until she got her degree to get her married.

They had agreed to all of those, only with the condition that she marry her father's business partner's son when she turned twenty-one. And she did marry, only to seek a divorce a month later.

Since then, it had been a constant battleground where her father and mother ganged up with her ex-husband to make her agree to remarry him.

"Hello, Ma," Anya greeted her mother, who was seated at the large dining table.

Even though her mother was home, she was dressed impeccably in an expensive dress with her full makeup on.

"Good God, Anya. What are you wearing? And why are your shoes dirty!"

Anya groaned inside. "I had to meet a client this morning, Ma. This is my usual business attire. There was mud onsite... so my shoes must have gotten dirty."

Anya didn't want to tell her mother yet about the visit to the Vardhaman Estate. There would be too many questions asked along with major drama which she wasn't prepared for, especially on an empty stomach. She pulled out a chair and sat opposite her mother at the dining table.

Her mother made a clucking noise. "It's a wonder that you get projects despite the way you dress. Why can't you dress prettily? Why do you always dress like a man with ugly shoes?"

"My dress and shoes are fine, Ma." Anya smiled at the maid standing next to the table waiting to serve. "Please get me an extra plate."

The maid immediately hurried to the kitchen to grab a plate. She was a new hire too. The staff were either fired or left their jobs constantly.

Anya recalled the kindly housekeeper from her early childhood who had worked for over ten years. Raji had been her substitute mother. She was the one who looked after her brother and her. She fed them, bathed them, put them to sleep and even consoled and put bandages on their wounds when they got hurt. Anya's parents were always away from home socializing.

And when Anya's father became suddenly rich, Raji was fired, and a younger and larger staff was hired. Anya recalled crying her eyes out at the time. Her best friend, Bobby, had consoled her at that time, wrapping her in his thin arms while she cried and raged in hurt. But a few months later, she had lost Bobby too.

"Do you really have to work even on a Saturday?" her mother continued as usual. "Papa and I thought it would be a nice hobby. But clearly it has taken over your life and cost your marriage too."

Ignoring her mother's hurtful words, Anya smiled and thanked the maid as she placed the plate in front of her and served food.

"Interior architecture is not my hobby, Ma. It's my full-time profession. I worked hard for my degree, and I love my job."

Her mother scoffed. "Women from decent families don't work, especially in jobs that require them to be in mud and construction filth all day. It's a wonder that Surya doesn't mind you working."

Anya sighed. "Surya is not my husband anymore. Even if he was, it's not up to him to mind or not about my job."

Her mother scoffed again. "Just because of a silly mistake, you can't break off a marriage like that."

"He slept with the hotel receptionist on our honeymoon. It wasn't the first time he cheated. He even slept with his personal assistant and many of his employees while he was engaged to me. They came to me with proof."

Anya's mother looked mildly annoyed rather than disgusted. "Men have needs, Anya. I told that to you so many times. You should be happy that a man can satisfy his lusts somewhere else. Wives are to be respected and protected and treated like queens."

Anya didn't bother arguing with her mother. She continued to eat lunch. The topic of her ex-husband didn't bother her like it used to. She wasn't even annoyed anymore and barely thought of her marriage or ex-husband.

"Don't eat so much rice," her mother scolded when Anya took a second helping. "You need to fit into the auction dress next Saturday."

"I'm on my feet most of the time during work, Ma. I get enough exercise." Anya not only took the second helping of rice, she even ate a generous portion of dessert, which must have been made for her brother.

The fact that her mother didn't say anything about the dessert made Anya suspicious.

Her mother wanted something.

"Let me show you the dress," her mother said when they were done with lunch. "I bought it from a new boutique."

With a sigh, Anya followed her mother. While they passed through the formal living room, her heart ached seeing some stunning antique pieces that once belonged to the Vardhaman Estate.

Growing up, she had hated seeing those pieces brought into her parents' house. It constantly reminded her of what she lost in a tragic way.

"The dress is royal blue in color," her mother stated as they entered a bedroom where a dress was kept on the bed. "I would have preferred pastels. But thanks to your job, your complexion is getting worse, and pastels will not suit you. I'll take an appointment at the salon on Saturday morning. You can get a facial done, and they'll even remove some of the tan."

"I'm not sure about my schedule on Saturday, Ma."

Her mother frowned. "You better make it to the auction, Anya. We need to maintain our status and network."

Anya wanted to collect the dress and leave right away.

She couldn't wait to get to her office so she could look up information on Bhargav Varma. Her mind was too occupied with thoughts about him and their visit to the estate.

"Papa needs our help too, Anya. This auction will help us put on a normal front."

That caught Anya's attention. "What do you mean? What happened?"

Anya's mother looked uncomfortable. "Papa has been losing a lot of money lately. He made some risky investments. Even now, he had to meet some people to see if they can help."

"What sort of risky investments?" Anya asked.

"I don't know," Anya's mother muttered. "Two months ago, he was excited about a deal that would triple our investment. It turned out to be risky for a reason."

Anya wasn't surprised by her father's decision to make risky investments. A couple of times, he had gotten to the point of bankruptcy and had to use his contacts to bail him out. One of the people who had helped was his business partner, which was why Anya had to be the sacrificial lamb and marry the business partner's son.

"Be there at the auction, Anya. Don't skip it."

Anya nodded, feeling trapped once again. But she knew she had to help her parents no matter how she felt. And it was only a few hours of evening.

"I will attend, Ma."

"Good."

Anya straightened from the bed. "All right, Ma. I have to get back to work."

Her mother let out a long sigh. "Fine. But you better not show up at the auction looking dull and tired. Remember, I'm booking an appointment at the salon on Saturday morning."

Groaning inside, Anya nodded in agreement. "Bye, Ma. See you on Saturday."

Collecting her dress, Anya stepped out of her parents' home. Although the dress was stunningly beautiful, she was not looking forward to next weekend.

***

Anya went to her office building.

Since it was a Saturday, the usual staff wasn't there. Only she or Trupti dropped by sometimes over the weekend to finish some pending design work.

She sat in front of her laptop and uploaded the pictures and entered the measurements taken that morning. She then sent an email with instructions to the 3-D graphic designer to begin working on the models.

As soon as she was done with work, she opened the internet. She entered Bhargav Varma's name along with the company listed on the email she had received.

Who are you, Bhargav Varma?

Several search results came back with the company name which owned several hotel chains worldwide. They were all luxury hotels. Most of them were skyscrapers but some of them were high-end resorts.

Then why the Vardhaman Estate?

He had asked her to restore the mansion to exactly how it had been before. Maybe it was because many international travelers enjoyed staying in old royal palaces.

She continued with her search about him, looking particularly for anything personal. There were no pictures apart from being featured in business magazines.

It was strange because most wealthy people she knew loved being in the public limelight.

Bhargav Varma doesn't like public scrutiny.

She read through one of the articles where he had made a passing reference about his family. He was based out of New York, where he grew up in a bad neighborhood. He began working at the age of fourteen at construction sites. And then, at the age of eighteen, he started a company with his older brother. While his older brother continued to expand business in real estate, Bhargav Varma got into the hospitality industry.

It was a typical rags-to-riches story.

She now understood the ruggedness that could been seen despite his elegant clothes and demeanor. He didn't grow up entitled.

That made her feel all the more drawn to him. Pushing away the attraction, she continued to read articles about him. Most of them didn't mention anything about his personal life. Only one of the articles mentioned that his mother was a schoolteacher and wasn't too happy with her sons quitting school to work in jobs at a young age.

She was just about to click another link when she heard a loud whistle.

"Whoa! Who's that hot dude you are stalking?"

Anya let out a short, embarrassed laugh and turned to see Trupti. She must have just returned from the final handover of a penthouse.

"He's the client I met this morning," Anya replied.

There was a stunned look on Trupti's face. "The hotel tycoon?" she asked.

"Yes."

"He's sizzling hot!" Trupti grinned. "Are you sure you don't want to take up the project even though it's a penthouse renovation?"

Anya laughed. "I have decided to take up the project. But only because he wants me to be a part of the team to restore the Vardhaman Estate."

Her friend blinked a couple of times, not understanding. "Vardhaman Estate? *The* Vardhaman Estate? The one you are totally obsessed with? Wasn't it seized by the banks nearly fifteen years ago and handed over to the government?"

Anya's heart ached listening to the last part. "Yes."

"Oh my God! But how? You said the government acquired it and wants to make it into a heritage site at some point in the future."

Anya had no idea how Bhargav Varma was purchasing the estate either. She hoped he succeeded because she badly wanted to see the estate restored to its former glory as soon as possible.

"We flew there this morning in a helicopter," she told her friend. "And he is already putting a team together."

"Wow, Anya! Then it's an awesome opportunity, and you love that place! I can't imagine how happy and excited you must be! Come on, let's celebrate! Let's go out for dinner, and you can tell me more about the sizzling hot client."

Anya laughed. "All right. Let's go."

It was already dark outside. She didn't realize it since she had been obsessively involved in uploading the pictures and then looking up information on Bhargav Varma.

There wasn't much she could tell her friend about Bhargav Varma. And whatever interactions she had with him wasn't something she wanted to share with anyone yet. Mostly because she didn't understand her extreme reactions to him either.

"Let's go to our usual place," Trupti suggested. "Thanks to the penthouse showing, I skipped my lunch. I'm starving now!"

They went to a place close to their office. It was a small restaurant, but the food was delicious. They took one of the few tables and ordered their usual.

"So how is he in person?" Trupti asked as soon as the waiter left with their order.

Anya tried not to blush at her friend's question. "What do you mean?"

Trupti grinned. "You are blushing. I don't think I've ever seen you like this before. I have a strong feeling you like this mystery client."

"I hardly know him. I... just met him today." She still didn't want to tell her best friend about meeting him in the club.

"So when is the next appointment?" Trupti asked.

"Monday morning. He asked me to be there at eight sharp."

"Ooh... he sounds bossy."

Anya laughed even as her face once again heated in a blush. "Maybe he is."

He did seem bossy. He had more or less ordered her to join him at the estate. Even his lunch invitation that afternoon sounded like a command.

Suddenly, images of him commanding her to other things flashed in her mind. Things she had fantasized about the previous night too.

Stop it! He is a client!

She pushed away those inappropriate thoughts about her client from her mind. Taking a deep breath, she smiled. "Enough about my day," she said. "Tell me, how did your final walkthrough go?"

Trupti was happy to talk about her work because she loved her job too.

Anya had met Trupti in the architecture college they attended. They both had a passion for designing homes when most people her age were choosing engineering or medical careers.

Trupti and she became best friend quickly. Anya felt lucky to have a friend who always supported her wholeheartedly, especially after she got divorced. The two of them began their company two months after the divorce and hadn't looked back since.

"So what did you find out about the hot hotel tycoon?"

Anya once again blushed. "Nothing much. He's from New York. He grew up there in a poor neighborhood. He quit school at fourteen and worked in construction with his brother. When he was fourteen, he began flipping homes. And then, he went into the hospitality industry."

Trupti listened with wide eyes. "Wow! That's so impressive."

"I guess so." It was quite impressive, especially because the men in Anya's circle were born with silver spoons and barely had to struggle for anything. They were way too entitled.

"How long is the project going to be?" Trupti asked.

"No idea yet."

She was going to put all her energies and everything possible into the restoration project. She only hoped that the attraction she felt towards Bhargav Varma would be gone soon.

CHAPTER FOUR

"Are you sure, Mr. Varma? You want two of us to attack at the same time?"

Bhargav was in a boxing ring at his personal gym with his trainers. He had changed out of his business suit and wore a t-shirt and track pants. He usually trained in the mornings. But after having spent time at the Vardhaman Estate, he needed an outlet.

"Yes. I'm sure," he replied.

The two men attacked him at the same time. Bhargav easily slipped into his fighter mode. Maintaining his balance, he easily blocked and deflected the blows. Since both his trainers were wearing protective gear under their clothes, he swung around and threw in punches and kicks, letting out his aggression.

His thoughts flew as he fought. He had visited the Vardhaman Estate a few weeks ago as well, but seeing it with Sukanya Kashyap's eyes made him feel things he hadn't felt in a long time. It reminded him of the confusion and hurt he felt as a child when his father had died. The grieving widow and three sons who were suddenly left to fend for themselves with no money.

His older brother had quit school and began working in construction for daily wages. Bhargav had wanted to follow in his brother's footsteps right away, but he had to wait a year until he grew tall enough not to be detected as underage. At fourteen, he was close to six feet. And since he was also on the broader side, he looked older than his age.

Living and working in a bad neighborhood meant being attacked. At first, he had fought back his attackers using his brute strength. But at the age of fifteen, someone took him under their wing and taught him to fight using the right techniques.

He had fought for money as a street fighter. He didn't tell his brothers or mother, but they suspected something was off when he often came back home with bruises. He had even broken his nose during one of the fights. With no healthcare, he hid it for a few days until his mother discovered it and dragged him to a hospital to get it checked.

Soon, he began polishing his technique well enough not to have any visible injuries.

And a few years later, even after he and his brother began a company and made enough money, he didn't stop the fights. He often slipped away during the dark of the night, eager to feel the power of his fists connecting with another's face. It was a high, an addiction which was hard to kick off.

Just like Sukanya Kashyap. It had barely been hours since he had last seen her and spent time in her company, but the restlessness and craving he felt to see her again was hard to control. He never thought he was weak, but his restraint was very weak when it came to her.

Sweat soaked his t-shirt as he continued to deflect the blows and fight with the two trainers. A few punches landed on him, but he didn't care. Ignoring the pain, his mind ran smoothly between finding the rhythm to fight as well as think about the woman who often haunted his thoughts.

The fight stopped nearly three hours later, only because he received a call from his younger brother. They were meeting to discuss the next steps in their plan.

***

It was midnight when Bhargav rang the doorbell to a penthouse.

His older brother answered it. "You are late," he said.

Bhargav shrugged. "Lost track of time with practice."

His brother frowned. Bhargav knew that his older brother didn't like being reminded of the time when Bhargav made money with street fighting. As the oldest brother, Yash Varma took his role of being the protector very seriously. He also hated that Bhargav hadn't listened and quit school to follow in his footsteps to earn money in construction.

"Aryan is on his way," his brother said as they went inside. "Let's sit outside near the bar."

Bhargav nodded, and they walked through a spacious living room. Unlike him, his two brothers preferred ultra-modern décor. They didn't want anything that reminded them of the past. He had been that way too, until he was faced with the truth. And now, he even chose the part of the plan that would throw him face to face with their past.

He recalled Anya's reaction when she had seen the painting called *The River*. It was a risk he took to place it in the living room, knowing she would see it. But the look on her face when she saw it was worth it.

"How was your visit to the estate?" Bhargav's brother asked.

"It was fine. I'm having a meeting on Monday with the architects. The engineering team will fly in next week too."

His brother nodded. "And the sale?"

Bhargav knew his older brother was impatient about how long the sale was taking. It was odd because Yash had taught him patience when it came to business.

But this wasn't business. It was entirely personal.

"The government is still insisting on keeping half of the land. I said it's non-negotiable, and we need all five hundred acres."

Yash frowned. "You think they'll agree to it on time?"

"They will," Bhargav stated. "The bureaucrats already accepted the gifts." The gifts were heavy bribes which the officials eagerly accepted in exchange for their cooperation.

They stepped out of the living room to the outdoor pool area and went to the bar. Bhargav noticed that his brother had been drinking.

"The usual?" Yash asked.

Bhargav nodded.

Just as his brother finished pouring the drink and handed him a glass, the French door to the balcony slid open.

"Stop hacking into my security system, Aryan," Yash scolded their younger brother.

Aryan was a computer whiz who expanded their empire by adding his billion-dollar software company to their corporation.

Aryan grinned. "Your codes are too easy to guess, big bro. You need to change them from Mom's birthday."

Aryan then greeted Bhargav. "Good evening, bro. After spending the day at the estate, I thought you'd spend the night hitting the shit out of your trainers."

"I already did."

Although his younger brother was smirking, Bhargav knew Aryan was affected by how things were proceeding, especially with the estate. Even after discovering the truth four months ago, it was hard for Aryan to digest everything. Aryan hated the estate and their past.

"Beer?" Yash asked Aryan.

"Nope. Need something stronger. I'll have what you two are having."

Yash poured another glass of scotch and dropped a couple of ice cubes into the drink before handing it to Aryan. The three of them met often. No matter how busy their schedules were, they always spent some time together, mostly with their mother. But things changed and would be that way until their plans were executed.

"Congratulations, bro," Aryan said to Yash. "Heard you got yourself engaged. So when is the happy day?"

Yash didn't seem too happy. "I gave two months' time," he replied.

Bhargav had expected his older brother to be coldly indifferent, but it was obvious that something was off. The sudden engagement was also not a part of the plan.

"Did Rajesh Mohan suspect anything?" Bhargav asked.

"No."

Which meant their enemy's greed was stronger than using logic or common sense.

"How did Rajesh Mohan's daughter react to the news?" Bhargav asked.

Yash shrugged. He looked indifferent while talking about the woman he was to marry. "She tried to hint she wasn't ready to marry. But she didn't mention anything about her boyfriend."

Aryan frowned. "According to the investigation, Divya Mohan hasn't met her boyfriend recently, but she is speaking to him quite often. She is also friends with that bastard Girish Shetty's daughter."

Bhargav noticed the frustration in Aryan's voice. His younger brother was having a tough time dealing with his part of the plan, especially Girish Shetty's daughter. Bhargav knew that Yash wasn't having the same problem with the woman he was supposed to marry. The trouble came from Yash's soon-to-be fiancée's sister-in-law.

"What about Rajesh Mohan's daughter-in-law?" Aryan asked, guessing the same.

Yash's expression was closed off. "What about her?"

Aryan frowned. "Would she threaten to tell your future bride about what happened in Milan?"

The first time Yash had deviated from their plan was two months ago when he took a huge risk by meeting one of their pawns directly rather than sending the man they hired. Bhargav noticed that since then, his older brother hadn't been much like himself. There was restlessness inside him rather than cold indifference.

"I think you should be careful with her, bro," Aryan advised.

"I'll take care of her," Yash replied.

The topic veered to the next course of plans and actions. With the sale of the estate almost being finalized and traps being laid out to all their enemies, things were proceeding rapidly.

"What about Ma?" Aryan asked. "Her cruise is going to be over in three weeks."

Their mother was on a three-month cruise when the plan was laid out. Now that she was returning, it would be hard to hide things from her, especially when the three of them were away at the same time.

Yash nodded. "I'll meet Ma when she returns."

"We should increase the security around Ma too," Bhargav suggested. "Just in case a nosy investigator manages to dig up her address or follow her to the school."

Their mother chose to stay independently in a gated senior community where she had many friends. So, it was easier to manage their ruse of the three of them not being in New York for a long period of time.

They decided to add two more security personnel to discreetly guard their mother. She had been teaching for nearly two decades and loved her job. Although all three of her sons were successful and billionaires, she still chose to continue the profession which she loved.

"What about Sukanya Kashyap?" Yash asked.

This time it was Bhargav who had a closed-off expression. "What about her?"

"Does she suspect anything?"

"No." Bhargav knew she didn't trust people easily. She must have begun looking up information about him, but not to the point of hiring a private investigator. She was too passionate about the Vardhaman Estate to think much of anything else.

Unlike him.

His thoughts ran to things other than estate and plans. His thoughts often ran to her.

"Good," said Yash. "I'll drop by the estate this week as well."

They continued to discuss the plans. It was close to four in the morning when they decided to disperse.

"I think all our plans are going smoothly," Yash stated. "Let's not risk it meeting again for a while."

Bhargav agreed.

Aryan didn't look very happy. He shook his head with a sound of disgust. "You both should have listened to my original plan. Bhargav should have gone after Mohan's daughter, and Yash should have tackled the estate. Now Narmada is close to sniffing out the truth, and it won't be long until Anya does too because there will be too many damn clues. Narmada and Anya weren't even supposed to be a part of our damn plans!"

Bhargav knew his younger brother's concern was legitimate. Their meeting at the gambling club hadn't been a part of the plan. But as soon as he discovered that Anya's brother had called her to the place, he risked it all and met her. Not just met her, he even pulled her into their game eventually.

Aryan looked at him. "We know Narmada is dangerous but don't underestimate Anya, bro."

"I can handle her."

Aryan didn't seem too convinced, but he nodded grudgingly.

Bhargav stepped out of the penthouse. Even as he headed back home, his thoughts ran to Anya as usual.

Anya loved the Vardhaman Estate. Her talent, experience and personal bonding to the estate would make her pour her heart into the project. He needed her to be that way. Because when things go wrong—which they would soon—she would be too committed to walk away.

He had seen the passion shining in her eyes as she looked at the place. Her eyes saw beyond what could be seen amidst the dust and cobwebs in the abandoned mansion. It had taken quite a bit of effort to stop himself from pulling her close to see if passion would continue to blaze in her eyes with his kiss.

The attraction between them was a live thing. But along with the attraction, he had seen the fight in her eyes—a fight to keep him at a distance.

A fight she would lose.

CHAPTER FIVE

Anya woke up to the sound of the alarm.

It was Monday morning. Even though she had barely slept the last two nights, she was pumped with energy. She had been working obsessively on the initial design plans for the last twenty-four hours. And when she finally crashed on the bed, expecting to fall asleep, thoughts of her new client stole her sleep.

No. Don't think of him again!

She knew it was impossible not to think of him, especially considering her dreams lately were of him, and her dream job also came with the condition of working with him.

But she hoped he would hand over the project to one of his managers after the initial meetings. That way, she wouldn't have to constantly fight the attraction towards him.

I badly hope he hands over to someone soon.

Anya took a deep breath and pushed away thoughts of Bhargav Varma yet again.

She got ready in record time. Then grabbing a glass of juice as breakfast, she stepped out of her house with her work laptop and printouts of the initial designs.

***

She reached the penthouse building. Bhargav Varma's assistant received her. But this time she was led to a different floor of the building.

"Sir should be here shortly, madam. He had asked you to wait in his office."

Some of the unsettling feelings reduced listening to that. It reminded her that Bhargav Varma was yet another entitled rich man who didn't value other people's time.

But he wasn't always rich and built his hotel empire from scratch.

She frowned at the reminder of why her fascination towards him grew. Pushing away her unruly thoughts about her client, she followed the assistant.

She was led into a spacious office area. There were workstations and closed rooms. They passed by what seemed to be a conference room. Towards the end of the floor was a large office room with a stunning view of the city.

"Sir should be here any minute."

"Thank you," she said and sat on a comfortable leather couch.

Her eyes fell on the clock inside the office room to see the time. She was taken aback when she realized she was early. There were ten more minutes before their meeting was to begin.

Her cheeks heated when she realized that in her eagerness, she hadn't even looked at the time until then.

"Would you like something to drink, madam?"

"Nothing, thank you." She was too excited and nervous to think of food right then.

The assistant nodded and stepped out of the office. Anya's eyes immediately swept over the office room looking for pictures or any personal items that would give her a hint of the man who fascinated her.

She found nothing. It was a beautiful office but coldly impersonal.

Why doesn't he have pictures of his brother or mother?

Maybe he wasn't close to them. Another thought came into her mind that shook her.

Did he have a girlfriend? Was he seeing anyone?

Her heart sank even as a strange hollow feeling filled her stomach.

She scolded herself. It was none of her business if he was dating anyone or was in a relationship. He was her client, and a critically important one. She needed to focus on that fact.

"Miss Kashyap," a deep voice greeted.

Anya jumped at the sudden interruption. For a big man, Bhargav Varma moved very quietly.

"G-good morning, Mr. Varma." She still felt shaken by her thoughts and his presence.

He was wearing a dark three-piece suit, and his hair appeared slightly wet. The subtle scent of his spicy cologne once again filled the air around him and her senses. Her cheeks heated as awareness towards him grew.

He was watching her. His eyes swept over her formal pantsuit and lingered on her lips. She had forgotten to apply lipstick in her hurry. Her lips tingled as his intense gaze fell on them.

Stop it!

But she couldn't stop. Instead, her eyes lingered on his lips. That's when she noticed something. "You are bleeding," she said, staring at the small trickle of blood at the corner of his lips.

His mouth twisted, and he rubbed his thumb against the edge of his lips, wiping away the trickle of blood. "I was distracted."

She was intrigued by his words. *Distracted by whom? And while doing what?*

But she refused to ask him those questions. Instead, she stuck to her job.

Pushing away her inappropriate reaction towards her client, she forced a small polite smile. "I've made a rough template of the initial designs of the rooms I took pictures of."

"I see." His voice turned deeper and huskier as he watched her with hooded eyes.

Her heart began to thump faster as she felt his stare. Once again, the strong pull of attraction crackled around them. She tried to look away, but she was unable to. She felt sucked into the dark intensity of his eyes.

A knock on the door cut through the tension in the room.

"Come in," Bhargav Varma instructed.

A middle-aged woman came in with a food cart. "Good morning," she said cheerfully.

The woman placed the cart in a corner where there was a small round table with two chairs.

"Join me for breakfast, Miss Kashyap," he said. "You can show me the designs while we eat."

Once again, the request to join him for breakfast sounded more like a command. And intimacy of having breakfast together sounded too much.

When she didn't reply, his mouth twisted. "I assure you, it's perfectly safe. Nina is a good cook."

Her cheeks heated. "I already had my breakfast, Mr. Varma," she lied. With the butterflies in her stomach, she could hardly think of food.

"Join me anyway," he ordered.

Feeling cornered since it would look foolish arguing about not joining him, she nodded and followed him as he sat on one of the chairs near the small round table. She took the chair opposite him and brought out the printouts she had taken of the initial designs.

He picked up the papers and looked at them. There was no expression on his face, but his eyes seemed to linger on them for many moments. She then saw his muscle ticking against his jaw.

Anya wondered what he was thinking. Was he upset? Did he like them? She had created those designs based on the original interior décor of the mansion. She was yet to add details.

Meanwhile, the woman named Nina placed two plates in front of them.

Anya smiled at the woman. "Just some coffee for me please," she requested.

Nina nodded cheerfully and poured some steaming, aromatic coffee into a cup before placing it in front of her. Along with cream and sugar, Nina also placed a vast selection of tiny cupcakes and croissants to go with the beverage.

Anya's mouth tingled as she did have a weakness for sweets. But she controlled herself.

She just took a sip of her black coffee and almost choked because it was too strong and bitter. She quickly added a generous amount of cream and sugar to make it palatable before taking the next sip.

Bhargav Varma finally finished looking at the designs. "You are quite good, Miss Kashyap," he said. "I wasn't expecting you to work on them so soon. And what you have done in just one day is quite impressive."

"These are high-level initial designs with the flooring, ceiling and dimensions."

He nodded before digging into what appeared to be a huge protein-rich breakfast. He ate in smooth moves. The long masculine fingers on his big hands moved efficiently. Dragging her eyes away from his hands, she focused on his eyes.

"The initial designs are only of empty rooms," she continued. "Since the furniture and artifacts were sold or stolen, I have suggestions to replicate most of the pieces."

He shrugged. "I don't want replicas. I want the originals."

She was taken aback. "What?"

He passed her the plate with the mini cupcakes. She automatically took one.

He then once again continued to eat his breakfast in smooth movements. "I already have a team working on retrieving most of the furniture and paintings. At least the ones that weren't destroyed in the fire."

Anya was shocked. "I see."

But why go through so much effort for a hotel?

"It's going to cost many times over to have the originals than having the replicas made, Mr. Varma."

"I know. I'm not too worried about the cost."

Anya frowned. "Why?" He was a businessman first. He would obviously look to make a profit.

His intense eyes bored into hers. "The estate and its history interest me, Miss Kashyap. And why settle for the fake when you can possess the genuine ones?"

Anya's heart thudded. Something about his words struck her deeply.

"I see," she said.

There was a brief silence, which was broken when the cheerful middle-aged woman returned. She cleared the plate in front of Bhargav Varma since he was done eating and placed a cup in front of him before pouring steaming coffee.

"Would you like another cup, madam?"

Anya was about to refuse, but Bhargav Varma's eyes caught with hers. "Have another cup, Miss Kashyap."

Anya paused before nodding in agreement. She wanted something to occupy her hands while the man who made her too self-aware sat across from her.

"I've set up a meeting with a few architects next Monday," he said. "Most of them are well-known. I want you to work with them and give them the input."

She nodded.

He handed her a sleek file. "Your contract," he said.

She took it and opened the file. When she saw the initial signing amount, her eyes widened.

Pushing away the shock at the ridiculously high amount, she briefly scanned through the rest of the contract. It would take some time to read through it.

"I'm flying out of the city in an hour to meet with the estate sale agents and should be back by six," he said. "Let's discuss the details or any questions you have during dinner. I'll pick you up at seven tonight."

Her heart leaped. "I-I have some pending work in the office that I need to finish tonight, Mr. Varma," she lied again. "But I can come back tomorrow morning."

His dark eyes flashed at her obvious lie. "I'm flying to Singapore tomorrow morning and will be back over the weekend."

Disappointment filled her. But she knew he had hotel chains spread worldwide that he needed to run.

"While I'm away," he continued. "I want you to read the contract in detail, especially the confidentiality and exclusivity terms. You can't discuss the details of the project with anyone else, and you also can't work with other clients while you are working for me."

A slight shiver racked her body. Although the terms were common enough for many high-profile projects, the words sounded ominous coming from Bhargav Varma's mouth.

"With the scale of the project, I would not be accepting new clients, Mr. Varma. In fact, I would be bringing in most of my team to work exclusively on the Vardhaman project."

"Good."

There was a heavy silence which increased the awareness again. Anya dragged her eyes away from him and looked at her coffee cup. She was done with her second cup of coffee. She also realized that in her nervousness, she even ate quite a few of the tiny muffins.

Her cheeks heated. The man was definitely not good for her health. He made her lose her mind.

"Thank you for the breakfast, Mr.Varma," she said. "Please thank Nina too. I will go through the contract and send the signed copy to your company email."

He didn't say anything.

"I should leave," she said, getting up from her chair. "All the best for the meeting with the estate agent. I hope the sale will be finalized soon. I'm looking forward to working on the Vardhaman project."

His mouth twisted at her overly formal tone. "I am looking forward to it too, Miss Kashyap."

Her heart thudded. Once again, the simple words coming from his mouth sounded ominous. She felt as though she were a fly who had willingly agreed to go into the spider's web.

Leaving the initial design printouts with him, she picked up her laptop. And then, she more or less ran out of his office room.

CHAPTER SIX

"Holy shit! This is your signing amount?"

Anya was still shocked by the amount. She was glad her friend was too.

"*Our* signing amount," Anya corrected. "Our entire team will most likely be working on the project during the coming months."

Trupti looked excited. "My God! I'm so excited for us! This is huge, Anya."

Anya smiled. "Yes, it is. But I still need to read through the contract just to make sure I'm not being asked to sign away my soul."

Even though she was joking, the feeling of being led into some sort of trap didn't entirely disappear.

"Don't be silly!" Trupti scolded. "This is what you have always dreamed about and worked hard for! You deserve this project and opportunity. And I'm sure you'll do an awesome job."

Anya relaxed slightly. It was silly to feel Bhargav Varma was out to get her for something. The man was a billionaire who was purchasing the Vardhaman Estate for his next hotel. All he wanted were her design skills.

She smiled at Trupti. "Thanks for the confidence. The first meeting with the other architects is next week. So, I'm going to be wrapping up my pending projects and do a hand over."

She only had two projects which luckily were at the tail end and could be easily managed by her team. She would be there for the handover.

"Let's celebrate tonight!" Trupti was excited.

Anya laughed. "It's Monday. And I still have a bunch of invoices to send. I also have to stop by the Pathaks and Mrs. Jain to check on the final touchups. There are two or three prospective clients I need to call and divert them to our other partnering firms."

Trupti waved her hand dismissively. "I can help with the invoices, and the other two should be done by evening."

Anya smiled. "All right. Let's celebrate. We can pick up a bottle of wine and order food from a good takeout—"

Trupti cut her off and shook her head. "No way! Let's celebrate properly. Let's go out to a club!"

Anya's heart jerked listening to the word 'club'. But she reminded herself that the clubs Trupti and she visited were bar lounges and nightclubs. Far from the slightly depraved gambling dens.

"Fine," she said, even though she'd rather catch up on her sleep. But seeing the excitement on Trupti's face, it rubbed off on her.

Putting aside the contract to read it carefully later, she continued with her task list.

She was excited to celebrate the biggest project of her lifetime later that night too.

CHAPTER SEVEN

"I'm sorry, Mr. Varma. We cannot sell the fifty acres. You already have four hundred and fifty acres along with the mansion. You should let go of the other fifty."

Bhargav was at a meeting with the estate agents, his lawyers and some mid-level bureaucrats.

"I want all five hundred acres," he stated.

"But Mr. Varma, like we said, those fifty acres are in litigation. Mr. Sampath is a powerful politician, and he wants to expand his factory area into those fifty acres."

"I want that factory shut down."

There were shocked looks on the men's faces.

"That's impossible, Mr. Varma."

Bhargav raised an eyebrow, knowing it was quite possible for him.

"The factory pollutes the surrounding agricultural lands," he stated. "It shouldn't have been permitted in the first place."

One of the men nodded. "That is true, Mr. Varma. Many farmers held protests over the years, but Mr. Sampath used his political influence to continue running the factory. The farmers were forced to abandon their lands eventually. Most of them are now workers in that factory even though they hate it."

"The factory is going to shut down in a month. Let those farmers know they can return to farming in a month."

There were shocked murmurs. "How, Mr. Varma?"

Bhargav raised his chin in a nod to his assistant who then placed a bag on the table. The men's faces lit up, knowing what was in the bag.

"The factory gets water from the river that passes through the estate. I want the main pipe cut off and the river water diverted."

There were gasps.

"B-but won't Mr. Sampath come after you?" one of the bureaucrats asked.

Bhargav's mouth twisted. "Let me worry about that."

He had dealt with many corrupt politicians all over the world. He knew how to tackle them. If bribe money didn't work, intimidation by dishing up dirt always worked. He already had enough dirt dug up on the politician who had illegally occupied a part of the estate land and the surrounding lands.

He slid his sunglasses on and got up. "All right, gentlemen. Get the papers drawn. Have the sale deed finalized for the pending fifty acres by next month. We'll be starting the work around the mansion next week."

He walked out of the meeting, leaving his lawyers to finish the paperwork.

His assistant followed him outside. "Sir, the old gentleman you wanted to hire as the head gardener is on his way to the mansion."

Bhargav nodded. "Let's go there."

For the rest of the day, Bhargav spent time at the estate, handling things that needed his presence. By the time he flew back to the city, it was later than he had expected.

His mouth twisted into a small smile thinking about Sukanya Kashyap. He wondered what she would do if he caught her in the lie of being busy that night and turning down his dinner invitation.

He called his assistant. "Ravi, I'd like you to make reservations for tonight."

CHAPTER EIGHT

"I'm so glad you talked me into celebrating tonight." Anya's voice was slightly slurred.

Trupti giggled. "I'm glad too. I've never seen you like this before."

Anya smiled widely. It was only her first drink, but combined with the lack of sleep for two continuous days, the single drink hit her like a punch. Luckily, they had taken the taxi like they always did when they visited a club or attended client parties where alcohol was served.

"I want to celebrate," she continued. "But I also want to forget Mr. Wicked so I can sleep better tonight."

Trupti was amused. "Mr. Wicked? I'm assuming you are referring to your scorching hot client, Mr. Varma."

Anya nodded before taking another long sip of the delicious drink.

"Why Mr. Wicked, though?" Trupti asked. "Is it because he makes you think wicked thoughts?"

Anya's cheeks heated as her friend guessed the reason correctly. "Yeah, but also because he scares me."

Her friend frowned. "What do you mean by scares you? What did he do?"

Anya shook her head. "He didn't do anything. It's just that he makes me feel so..." She didn't know how to finish the sentence.

He made her feel conflicted. She was strongly attracted to him and felt a connection that she had never felt before towards any man. It was odd, and it terrified her.

"Hmm... I think you are falling for the hot client."

Her heart jerked at Trupti's words. "I only met him properly twice! How can I be falling for him?"

Trupti latched on to her words. "What do you mean by properly? When did you meet him improperly before?"

Anya's cheeks heated.

"My God! You met him sometime before too! Tell me when!" Trupti demanded.

Maybe it was the drink or simply because she needed to tell her secret to her friend. "I met him two months ago at the club when I went to drop off the papers to my brother."

Trupti's eyes widened. "The gambling club?"

Anya nodded.

"Holy shit! No wonder you seemed distracted after meeting him again. What exactly happened in that club?"

Anya blushed. "Nothing. He just rescued me from a drunken man. We barely interacted."

And yet, the spicy scent of his cologne continued to fill her senses along with the feel of his hard chest and the impact of his darkly handsome face. And then there were forbidden thoughts she had of him, and forbidden things she did while holding his shirt button.

"Ooh. This is so exciting! Now that you will get to work with him for at least one year, I'm sure there will be something more for sure."

Anya shook her head. "There can't be more. He's a client now."

"So what?" Trupti demanded. "We don't have a rule not to date clients."

A couple of Trupti's ex-boyfriends had been their clients. Anya didn't have a problem with it.

"Has he asked you out?" Trupti asked. When Anya blushed, Trupti clapped excitedly. "Oh my God!"

"Those invitations were for discussing business."

But his hooded eyes made it obvious they weren't entirely business-related.

"That's it!" Trupti more or less shouted. "The next time he asks you out for dinner, you better accept it!"

Anya shook her head. "I don't think I can."

Trupti made a noise of frustration. "Why not? It's not like you have to marry him or even have a relationship with him. If you enjoy his company, simply enjoy it and see where it goes."

Anya was taken aback. After her very brief marriage, she was busy building her business to prove to her parents that she can live her life on her terms. She hadn't given much thought to dating or relationships. She had always felt content with what she had.

Until she met Bhargav Varma.

After meeting him, a strange restlessness had taken over her. She felt as though a part of her was missing. And when she met him again in the penthouse, she gravitated towards him as though he were the missing part.

That's what terrified her the most—the strange, imagined connection.

She knew it was all in her imagination. Things like feeling connected to a complete stranger did not occur in real life.

"Yeah, maybe I should just kiss Mr. Wicked. It'll prove that the attraction was just hyped up in my head."

Trupti's eyes widened. "Bhargav Varma."

Anya laughed. "Yeah, Bhargav Varma. Mr. Wicked or maybe I should call him Mr. Bossy because he always commands rather than requests. *Have breakfast with me, Miss Kashyap. I'll pick you up at seven for dinner tonight, Miss Kashyap.*" She imitated his deep, commanding voice.

Trupti's eyes continued to remain wide. Anya squinted at her friend's odd expression. "What?"

Anya then realized that her friend wasn't looking at her. Trupti was looking at something behind her. Even through her drunken haze, Anya belatedly felt the prickling sensation behind her neck.

"I prefer being called Mr. Wicked rather than Mr. Bossy, Miss Kashyap," a familiar deep voice said from behind her.

Anya slowly turned around until her eyes clashed with dark, intense eyes that belonged to her client who she had just been imitating.

***

Anya stared at the darkly handsome face for a few moments. Then blinking rapidly, she frowned. "Am I dreaming of you again?" she asked, her voice slurring slightly.

His mouth twisted in amusement. "Again?"

Oh shit!

She knew she wasn't dreaming. The man in front of her was real. And he also heard her calling him Mr. Wicked and Mr. Bossy and imitating him. And he also caught her red-handed in the lie of being busy with work that night. Her entire face heated in embarrassment. Trupti's loud clearing of her throat cut through the haze. Anya dragged her eyes away from her client's intense gaze and looked at her friend who was watching him with a mix of awe and curiosity.

"Mr. Wicked... I mean... Mr. Varma is our new client," Anya hurriedly told Trupti, even though her friend knew it already. With her face still burning, Anya turned to him. "Mr. Varma, this is Trupti Gupta, my business partner and friend."

There was a look on amusement on Bhargav Varma's face as he nodded with a small smile. "I heard your specialty is designing penthouses, Miss Gupta," he said. "On our first meeting, Miss Kashyap had given me an ultimatum to either avail your services or to find a different company."

Oh God!

She recalled saying that to him. She had been too shocked and shaken to see him at the time.

Trupti laughed. "I heard a lot about you too, Mr. Varma. And I also heard that wasn't the first time you and Anya met."

Anya's face blazed at her friend's words.

Bhargav Varma's eyes hooded slightly. "Yes, it wasn't our first time."

Anya's heart thudded as their gazes locked for a few moments.

"Are you here alone, Mr. Varma?" Trupti's voice cut through the staring.

Anya blinked, and then she frowned slightly.

How did he know I was here? Was it a coincidence again?

Once again, she felt as though she was being led deliberately into a trap.

"I'm here with someone," he said, raising his chin slightly to point at a table. "I just came by to say hello when I saw Miss Kashyap."

Anya slowly turned to see who he had replaced her with for the dinner invitation. When she saw a beautiful, elegant woman, disappointment hit her hard. He was on a date.

Then why the hell does he still look at me that way? Maybe he looks at all women that way.

But he wasn't looking at Trupti with hooded eyes. He appeared polite and distant. Anya sucked in a deep breath not knowing what to think or feel.

His mouth twisted into a small smile while his eyes continued to remain hooded as he watched her. "I'll see you next week, Miss Kashyap. Enjoy your... work tonight."

Her cheeks heated when he called out her lie to turn down his dinner invitation for that night.

Before she could say anything, he nodded at Trupti and joined his date, leaving her confused once again.

CHAPTER NINE

The rest of the week went by in a blur of catching up with paperwork and handovers.

"The cottage looks very cozy and inviting, Anya. Thank you so much."

Anya smiled at her client. "You are welcome, Mrs. Jain. You have a beautiful cottage."

The older woman looked excited. "I can't wait to invite my grandchildren here. They would have so much space to play and you did a wonderful job with the playroom."

Anya had enjoyed working on the project, mostly because of the older woman's enthusiasm and excitement. The theme of the décor was low-key elegance along with the practical aspect of having children visiting often.

"Please drop by anytime you wish," the woman invited.

"I will, Mrs. Jain."

Thanking the woman and getting the final sign-off, Anya headed back to her office. She had way too much work pending before she could begin focusing only on the Vardhaman project for the next year.

Her heart leaped at the reminder that she would be working for Bhargav Varma for that long. Despite trying not to, the man distracted her and occupied her thoughts way too often. Even though she knew he was dating other women and was most likely a playboy, her mind refused to stop thinking about him.

Stop distracting me!

Feeling foolish that she was talking to the man inside her head, she sighed out loud and continued to head to her office.

It was a little before lunchtime. Since it was Friday afternoon, she wanted to order lunch for her team. She hadn't yet announced to any of them regarding the Vardhaman project. She was waiting until she finished signing the contract.

But she still wanted to throw a mini celebratory treat for landing the project.

She parked her car behind the office building and went in using the back entrance which was closer to her office room. But just as she neared her work area, she could hear Trupti's upset voice.

"She doesn't want to speak to you!" Trupti yelled at someone. "How many times should she make that clear?"

Frowning, she hurried inside. She could see finally Trupti's angry red face. A man stood in front of Trupti. Anya could only see his back. He was wearing a designer t-shirt and jeans and was of medium height.

Suddenly, Anya felt her skin crawling as her steps faltered slightly as she neared her office room. Trupti saw her first but didn't call her out.

It was Anya who had to take a deep breath and speak out. "What are you doing here, Surya?"

At her question, the man turned back and looked at her. The smile he had on his face made her skin crawl even more.

"Hello, darling. Can't a man visit his wife?"

***

Anya looked at Trupti, who glared as if she wanted to slap Surya. Fortunately for Surya, Anya didn't feel the same. He didn't invoke any strong emotions in her, apart from disgust. She had been indifferent to him even during the brief period they were married.

"I'm not your wife anymore, Surya," she reminded him for the hundredth time. "We got divorced five years ago."

Surya's face tightened in anger at her indifferent tone. "I only divorced you because you wanted to try out some kind of career for a while. You already wasted enough time. You are not getting any younger, and I want children."

Her disgust grew, and she nearly wanted to throw up.

Trupti was outraged. "How dare you! Get out of here before I call security."

Anya agreed with her friend. "You should leave now, Surya. I already told you enough times I'm not interested."

He looked furious, but there was a strange, creepy victorious look on his face. "Oh. You will be interested when I tell you that your family is going to be on the streets soon."

Anya frowned at his dramatic words. "What?"

"Your father is desperate for money. He is on the verge of losing it all."

Anya recalled her mother telling her about the financial crisis they were having. But her mother hadn't given her any details. Her parents always kept their investments hidden from her. They only shared it with her brother.

"I don't see how my parents' financial situation is related to me."

His eyes narrowed. "I can save your family from this situation."

Her heart jerked sickly when she understood where he was going. When he saw her face, his creepy smile got wider. "I'm sure you can now see things clearly."

Trupti was once again outraged. "You are the last man she would ever be with. She already has someone."

Surya's head whipped as he glared at Trupti. "What the hell are you talking about?"

Anya stared at her friend, wondering what story Trupti was spinning.

Trupti had a satisfied smile on her face. "Anya has a boyfriend."

Surya looked furious. "You are lying," he hissed out. "There is no way she is seeing a man. She hasn't been with anyone since the divorce. What is this imaginary man's name?" he demanded.

Trupti smirked. "His name is Bhargav Varma, a billionaire hotelier who is richer than you several hundred times over."

Anya was shocked. Her heart thudded as she had no idea how to react.

Surya shook his head. "I still don't believe you. She doesn't ever date!"

"Anya met her handsome boyfriend in a club. It was love at first sight. Unlike with you, she is not forced into being with him. She chose him out of her heart... and of course his scorching hot looks and body."

Anya blushed at her friend's words. Although Trupti was lying, most of her words were still the truth.

Surya turned to Anya. Seeing her blush, his face turned red with fury. "You bitch! You are cheating on me with some bastard!"

Anya was now annoyed. "Stop using that language on me," she said icily. "I am not cheating on you because we are not together. And you, of all people, shouldn't accuse someone of cheating."

His face turned a darker shade of red. "I told you those women were just cheap lays! You wanted us to wait to have sex. What the hell was I supposed to do!"

"You were supposed to wait until we got to know each other better," Anya replied. She shook her head. "Frankly, I don't care what you do now. Just leave me alone."

Two security guards showed up right then.

"Is there a problem, madam?" one of them asked.

"Yes," Trupti said with a smile. "This man has a problem finding his way out of the office. Please escort him out."

Surya burst out angrily. "I'll see how you won't agree to marry me! Very soon, you'll be begging me marry you."

"Not even in your dreams, buddy," Trupti taunted. "Get lost now!"

He glared at Trupti and then at Anya before he walked away with a huff. The security guards followed him out.

"God, that man is so hard to get rid of!" Trupti huffed out a sound of disgust. "Why does he keep stalking you?"

Anya sighed. "His ego was hurt that I divorced him."

Trupti shook her head. "I think his ego was more hurt that you didn't sleep with him when he seduced half the women in town. The slimy bastard thinks you owe it to him!"

Anya knew that too. "Forget about him," she said. "I was planning to treat the team for lunch. Let's order something special. How about Thai food?"

Trupti grinned. "Oh yeah! A little pre-celebration for getting the contract with your boyfriend?"

Anya blushed and whacked her friend playfully. "Stop it! Someone might hear and think it's true."

Trupti laughed. "Oh. I somehow feel it will be true soon."

Shaking her head at her friend's outrageous remark, Anya went on with the rest of the day as planned. And as usual, her so-called imaginary boyfriend with dark, intense eyes and his imperfectly perfect face haunted her thoughts often.

Stop distracting me!

CHAPTER TEN

The sound of the phone ringing was loud.

Anya groaned and wanted to ignore it. It was Saturday, and she wanted to sleep in. After a long while, she had just begun to catch up with a good night's sleep.

The phone continued to ring.

Hoping it was a short call, she reached for it. But when she saw the number flashing, she groaned again.

"Hello, Ma," she answered in a croaky voice.

"Anya, the auction is tonight!" her mother more or less shouted into the phone. "I hope you are on your way to the spa appointment."

Anya winced. She had forgotten about the spa appointment.

"What time, Ma?"

There was an annoyed shriek. "Sukanya Kashyap! Get up right now and go! The appointment is in a half-hour. The place will be packed because everyone will be preparing to get ready for the auction tonight. Go right now!"

Anya groaned inside. The place would be packed because most of the rich elite would want to be seen at the charity event.

"All right, Ma. I'm going. I'll see you this evening."

"Go! And I'll call you again to check when you are done."

Anya ended the call, knowing her mother would also call a few more times to check until she reached the event's venue that evening.

She groaned again. This time loudly.

She called her friend's phone and Trupti answered within a couple of rings. And she sounded bright and fresh, unlike her groggy and drowsy self.

"Hello, my dear partner. What's up?"

"I have a spa appointment this morning. Do you want to join me?"

There was laughter. "Sorry, my friend. I would have loved to join you, but I'm spending the weekend with Rishab." Rishab was the guy Trupti was currently dating.

Anya sighed. "Have fun and say hello to Rishab from my side. God, I can't wait for this weekend to be over."

There was an amused chuckle. "Oh. Is it because you can't wait to see Mr. Wicked again?"

Anya blushed. "Stop it!" she scolded her friend.

"Yeah, yeah. Deny it all you want, but it's obvious you like him."

"Have a great weekend with Rishab!" Anya hurriedly said. "Bye!"

She could hear her friend's laughter before she ended the call.

Anya shook her head.

He is only a client. Nothing more.

She repeated it in her head until her mind and body understood that fact.

***

"Anya! Everyone is here already! Where are you?"

Anya could hear the noise from a large crowd in the background.

"I'm ten minutes away from the place, Ma."

Anya was driving to the event location in her uncomfortable dress. The heavily embroidered, dark royal blue dress had a narrow waist with a dramatic puff. Her high heels didn't help with the driving either.

"All right. Come soon!" her mother scolded before ending the call.

Anya sighed once again, wondering why she couldn't just donate to the cause rather than attend a fancy dinner party when she had so much pending work to do.

The auction was just a ruse. The items put up for auction were mostly for vacations in exotic places around the world. She didn't mind donating to the cause, but she didn't have the interest or the time to make use of any exotic vacations.

Unless the Vardhaman Estate would be ready to be occupied.

Her heart ached in longing to be able to stay in the mansion. The memories she had of the place were bittersweet.

Soon, I'm going to help bring back the mansion to its former glory.

It might not belong to her, but she was determined to put everything she had in restoring the mansion. She wouldn't just put in her time and effort, she would pour her heart and soul into it.

"Good evening, madam," a uniformed valet received her as she pulled into the venue.

Smiling, she got out of her car and handed the man her car keys. "Thank you," she said.

Her smile widened, seeing how her small car stood out like a sore thumb among the sleek high-end cars. Her mother hated the car and had demanded many times that she change it. But Anya stood by her tiny car as it was practical in the city to navigate narrow streets and heavy traffic.

A doorman greeted her with a smile. Smiling back at him, she took the itinerary card he handed to her. Usually, there were a few musical recitals, but most of those were from the children of the rich and elite. Some of them were genuinely talented, but the rest weren't.

Hoping she could miss the recitals, she went directly to the main hall.

"Anya!" her mother spotted her right away. "What took you so long? You missed a few recitals."

"Sorry, Ma. Traffic."

Her mother waved away her explanation. "Come on. Let's meet everyone. They have been asking for you."

Anya let her mother lead her around a sea of glittering diamonds and the expensive yet overwhelming smell of perfume. Pasting a polite smile on her face, Anya greeted the people. She recognized most of them because her parents socialized a lot and formed many connections over the last fifteen years. Most of the social gatherings, including the current event, were purely to make influential connections.

"Hello, darling," a woman greeted. "My friend, who is the chief minister's niece is looking for an architect. But I think she wants someone more... high-end."

Anya widened her fake smile. "I'll be sure to pass on the suggestion to more high-end architects."

Anya's mother's grip on her arm increased. Ignoring the pain, Anya continued to greet. Some people were genuinely polite and affectionate, and some weren't.

"We were at the Voras' home last week. What an amazing job you've done, Anya."

"Thank you, Mr. and Mrs. Tripathi." This time Anya's smile was genuine.

There was also conversation about the Vardhaman Estate.

"Have you heard?" a woman asked Anya's mother. "There are talks that an international buyer is planning to purchase the Vardhaman Estate."

Anya's mother shook her head dismissively. "It must be a rumor. The estate is under government control. And besides, who would want to put their money into a crumbling mansion?"

Anya didn't react to the conversation. But she did look forward to her parents seeing the mansion once it was fully restored.

She kept her face blank and pasted a small smile.

The introductions went on for close to thirty minutes. Although the venue was packed, the well-landscaped garden area outside didn't have a lot of people. Anya wanted to step out for some fresh air.

"Surya and his family are here too," her mother said to her. "They are in the auction hall. Let's go there."

Anya was determined to put off the meeting until much later. "I just got here, Ma. Let me grab something to drink, and I'll join you in a while."

Anya's mother's eyes narrowed in suspicion. "All right. Come back soon. I'll let Surya know you are here."

The last thing she wanted to do was face that man. His presence would churn her stomach, especially after the previous day's confrontation.

She headed outside hurriedly towards the manicured garden. She did grab some water first near the beginning of the lawn. And then, she went towards the back. She nearly broke into a run. Just when she was about to cross the lawn area and disappear into the dimly-lit trees, her high heel caught over something, and she tripped.

Shit!

She was sure she was going to fall. She only hoped she didn't sprain her ankle or get hurt badly before her upcoming critical week.

She braced herself for the ground to come crashing when something hard wrapped around her waist and pulled her up. She then crashed into a hard chest instead. The man's spicy expensive cologne filled her senses immediately.

"Thank you so much. I wasn't looking. I was—" She broke off in a gasp when she saw who her rescuer was. Again.

"B-bhargav? I-I... mean, Mr. Varma, what are you doing here?"

The lighting wasn't bright, but it was just enough to see his face clearly. His mouth twisted into a familiar dry smile. "I was invited to the event, Anya... I mean, Miss Kashyap."

Anya's cheeks heated at his deliberate teasing. Her name sounded sinful coming from his mouth, making a burst of heat flare deep inside her stomach. Some of her heated fantasies featuring him flashed through her mind.

Stop it! He's a client!

But he's a client you often fantasize about. What's the harm if he doesn't know?

Her cheeks heated even more as more graphic fantasies flashed into her mind. Her heart began to beat unevenly, seeing his darkly handsome face after nearly a week.

She was about to take a step away from him and make a polite excuse to escape from his magnetic presence when she heard someone calling her name.

"Anya!" It was her ex-husband.

Dammit.

She had forgotten why she had been running away in the first place. She had wanted to escape her ex-husband. But now, not only would Surya catch up to her, but Bhargav Varma might witness the drama between her and Surya.

Suddenly, an idea struck her.

It would sound silly, but it was the only thing she could think of right then.

She placed her slightly trembling palms on Bhargav Varma's hard chest. "Mr. Varma," she whispered hurriedly. "I'm sorry to put you in a situation. But I need an urgent favor from you."

Bhargav Varma didn't react to her touching him. He only raised a masculine brow.

She forged on hurriedly. "My ex-husband is following me," she said while Surya's voice got closer. "I don't want to talk to him. Can you... pretend to be my... boyfriend?" she asked.

Her face was on fire. She was touching her client and asking him to pretend to be her boyfriend. It was hardly professional, but she had no other choice.

Bhargav Varma didn't seem surprised or annoyed by her request. His mouth twisted into a small smile, and he shrugged. "Sure, Miss Kashyap."

"Thank you, Mr. Varm—" She broke off in a gasp when his slightly roughened warm fingers moved from her waist and wrapped around her neck.

Before she could figure out what he was trying to do, he bent his head and captured her mouth with his.

Anya's mind turned completely blank, and there was a roaring noise in her ears as blood rushed into her head. All thoughts shut down, and all she could do was feel.

She felt as though she was caught up in a raging storm with no shelter in sight. She was instantly blown away.

It wasn't a sweet kiss. She somehow knew it wouldn't be. His heated mouth possessed hers, taking everything and demanding even more. His rough fingers tilted her head, holding her at an angle where she had no choice but to give in to the passion. His tongue conquered.

A low moan escaped her throat at the intense pleasure she felt with his invasion.

His fingers tightened, and he dragged her even closer until her chest rubbed against his hard chest. She felt the heat of his body even through the several layers of their clothes. Her nipples tightened under her dress and her stomach fluttered hard while her legs shook beneath her.

She clutched his suit jacket for support.

The kiss went on and on, and she never wanted it to end. She was consumed by him. The taste of him was warm, rich and completely addicting. She rubbed her tongue against his, drawing out his rich, warm taste even more.

He let out a deep masculine groan that vibrated against her chest. But the next moment, his mouth pulled away from hers.

At the sudden loss of his heat and taste, she slowly blinked open her eyes. Their gazes clashed. His fingers still held the back of her neck, and he was watching her with hooded eyes while she stared up at him in a daze. They were both breathing heavily

She didn't know how long they stared at each other, but sudden loud music from inside the event hall jerked her back to her senses. Slowly, her eyes widened as she realized what just happened.

"We kissed," she said in a whisper.

His mouth twisted into a smile. "Yes, we did."

Her cheeks heated at his obvious tone. "But we can't kiss," she said.

"Why not?"

"You... you are my client. And I... I... am not supposed to touch or think of you like..." She couldn't finish her sentence.

His eyes remained hooded as he watched her with a slightly amused smile. "I thought you asked me to pretend to be your boyfriend, Miss Kashyap. Your ex-husband seems to have believed it. He left."

Anya stared at him and had to blink a couple of times to recall what had happened moments before their kiss. Surya had come looking for her outside, and she had begged Bhargav Varma to pretend to be her boyfriend.

And he complied.

Her blazing cheeks heated even more. "I didn't mean for us to kiss! I just meant for you to *pretend* to be my boyfriend."

His mouth twisted more. "A boyfriend kisses his girlfriend, Miss Kashyap."

She didn't know what to say. Her mind and body were in turmoil. Her body was heated from his proximity and their kiss. Unconsciously, she leaned against him, wanting to feel his hard chest against hers again.

Oh God! What am I doing!

Immediately, she dropped her hands from his hard chest and took a step away from him. He released the grip around her neck and let her go.

"I... I... need to go," she stammered, feeling completely at a loss. "My parents are inside."

She turned away from him and began walking. She knew she was coming off as strange by more or less running away, but she needed her mind and senses to be back again.

Her lips tingled and felt swollen. Her stomach wouldn't stop fluttering, and there was a dull throbbing in between her legs deep inside her core. The kind she had felt over the last two months when she held his shirt button and fantasized about him.

Oh God!

Placing her hands on her blazing cheeks, she hurried into the event hall. She didn't know where to go. She simply needed the safety of the crowd, so she didn't make a complete fool of herself by throwing herself at her client again.

"Anya!"

It was her mother.

"Where did you go for so long?" her mother demanded. And then, she frowned. "What happened to your lips? They look red and swollen"

Anya hoped her cheeks weren't visibly flushed. "I think I had a slight allergic reaction to my lipstick. I just wiped it away with cold water."

Her mother shook her head. "That's why you should invest in good makeup. Buy some expensive brand."

Anya's lipstick was a decent brand made of organic products. That night she had applied a strawberry-flavored lipstick.

Bhargav Varma must have tasted it during their heated passionate kiss.

Oh God.

She didn't know how she was going to face him again.

"Come on, let's go," her mother said. "The auction is starting."

Anya followed her mother blindly.

The auction was just about to begin, and people were preparing to bid on the exotic vacations. Anya was only half-listening and barely focusing on what was happening around her. All her thoughts were on the kiss.

Her body was still humming in an excited yet unfulfilled buzz. She slowly and subtly began to look around the hall for a tall man with broad shoulders and a darkly handsome face. She couldn't see him anywhere.

She was half-relieved he hadn't followed her inside.

She wasn't ready to face him yet.

Just as the rules for the auction were beginning to be announced, she heard her mother greeting in an exaggeratedly exciting way.

"Hello, Surya! Come join us."

Cringing, Anya turned to see her ex-husband and his family. She greeted his parents politely and ignored Surya's glare.

"You should bid for a Switzerland vacation, Surya," Anya's mother suggested. "It's a beautiful place this time of the year."

Anya wasn't surprised by her mother's not-so-subtle hint. But this time, she didn't bother saying anything. Neither did Surya.

Anya's mother looked somewhat puzzled at Surya's silence. He had always leered possessively at Anya and spoke as though they were still married, or it was only a matter of time until they remarried.

This time Surya glared at her with rage.

Thanks to the mind-numbingly passionate kiss he witnessed a while ago, he really believed she had a boyfriend.

Knowing him, he would be too proud to mention she had a boyfriend to either her parents or his.

Thankfully, the auction bidding finally began. The next few minutes were a blur as bidding continued.

Anya excused herself. "I need to drop my check," she said.

She went towards the entrance of the room and placed her check into one of the drop boxes. She didn't write any destination name on the auction slip.

Hovering a few more moments near the entrance, she wondered whether to go back and join her parents or step out. Biting her bottom lip, she decided to step out.

She wanted to speak with Bhargav Varma. It was silly of her to have run away without an explanation. Half hoping he had left and half hoping he was still there, she stepped out into the manicured garden.

She didn't have to search for long. He was standing outside the building but away from the crowd. This time, he wasn't alone.

He was talking to a beautiful woman. Anya recognized the woman—it was the same woman he was with at the restaurant bar.

A sharp, piercing ache poked into her heart followed by anger.

How dare he kiss me when he is dating another woman!

She latched onto that fact.

She hated men who cheated. She had been briefly married to one. But even though she and Bhargav Varma had no relationship, she still considered him to be cheating on that woman.

Sharp disappointment hit her along with anger. She had thought him to be different because he was a self-made man and was restoring the Vardhaman Estate without spoiling its original beauty for profits.

But he turned out to be yet another rich playboy like her husband, who thought women were only to be used for lust without any emotional connection or fidelity.

As though sensing her glare, he looked up, and their eyes clashed.

"Miss Kashyap, come here," his deep voice commanded.

She wanted to ignore his order. But since she wanted to work on the Vardhaman project and he was her client, she went to him.

The beautiful woman who was his date looked at her with a smile. The smile appeared genuine and sweet, which only made Anya more furious that Bhargav Varma was cheating on such a nice woman. And even if the woman were rude or obnoxious, it would still be damn wrong.

"Ritu, this is Sukanya Kashyap. The lead architect for the Vardhaman project."

The woman's smile widened. "Hello, Anya. You must be quite excited."

Despite her personal feelings towards her client, Anya slowly smiled back. "Yes, I am very excited."

Bhargav Varma's eyes hooded as he watched her. And then, his gaze dropped to her reddened lips.

Anya hated that her lips began tingling again. Feeling angry, she pressed them together.

There was a small flash of amusement in his eyes. "Miss Kashyap, this is Ritu Kapadia. She will be helping with the repurchase of antiques for the mansion. I showed her the drawings and photos you had given me."

Ritu Kapadia smiled. "Oh yeah. Bhargav showed them to me on Friday. Coincidentally, we saw you at the place during our dinner meeting. But you were having fun with your friend, and we didn't want to pull you away for work on a Friday evening."

Anya was stunned.

She had not expected the woman to be a part of the Vardhaman project. Before she could say anything, they were joined by a grinning man.

"Darling, I won us a trip to Paris," the man said.

Ritu Kapadia laughed in delight. "I'm so glad. I was hoping you would."

The man slid his arm around the woman.

"Keshav, this is Anya Kashyap. She is the lead architect of the Vardhaman project."

The man's eyes crinkled in laughter. "Nice to meet you, Anya. You must be quite excited too. My wife wouldn't stop talking about the project over the last month."

Anya felt the tight knot of anger and disappointment inside her stomach beginning to disappear. She smiled, and this time, it wasn't strained.

"Thank you. Yes, it is an exciting opportunity," she said.

Bhargav Varma hadn't been on a date with Ritu Kapadia. They were at a business meeting on Friday night.

Anya turned to him. Her stomach fluttered when their eyes met while he continued to watch with hooded eyes as though gauging her reaction.

Anya tried not to let her relief about him not dating anyone show on her face.

"Why don't we go inside?" Ritu suggested. "I have a feeling most of our antiques purchased would be from the crowd inside."

Dragging her eyes away from Bhargav Varma's hypnotic gaze, Anya nodded at Ritu. "My family has quite a few pieces as well."

There was excitement along with a flash of curiosity in Ritu Kapadia's eyes. "Oh, yes! Bhargav had mentioned the connection. I hope I can convince your parents to sell a few pieces."

Anya smiled but didn't say anything.

She wasn't sure if her parents would sell those pieces. It wasn't due to sentimental value, but more of prestige for them to have something from the Vardhaman mansion.

"Good luck with the negotiation," Bhargav Varma's deep voice rumbled.

"Oh. You aren't joining us inside?" Ritu asked.

"No. I have another event."

Anya was disappointed.

"Oh. Have a pleasant rest of the evening then," Ritu said cheerfully.

Bhargav Varma nodded. "See you two on Monday," he replied, his gaze on Anya.

"Good night, Mr. Varma," Anya murmured.

Once again, dragging her eyes away from his hypnotic gaze, she followed the couple inside. She could feel the heat of his stare on her back until she disappeared inside.

The rest of the night continued in an uneventful way. Knowing Bhargav Varma had left, the night didn't hold any interest.

Anya introduced Ritu Kapadia and her husband to her parents. Since, according to the contract, she or Ritu couldn't discuss the project with anyone, Ritu introduced herself only as an interested antique dealer.

The charity auctions continued, and a sea of people laughed and conversed around her. But all Anya could do was paste a smile while a single thought kept repeating in her mind.

I kissed my most important client. And I more than just liked it.

CHAPTER ELEVEN

"You are playing with fire, bro."

Bhargav was at his penthouse with his younger brother. Aryan was sipping a beer while Bhargav decided to skip drinks that night.

Aryan was frowning. "Something could have easily gone wrong if you were discovered at the auction!"

Something had already gone wrong. But not for the reason Aryan thought.

Bhargav could read people easily and guess their motives in advance. He had known he wouldn't be discovered at the auction. It was simple to dodge people, and no risk was involved.

But what actually went wrong was when he kissed Sukanya Kashyap.

He had been addicted to her even from a distance. But holding her in his arms while feeling her passion and tasting her lips was like a powerful drug he could never get rid of.

He wanted more of it. All of it.

Aryan shook his head. "Dammit, bro! You should have switched with Yash like I had suggested right from the beginning. There is no way you can go through this with Anya. It's obvious you can't stay away from her. And from now on, she's going to be bloody working for you!"

Bhargav shrugged. "Our mission is to find the truth. How we go about it shouldn't really matter. Let's discuss the progress of that and leave the things that don't matter."

Aryan scowled. He was clearly not happy about letting go of the topic. But Bhargav knew his younger brother wouldn't oppose him.

Right from their childhood when their lives had been rosy to the time when things went dark, he and his brothers stuck by each other and their decisions.

When Yash and he quit school, Aryan had wanted to follow their footsteps. Aryan wanted to help the family financially too. But he was told to finish his education to fulfill their mother's dreams. Ultimately, Aryan had done so by graduating out of a top university and starting an IT software company right away.

"Things are nearing for you," Aryan reminded. "You are close to ruining the bastard. I'm not sure how you can go about the rest of the plan with this new development."

"What I do for mansion restoration won't be impacted by the rest of our plan."

Aryan frowned. "Why not? Why do you think she'll continue to help even when you—"

"She will."

Aryan scowled and shook his head. "I still don't get it. You and Yash have always been the most rigid, stubborn asses all your lives. Both of you would give me a hard time if I didn't follow the rules and deviated even a little. And now, both of you are off your plans. That too for women from the enemies' side. You have never been this way with any woman."

Bhargav didn't comment.

Aryan let out a sigh. "Well, at least the designs that Anya made are really good. I can't believe she got all of that done in such a short time."

"She remembers the place well."

Aryan nodded.

Bhargav handed another beer to his brother. "How are the bank statements coming along?" he asked.

"I could only hack into one of the systems. The other bank doesn't have data fed into software. I need to get those manually."

"What about the individual bank transactions?"

Aryan frowned. "I was able to hack the accounts for all three. But the bastards are stashing money in multiple accounts not just here but also abroad."

They discussed the details of those transactions—some of the recent ones and ones that happened fifteen years ago.

"We need to build more contacts with the top officials in law enforcement," Aryan suggested. "The bribes might not always work. And this is a cold case from fifteen years ago."

Bhargav nodded. "Yash has met some officials, and so have I. There won't be a problem digging up an old case."

Bhargav wasn't entirely satisfied with the progress he and his brothers were making. They were close when it came to destroying their enemies, but that wasn't their main objective.

They wanted to know the truth of what actually had happened fifteen years ago when their family was completely destroyed and torn apart. Nothing could compensate the loss they had suffered, but it would bring some amount of peace to their mother.

"All right," said Aryan, getting up from the bar stool. "I guess it's time for me to return to my studio apartment." He shook his head. "I wish Shetty's daughter was a damn gold digger. Then I could please the damn woman with gifts or money rather than slaving in a bloody cramped apartment."

A smile broke on Bhargav's face seeing his brother riled up. His younger brother was their mother's favorite pampered son. With him achieving success from a young age, he was used to the finer things in life. From a sprawling penthouse in Manhattan, Aryan had to now live in a studio apartment to impress the enemy's daughter.

"Join the call tomorrow morning," Bhargav reminded him of their weekly touch point.

"Fuck, I forgot about it. Can't we change the call time to sometime after ten in the morning? Who the hell sets up an important phone call at seven on Sunday morning! You and Yash are deliberately torturing me because Ma loves me more."

Bhargav's mouth twisted in amusement. "You'll live through the torture, don't worry."

Aryan shook his head. Then picking up his motorbike helmet from the empty barstool next to him, he got up to leave. He waved right outside the main door before getting into the private elevator. "See 'ya, bro. Goodnight, and try not to dream of the beautiful Anya Kashyap. Remember, she's just a pawn who is going to hate your guts soon."

Bhargav didn't respond.

But as soon as he closed the door and went back into his penthouse, his thoughts continued to run over his beautiful pawn and their kiss.

He recalled the feel of her. And the taste of her. Sukanya Kashyap had clung to him and melted against him while moaning in passion during their kiss. She had kissed him back, tangling her sweet tongue with his and giving in to the need they had both felt since the moment they met.

And now that he had tasted her lips and mouth, the need for her only intensified. He now craved to know how she would feel like when he was buried deep inside her.

Would she cling to him? Or fight him?

He knew she was still fighting her feelings towards him inside her mind. She couldn't meet his eyes right after their kiss and ran away soon after. But he also saw the relief in her eyes when she discovered who Ritu Kapadia was.

She wanted him, but something was holding her back. Maybe she could sense the predator in him due to her excellent instincts. She sensed she was being hunted by him.

Yes, she would hate him soon.

Yes, it was beyond redemption to draw her into something she wasn't a part of.

But none of those facts were going to stop him in any way.

He wanted her and craved her. And he would ultimately claim her.

CHAPTER TWELVE

It was Monday morning, and Anya felt nervous and embarrassed as she took the elevator up to her client's office building.

After the kiss on the night of the auction, she would be facing Bhargav Varma for the first time in the light of the day. All of Saturday night and most of Sunday, she had been embarrassed, aroused and most of all, obsessing about their kiss and how she would face him. She had not only kissed her client back, she literally had rubbed her body against his, begging for more.

No! The kiss didn't happen.

She told herself that because she decided to behave as though the kiss had never happened. She would brazen it out.

He is just another client.

The elevator stopped, and she stepped out before walking to the office she had been to the previous week.

"Hi, I'm Sukanya Kashyap," she told a woman seated at the lobby desk.

The young woman checked her computer before smiling. "Hello, Miss Kashyap. I was asked to have you seated in the office room."

Anya followed the young woman to the office room. On the way, she saw preparations being made in the conference hall where bottles of water and breakfast carts were being set up.

There were still forty more minutes before the meeting would begin.

"Sir will be here shortly," the woman said as she opened the corner office room.

Anya thanked the woman and sat on the chair opposite the office desk.

After the woman left, she pulled out her laptop from her bag. She was asked to come early before meeting with the rest of the architects and team. She assumed it was because Bhargav Varma had a few doubts or questions about the updated designs she had sent.

She quickly looked through the designs and checked her notes and suggestions. The team would have senior architects she would be required to consult with on certain things. She even got a few printouts she wanted to share with them.

She reached inside her laptop bag and pulled out the printouts to check them. She must have pulled the papers hard because one of the clips holding them together snapped.

Shit.

She looked around quickly to see if there were additional paper clips on Bhargav Varma's desk. There were none. His desk was clutter-free except for a sleek penholder.

Hoping she could find something inside it, she pulled it closer. There were just three pens of different colors. But when she looked inside, she saw something at the bottom. It was dark pink in color.

Hoping it was a paperclip, she fished it out. It was a clip but didn't seem to be the type to be used for papers. She frowned when she saw how familiar it appeared.

Suddenly, she remembered.

Oh my God!

It was the hairclip she had worn to the gambling club. She thought she had lost it that night on the floor somewhere.

Then how did Bhargav Varma get it? And why did he keep it?

Her heart thudded as she stared at it.

Maybe it isn't my clip.

But the dark pink shade with light glitter was hardly the kind Bhargav Varma would keep around for personal use.

She was still holding the clip and trying to figure it out when she felt the back of her neck prickle. A light whiff of familiar spicy cologne made her heart thump harder.

"Good morning, Miss Kashyap," Bhargav Varma's deep voice greeted.

She turned to see him. He was dressed in one of his dark business suits and his hair appeared slightly damp indicating he must have stepped out of the shower minutes ago. Her mouth tingled along with her nose when she saw how devastatingly handsome he looked.

"G-good morning, Mr. Varma," she greeted back, trying hard not to stare and blush.

His mouth twisted in a familiar way. He came closer, and then leaning slightly towards her, he smoothly took away the small pink hairclip from her hand and dropped it back into his penholder.

Anya's face heated all the more. She hoped he didn't think she was snooping in his things.

"I was looking for a paperclip," she hurriedly explained.

His mouth remained twisted into a smile. "I'll ask someone to bring a few." He straightened. "Come join me for breakfast," he ordered as he went to the seating as last time.

Biting her lip, and feeling confused, she went towards him.

"I already ate," she once again lied.

He raised his eyebrow. "Then join me for coffee."

Her cheeks heated again as she was reminded of their last breakfast when she refused to anything at first but helped herself to delicious cupcakes later. Pushing away her embarrassment, she sat opposite him.

"So did you go through the contract and sign it?" he asked.

She nodded. "I brought the signed copy." She handed him the folder.

She had read through the contract once and didn't find anything glaring that would stop her from signing her dream project.

His eyes flashed with satisfaction. "Good."

Before Anya could speak about the updates she made on the designs, the same woman as last time brought in the breakfast cart. Anya greeted her with a smile. "Hello, Nina."

The woman smiled back as she served breakfast and poured coffee.

Bhargav Varma began eating. "The team I put together is not final," he said.

Anya was surprised.

He watched her closely. "Although there are architects who are more experienced than you, you will have the power to decide on certain things. If anyone gives you trouble or is difficult to work with, then feel free to have them replaced. I need the project to be efficient."

Anya nodded. "Thank you. I will ensure the project goes on smoothly."

There was momentary silence while he ate breakfast. She sipped her hot coffee and took a small bite from a cupcake. Her heart raced when she looked up to see him watching her with hooded eyes.

"Did he trouble you again?" he asked.

Anya had to drag her mind away from his hypnotic stare and blink. "Who?"

His mouth twisted into a small smile. "Your ex-husband, Miss Kashyap. The man you were running away from and asked me to pretend to be your boyfriend to get rid of him."

Anya's cheeks heated at the reminder. She was also reminded of what that request had led to. "No, he didn't trouble me again," she murmured quickly.

She was supposed to pretend the kiss never happened. But it was hard when awareness was buzzing so strongly between them. She lowered her eyes, hoping the impact of his dark, intense gaze would disappear. But her eyes automatically fell on his strong, tanned hands as he held a fork and ate with smooth, efficient moves. Her cheeks heated recalling the heat of his slightly calloused fingers while he gripped the back of her neck to kiss her.

She tore her eyes away from his hands and quickly looked up at him.

He was still watching her. "Arrangements will be made for the team to travel to the site on a regular basis," he said. "But I would like you to personally accompany me to the estate during updates."

Her heart jerked at his order. "All right."

The rest of the breakfast was spent in thick silence. She tried not to squirm.

How the hell can I work for him if I can barely sit still without feeling drawn to him?

She was passionate about her work. But it was the off-work moments with him that made her completely flustered.

She drank more coffee and ate two more cupcakes when he was finally done with breakfast.

He put away his cutlery and reached for the folder placed next to him.

He opened it and pulled out her contract. He then flipped through it, verifying her signatures. And when he was done, he looked up at her.

His dark eyes flashed, making her heart thump even harder. "Welcome to the project, Miss Kashyap."

The simple statement made her shiver. Whether in excitement or something else, she didn't know it yet.

*****

"Mr. Varma," a man interrupted. "A project of this scale cannot have someone this young leading it. I think you should reconsider Sukanya Kashyap—"

The meeting with the project team began a couple of hours ago. Anya had already met some of the architects before. Two architects among them were well-known and had done many high-profile projects. One of them wasn't sold on the idea of her leading the project.

Bhargav Varma cut off the senior architect midway. "The contracts you have signed state that I would decide any changes in the project. Miss Kashyap is the lead I have chosen."

There was a momentary silence.

Anya knew that the senior architects would try to grab control of the project. She had been in similar situations a few times before and handled it. But she hadn't expected Bhargav Varma to bluntly cut them off while coming to her rescue.

"Mr. Satish," she addressed the slightly disgruntled senior architect with a smile. "I have spent my childhood holidays often at the Vardhaman Estate before the fire tragedy. I am very excited to work with you and the team to bring it back to its former glory."

The older man relaxed slightly. "Oh, I see."

She took the opportunity to show them the initial designs and pictures she had of the mansion. There were several murmurs of approval along with a few questions. Anya replied to them all.

"I want the restoration to finish within a year," Bhargav Varma stated. "When the final sale and permissions are completed, the work needs to begin on a war footing."

One year was too aggressive for an estate of that scale. But the budget Bhargav Varma was pouring into the project would make it possible.

"I will not be directly involved in the project," he further added. "I travel often and have other businesses to take care of. Miss Kashyap would be the only liaison between the team and me. Any issues or grievances should be conveyed through her." His eyes met hers. "I'll see you soon, Miss Kashyap."

He got up and nodded at the room in general before walking away.

Even as the rest of the meeting continued smoothly without a glitch, there was a new thought it in her mind.

How often do I have to meet him in person?

CHAPTER THIRTEEN

"Anya Kashyap, you are getting way too obsessed!"

Anya looked up from her laptop to see her friend standing in her night dress with her hands on her hips.

"What happened?" Anya asked, blinking lightly to get the fatigue out of her eyes.

Trupti shook her head. "This is the third night this week you are staying up all night to work! Get some sleep, woman!"

It was actually the fourth night, but Anya didn't want her friend to know.

The week had sped by in a blur. She and the team of architects were flown to the mansion right after the meeting. Since the time they flew back, she had constantly been working with them on the designs.

The previous night, Anya had gone to Trupti's apartment to crash in the guest bedroom. After week-long meetings during the day and catching up with the design planning in the evenings and nights, she had felt too exhausted to drive home the previous night.

Although she had gone to bed on time after dinner with Trupti, she was reminded of yet another detail from her childhood memories that she wanted to include in her design. So, she had woken up again to update it.

"We'll be finalizing the designs in a few weeks. The other main architects are at it as well."

Trupti raised her eyebrow. "I highly doubt if they are pulling all-nighters and obsessively working all day and night."

Anya smiled. "I'll sleep tonight, I promise."

Her friend scoffed. "You broke your promise last night and the night before that too!"

Anya laughed, knowing it was true. But the time spent was worth every bit of her sleepless nights over the week. "Look at the designs the team and I are putting together. Aren't they stunningly close to the mansion pictures from my childhood!"

Trupti looked at the designs and then at Anya's face before grinning. "I think you'll want to live in that mansion when it's done and restored! Mr. Wicked is going to have a tough time getting rid of you at the end of the project."

Anya blushed. "It's going to be a hotel after the restoration. I can rent the rooms anytime."

"Or you can convince that hot owner in other ways to let you have a private bedroom suite in the Vardhaman mansion."

"Trupti!" Anya's cheeks were on fire.

Trupti laughed. "What? Imagine staying in your dream place and having that hottie to set you on fire between the sheets."

"Stop it! I have to meet him often to provide him updates!"

Her friend grinned. "Ooh. Then maybe you should drop some heavy hints of your future plans. Corner him and kiss the hell out of him. Show him you are worth giving up a suite in the mansion."

Anya shook her head at her friend's outrageous remarks. "There will be other employees and workers!"

Trupti smirked. "Ah. So if there weren't other people, you wouldn't have minded kissing him?"

"I already did."

There was a sudden silence as Trupti's eyes slowly widened.

Anya realized what she had just confessed to her friend. She had intended to pretend that the kiss had never happened. But thanks to her lack of sleep and her friend's constant teasing, she ended up blurting it.

"Oh my God! You kissed Mr. Wicked? When!"

Anya's face heated. "It isn't like how you are imagining it to be. It was just... pretence and... and... didn't mean anything."

Trupti didn't let it go. "How can a kiss be pretence? And of course, it meant something because your face is the color of a tomato right now."

Oh God.

"What else happened that you didn't tell me yet?" Trupti demanded.

"Nothing. Surya was chasing me at the auction when I bumped into Bhargav Varma. I just asked him to pretend to be my boyfriend to get rid of Surya."

Trupti slowly grinned. "And he kissed you?"

Anya blushed. "He was just pretending."

"But the kiss happened. And I bet there was a lot of tongue involved and some hair pulling too. Bhargav Varma definitely looks like a man who would take charge and kiss the hell out of a woman."

All week Anya had been drowning in her work, trying not to think of her darkly handsome client or their passionate kiss. But now, thanks to her friend, the memories of the kiss and the forbidden feelings she felt for him rushed in.

Her scalp above her neck began tingling, recalling how it felt when he gripped her hair while his tongue ravaged her mouth. Liquid fire shot through her bloodstream.

"He's just a client," she insisted. "There's nothing between us."

"Uh-huh." Trupti clearly didn't believe her. There was another smirk on her friend's face. "Do you remember the sports star whose penthouse I redecorated last year?"

Anya nodded. "Of course. The décor was one of your best."

Trupti laughed. "It wasn't easy at first. I had felt similar sparks with that guy, and it was highly distracting. I couldn't focus on my job."

Anya's heart thudded. Although she was able to focus on her job, the strong attraction she felt towards Bhargav Varma was highly distracting.

"What did you do?" she asked.

Trupti's smirk became wider. "I gave in to the attraction. I had sex with him. And you know what happened? The magic was gone, and I realized he was selfish in bed and quite the narcissist outside it. He bored me to tears with his constant bragging. He was no longer the hot client who distracted me." Trupti grinned. "Maybe you should try it too. You might realize Mr. Wicked is just another annoying narcissist billionaire with nothing else going on for him."

Anya shook her head with a laugh at her friend's suggestion. "No thanks."

Trupti shrugged. "Your loss. But if you are not interested in him, then maybe I can..."

A sudden bolt of possessiveness and jealousy hit Anya hard. "No!"

Trupti slowly smirked. "No?"

Anya was shocked by her reaction. She had never felt that way before about anyone.

"I... I... meant he's usually very busy. He's always travelling. It won't be that easy to meet him and... date him."

Trupti grinned. "I see."

"And... and... you like Rishab," Anya reminded her friend. "He's definitely a nice guy." Taking a deep breath, Anya pulled herself together. "All right. I'll get going now. I have to stop by my parents' home too."

Trupti looked amused. It was obvious Anya was running away from the uncomfortable conversation.

"See you on Monday," Trupti said. "And if you kiss Mr. Wicked again, you better tell me everything!"

Anya heard her friend's laughter as she hurried out of the apartment.

God! What's wrong with me?

Why did she suddenly feel so possessive and jealous about Bhargav Varma? The thought of him locked in a passionate kiss with her beautiful friend filled her with anger and jealousy.

Ugh. I need help.

Or maybe a good night's sleep would straighten her brain and stop her from thinking irrational thoughts about a man she had no right to feel jealous or possessive about. Letting out another sigh, she reminded herself yet again to continue repeating a fact in her head.

He's just a client.

***

Anya's parents weren't home when she dropped by. It was Friday morning, so she had expected at least her mother to be home until afternoon.

But her brother was surprisingly there.

Her brother lived in the middle of the city in an apartment which was close to the most popular clubs and restaurants. He also didn't usually get up before noon since he partied until dawn.

Anya smiled. "Wow. Didn't expect to see you here this early in the morning. What's up?" she asked, sitting across from him in the family room.

"Didn't Ma tell you? I live here now."

Anya was taken aback. "Here? Why? What happened?"

Her brother looked annoyed. "Nothing happened. I just live here. Why can't I live in my parents' house?"

Anya shook her head at her brother's reaction. Clearly, something happened to make him feel that sensitive. Also, he wasn't that attached to their parents to want to move in with them. He preferred the privacy of his own place. She frowned, wondering what it could be.

"Oh no, Sohan! Don't tell me you lost that apartment!" She recalled handing him the apartment papers which he had used as collateral during gambling.

"None of your business!" he snapped.

Anya felt angry at his words. "It is my business. You are my brother, and I was the one you reached out to for help when you needed those apartment papers."

His jaw clenched, but he didn't say anything.

"Tell me what happened," she insisted.

There was nothing she could do, but she wanted to know if her brother needed help. She had begged him the last time to go to therapy and get professional help for his alcohol and drug addictions. Although he somewhat got over alcohol and drugs, he was now addicted to gambling.

"Nothing," he said irritably. "I lost the apartment and my cars. I asked Papa for help, but he refused to pay my loan amount or give me money to rent an apartment in the city. I don't know why he's become so cheap. It's not like he's going to save that money and give it to someone else. I'm going to inherit everything anyway."

The sense of entitlement in her brother's words was too evident. But Anya didn't want to call him out right then. She knew it would be of no use, and her brother would only get more defensive.

Maybe it was a good thing that her brother would be staying at her parents' house. It would stop him from gambling again.

"Why do you look so tired?" he asked with a frown.

She smiled. "I have been busy with a new project. I spent the night at Trupti's place and am heading home."

She didn't want to tell her brother about the Vardhaman project because of the contract terms. But she did wonder how he would react. Her brother hadn't been close to any of the Vardhamans, but he used to spend his holidays at the estate during childhood.

Her brother shook his head. "If you marry Surya again, you needn't have to work."

Anya sighed. "You are starting to sound like Ma and Papa."

Her brother shrugged. "They are right. Why can't you just marry him and enjoy life? Why do you need to keep trying to prove you are independent? Surya is willing to lend me money too if you agree to his proposal."

A bolt of anger and disappointment hit her, listening to her brother's words. She didn't know why she had expected her brother to come to her defense or understand her. There was a brief time when her brother had supported and consoled her. It was when she lost her best friend during childhood.

She and her brother had been each other's support system then, until he got pulled away into the fast life and bad company.

"Well, I'm sorry that me not marrying an egoistic serial cheater is spoiling your life," she said, unable to hide her disappointment.

"Don't be dramatic, Annie."

Anya's heart jerked. Her brother rarely used that pet name for her. He knew it made her feel sad and nostalgic.

"Fine," he said. "If not Surya, why don't you marry some other rich dude who can loan me money?"

She shook her head with a short laugh. "Why don't you do the same thing?" she asked. "Marry a rich heiress. Then you don't even need to take a loan."

As she predicted, the expression on her brother's face closed up.

Anya knew why. Her brother was in love with a woman who unfortunately was not rich enough for her parents. Her parents would be horrified and would never agree to her brother marrying someone who wasn't of the same social status. It didn't matter that her parents had belonged to a similar social class until fifteen years ago.

Anya sighed. "I like Pooja," she said. "She's a beautiful, sweet and hardworking woman. I can speak to Ma and Papa about you two."

Her brother shook his head. "Don't," he warned. "I know they will be disappointed."

"So what?" Anya demanded. "You can't stop being with someone you love just because your family doesn't approve of that person!"

"Leave it, Anya. Things are not that simple when it comes to love. You won't understand because you never fell in love."

Anya wanted to argue, but looking at the shut expression on her brother's face, she kept quiet.

"Fine," she said, getting up from the sofa. "I'll get going. I have to catch up on some sleep and work."

She kissed him on his cheek. Her brother just nodded, looking lost and unhappy.

Letting out another sigh and wishing that her brother was willing to take her help, she left her parents' house.

Her brother was wrong.

Yes, she had never been in love. But if she did love someone, nothing would stop her from being with that man. And she would expect the same in return. She would expect the man to do everything possible for their love and fight for her.

A darkly handsome face flashed into her mind, making her heart race suddenly.

She shook her head to push away thoughts of him. It was irrational. She was not in love with Bhargav Varma. She wasn't that foolish because she knew a man like him would break her heart to pieces.

He's just a client.

"Their assets will be frozen in exactly two weeks, Mr. Varma."

Bhargav was at a guesthouse in a secure area. All the cameras and surveillance of the place were turned off.

"Are the offshore accounts included in it?"

"Yes, Mr. Varma. We sent information and placed the request for those accounts to be frozen as well."

"Good."

Bhargav's assistant placed a bag containing a small 'gift' to the officer. The man smiled widely.

"And I remember the instructions about the auction of their assets as well, Mr. Varma. I have requested it to be silent."

Bhargav was prepared for it as well. Aryan would hack into the system and ensure that all assets would be auctioned and purchased by Ventura Holdings.

"Thank you, Mr. Varma."

Bhargav nodded.

The officer grabbed the bag greedily and left the guesthouse.

Bhargav sat back while flipping through the papers the officer had got for him. It contained all the information of the various bank accounts that would soon be frozen.

"Has he contacted any other banks for loans?" he asked.

Ravi shook his head. "No, Mr. Varma. He was turned down by all of the banks."

"Good. Get the loan sharks to contact him this week."

"Yes, Mr. Varma."

In barely two weeks, Bhargav's target would be trapped completely. But instead of satisfaction, Bhargav felt strangely restless.

It was his beautiful prey who was the cause of his restlessness and many sleepless nights. He hadn't met her all week. He had deliberately stayed away to see if his obsession could be tamed.

But he discovered that his burning need only grew.

"Ravi," he said. "Have the helicopter readied tomorrow morning."

CHAPTER FIFTEEN

Anya was a little early. And there was no one to receive her downstairs to take her up to the penthouse.

It was Saturday morning.

She had finally managed to catch up on her sleep. The moment her head hit the pillow after lunch, she fell into a deep sleep only to wake up the next day morning at five. Feeling refreshed, she had checked her messages, only for her heart to begin racing seeing a message from an unknown number.

Unknown number: Update meeting tomorrow at 8. -BV

Feeling excited and slightly nervous, she got ready for her appointment right away. She ended up reaching the penthouse building a few minutes early. It was only seven thirty, and the appointment was at eight.

Dammit!

Hoping someone could still help her, she went to the lobby where a woman was seated at the reception area.

"Hi. I'm here to meet Mr. Varma."

The young woman smiled back. "Oh yes. I was asked to send you to the fifteenth floor towards the training ring."

"Thank you."

What was a training ring?

Anya imagined it to be some sort of new employee training area. She had signed a contract with Bhargav Varma's company and was technically working for him. She supposed there were a few things that he wanted her to be oriented in.

Stepping into one of the elevators in the lobby, she pressed the button to the fifteenth floor.

Her heart began to thud. It had been less than a week since she had last spoken to him. But it felt much longer. He had asked her to update him personally, but he hadn't contacted her the entire week while she was immersed in designing along with the team.

I wonder when we'll visit the estate again.

She hadn't had her fill the last two times she had been there. She had only stayed a couple of hours to take pictures and measurements of the rooms. With the inspection and other clearances completed, she hoped she and the team could visit the place frequently.

She let out a sigh.

The elevator stopped with a sound of a ping, and doors opened on the fifteenth floor. As soon as she stepped out, the smell of the antiseptic invaded her senses.

She frowned in confusion.

Instead of an office area, she could see the huge gym area through the glass wall where many building residents were working out.

She stopped and asked a man who was passing by. "Excuse me. Where is the training ring?"

The man looked at her strangely. Maybe because she was wearing her work clothes and holding an oversized bag in the gym area.

"It's at the end of the corridor. But it can be used only on a reservation basis."

She nodded and went as directed.

A strange feeling of déjà vu filled her senses. She was reminded of her visit to the club two and half months ago. A strange sizzle and undercurrent filled the air.

Pushing away those memories and feelings, she stopped in front of the door that said training ring. Pulling the door open, she stepped inside, only to be completely shocked.

It was a big training ring. Or rather a boxing ring. And Bhargav Varma was boxing with two other men. Her mouth fell slightly open as she stared at him. His hard, muscular body was nearly bare and glistening with sweat. And his darkly handsome face looked brutally ruthless as he hit out at his opponents.

Her stomach fluttered and her cheeks heated, because although she had fantasized about him many times over the last two months, she had never imagined his bare body.

He was like a beautiful sculpture she sometimes commissioned for her clients. But no sculpture emitted the raw energy and aura that Bhargav Varma had around him.

He held her completely captive.

She didn't know how long she stood there staring at him in rapt attention when vaguely she heard a voice calling her.

"Miss Kashyap? Excuse me, Miss Kashyap."

Blinking slightly, she turned and saw the personal assistant, Ravi.

"I'm sorry for the confusion, Miss Kashyap. The receptionist had meant to send me up here. You were supposed to go to the penthouse."

The PA's words slowly sunk into her brain and cleared away the fog. She blinked again, only for her to feel embarrassed. "Oh."

The assistant shook his head. "The receptionist is new. I apologize."

"Uh... it's okay."

Hoping that Bhargav Varma hadn't noticed her gawking like a schoolgirl at his bare body, she turned towards the fighting ring where the sounds of the fight were ongoing. This time, his blows were less intense as he smoothly moved to dodge the blows from his opponents.

Her heart jerked when she noticed that his mouth was twisted slightly in a small smile. And then, for a brief moment, his dark, intense gaze clashed with hers.

He had noticed her presence.

Oh God.

Feeling completely embarrassed, she hurried out of the training room.

With her face on fire, she went towards the elevators and waited. Ravi stepped in and pressed the penthouse floor along with a code. While the elevator took them up, she leaned her back against the elevator wall.

Oh God. Why is this happening to me!

It shook her.

In her line of work, she had met many good-looking men—movie stars, sports stars, rich businessmen. Some of them even hit on her. She had never felt flustered. But she was always flustered with Bhargav Varma. She didn't know why.

How can I face him now!

Even though she was tempted to hide from him, she knew she couldn't. Not when so much was at stake. All that mattered to her was the Vardhaman Estate. Taking a deep breath, she once again decided to stick to her plan and pretend she hadn't been staring at his nearly naked body a while ago.

The elevator stopped. Ravi led her to the penthouse and asked her to wait in the living room. "Sir will be joining you shortly."

Anya nodded but didn't sit on the couch. Instead, she decided to look at the painting she had seen the last time in the penthouse.

The River.

As she neared it, her heart began thumping. It was from the Vardhaman Estate, one of the many things that had been sold during the property seizure. She recalled now how she had begged her parents to buy the painting or acquire it fifteen years ago, but they hadn't been interested in buying something so ordinary-looking.

Would Bhargav Varma be willing to sell?

She wanted the painting quite badly. She wondered if she could negotiate the terms of her payment to include the painting in it. To him, it would only be a part of the hotel he was building. But to her, it meant a lot.

"You seem fascinated, Miss Kashyap," a deep voice spoke from behind her.

Jumping slightly at the sudden intrusion, she turned around. Bhargav Varma was watching her with a small smile.

"What?"

His smile grew slightly. "I was stating that you seemed fascinated. With the painting."

Her cheeks grew warmer as she recalled how she had been fascinated by him a while ago when he was nearly naked and fighting inside a boxing ring.

"Uh yes. I know this painting from my childhood."

He didn't say anything and continued watching her.

Once again, awareness and thick tension grew around them. She held her breath to stop the addicting spicy cologne from filling her senses. She even had to fist her palms to stop the sudden urge to run her fingers through his freshly washed and combed thick hair. She wanted to touch the rough stubble on his hard jaw and run her fingers over his imperfect nose and feel his hard yet sensuous lips on top of hers.

What the hell am I thinking!

She cleared her throat noisily. "I've brought the updated designs the team and I put together, Mr. Varma."

His eyes flashed in amusement at her formal tone. "You can update me during breakfast, Miss Kashyap."

Before she could say anything, he began walking away.

She followed him as he stepped out of the living room and sat on the large balcony where breakfast was readied.

"Coffee?" he asked.

She shook her head. She didn't need any caffeine for her already alert and jumpy nerves. The man made her way too aware of him.

"Have a cupcake then. Nina made the dark chocolate chip ones that you like."

Her heart jerked that he had noticed it from their earlier breakfasts.

"Thank you," she murmured and took one and placed it on her plate.

"Ritu mentioned about your meeting last week."

She nodded. "I couldn't meet her in person. I've been on the phone with her and sent her the updated designs. I'm meeting her next week to go through the list of items we'll have commissioned."

He glanced at her. "She mentioned that you wanted to use the reclaimed wood from the damaged items."

"Yes." Anya's heart ached at the thought of throwing away the damaged furniture. She wanted to cling to every piece possible. "There should be several teak and rosewood trees at the estate. If the trees are in good condition, we can use their wood."

There was a thoughtful look on his face. "Good idea. I'll have someone go and assess if the wood can be used."

"I can help," she suggested. "I know of a few places where those trees were planted."

He raised his eyebrow at her request. "Sure, Miss Kashyap."

Anya's cheeks heated. She knew she was sounding pushy, but she wanted to explore the estate badly. Lowering her eyes, she finished eating her cupcake.

She was about to pull out her laptop to show him the updated designs when she heard him speak.

"Not now," he said. "You can show them to me while we are on our way to the estate."

Her eyes flew up as her heart jerked in excitement.

His mouth twisted into a small smile, seeing her excited face. "Do you have other plans for the day, Miss Kashyap?"

She shook her head. "No, Mr. Varma. I'm free all day." In fact, she was free all weekend. But she didn't want to tell him that as she would come off desperate.

"Good. Then I guess we'll be spending the day at the estate."

Her heart raced in excitement. And it wasn't entirely due to the estate. Looking at his hooded eyes as he watched her while he ate his breakfast, she knew she would have to once again keep repeating the words.

He's just a client.

***

Anya's heart thumped as she looked out of the helicopter window. She could see that the area around the mansion had been cleared. When she and the team had visited the place five days ago, the work was still ongoing. They weren't allowed to go outside the mansion.

Anya turned to look at Bhargav Varma seated next to her. "Can the team and I visit the place again?"

"Yes. I've asked Ravi to arrange for an exclusive bus for the team to visit the mansion whenever required. If it's an emergency, you can use the chopper as well. Just let Ravi know, and he can contact the pilot."

Excitement drummed through her. "Has the sale been finalized?" she asked.

Since Bhargav Varma was already spending a lot of money on the designs, artifact acquisitions and many other things, she assumed the estate sale was completed.

"Not yet," he replied. "But it will be next week, including the fifty acres next to the factory."

She was surprised but very glad that he was acquiring the disputed land as well. To lose even an inch of the land would be equivalent to losing a part of her heart and memories. The estate might not belong to her, but she wanted the entire area restored, including the beautiful rivers, orchards and vast open areas.

"We will be landing shortly," the pilot announced.

Anya continued to look out the window while the helicopter landed in front of the mansion.

This time, when she got out of the helicopter, she didn't have to wade through thick weeds since the path had been cleared. She recalled the designs she had put together to lay the beautiful stone pathway around the marble fountain that resembled the original design.

She smiled as the place began coming alive in her mind. She recalled the laughter and shrieks while she and her best friend ran around the fountain chasing each other.

"Good morning, Mr. Varma!"

Anya turned to see a smiling old man who appeared somewhat familiar. It was Saturday, but a few workers were still working. Bhargav Varma greeted the old man with a wave while continuing to walk towards the mansion.

Anya frowned, wondering why the man appeared somewhat familiar.

"The engineering team has given out all the clearances," Bhargav Varma stated. "There are a few patchworks pending on the second floor which will be completed this weekend."

Anya dragged her mind back to the mansion. "The team and I were able to take pictures and measurements of the second floor as well," she said.

"Good."

They walked into the mansion. A few workers were fixing minor structural issues. Bhargav Varma gave out a few instructions while Anya made notes. They went into one of the bedrooms on the top floor.

"My family and I used to stay here during our visits," she said. "This used to be my room."

The room was nearly barren except for the heavy bed that still looked sturdy even after many years.

Bhargav Varma looked at the bed. "The wood seems to be of good quality."

She nodded. "Yes, it is. This is rosewood. Most of the furniture in the mansion is made from rosewood trees on the estate."

Bhargav Varma nodded. "I've asked for a car to be brought in to drive us through the estate. But we won't be able to go far since the paths are blocked."

Anya shook her head. "We won't need a car. We can walk."

Bhargav Varma's eyebrow rose at her suggestion.

"I... meant I don't mind walking however long. But we can stop if you get tired—" She broke off in embarrassment when she saw his small, amused smile.

"I think I can catch up with you, Miss Kashyap."

Her face heated.

Dammit!

She was reminded of earlier that morning when she had seen his muscular body and his raw energy while fighting two men at a time. Of course, he was fit enough to walk as much as her if not more.

She blushed. "I can guide," she suggested. "I remember the location of the trees quite well." Anya recalled that the teak and rosewood trees had been planted near the river.

He nodded with a smile. "Then, let's go."

They stepped out of the mansion. Grabbing a couple of water bottles, they set out to explore the estate by foot.

Most of the area was still covered with thick weeds, but she visualized how it had been at its peak glory. Native and exotic flowering bushes, vegetable gardens and fruit orchards had been carefully placed around the mansion and all over the estate.

"So, tell me more about this place," he asked. "Did you enjoy your time at the estate during your childhood?"

She smiled at the memories. "I loved it here." She spoke about the beautiful river and several ponds that she swam in during summers. She also told him how she and her best friend snuck out during the nights for a secret swim.

Bhargav Varma looked amused. "I didn't think you had a wild side hidden in you, Miss Kashyap."

She blushed. "Why not?" she challenged. "Everyone has a wild side, Mr. Varma. So do I."

His eyes hooded. "Is that so?"

Anya's face heated at his question, which made her statement about her wild side appear suggestive.

Clearing her throat, she continued with her narration of her childhood memories. "We used to go fishing in the river," she said. "The people from the nearby village also fished in the river."

He didn't call her out for changing the topic. He walked along with her with a small smile on his face.

They stopped after nearly an hour when they reached the narrow river.

She pointed to the thick trees that looked lush even after so many years. "Some of these trees were there even during my childhood."

Most of the trees lining the river ends were rosewood and teak. Whenever Ashok Vardhaman cut the trees to use the wood for furniture, he had made sure more trees were planted. Anya had planted some of those trees as well.

Bhargav Varma was silent. He went to the river and began inspecting the place.

Meanwhile, Anya went in the opposite direction looking for one of the trees she and her best friend had planted over fifteen years ago. She found it within a few moments.

Her heart squeezed painfully when she saw it. It had grown into a tall tree and was right behind another big tree which she and her best friend had used as a landmark to identify the planting at that time. She went closer to that tree and ran her fingers gently on the thick trunk that still held hints of a deep carving after many years.

"That looks like a heart-shaped carving," Bhargav Varma's deep voice stated.

Anya's heart jerked at the sudden interruption.

When she turned around, he was standing close and watching her with an expression she couldn't read. His eyes were hooded and darkly intense.

The top two buttons of his shirt were open, displaying tanned skin. His shirt sleeves were rolled up to show more of the tanned skin dusted with masculine hair over his muscled arms.

Her heart began to thud loudly.

Suddenly, from fond nostalgia, the air around her thickened to something else. It practically vibrated with electricity. She became extremely aware of how she was once again alone with the man she found irresistible right from their first meeting.

His dark eyes flashed with heat and desire, making her heart pound loudly, drowning out any sane thoughts.

She didn't know who moved first, but suddenly she found her back against the thick tree with his hard body covering hers while their mouths fused together. Heat and excitement exploded inside her, turning her mind and body into liquid.

His mouth ravaged hers while she clung to his broad shoulders and kissed him back as though she were starving. She wanted more. She wanted his wicked mouth and touch everywhere.

As though he could read her mind, she felt pressure on her top and heard a small ripping sound. A cool breeze fell on her chest and stomach before his rough, calloused hands enclosed over her breasts.

She moaned at the sensation. Her hands slid from his broad shoulders to his shirt. Grabbing the ends, she dragged it apart until the shirt opened slightly and she could feel the heat of his hard, muscular body. She ran her palms under his shirt over his bared skin.

He groaned and then growled before yanking on her bra until she was completely bared. And then, he dragged her closer, crushing her against him.

Another moan escaped her as the tips of her aroused breasts rubbed against his hard chest.

His hands gripped her hips and lifted her against the tree. Before she could think or miss his kiss, his hot mouth closed over her breast and sucked with a ferocity that made her cry out.

He was devouring her, just like his hooded eyes had promised. She gasped out his name and clutched his head as a desperate need rose inside her that she couldn't contain. With each fierce tug of his mouth, she felt herself falling deeper and deeper into an abyss.

She cried out his name again and again.

His mouth left her breasts, and he lowered her again to capture her lips in a fierce kiss. The world continued to spin in heat and desire.

Only when her breath escaped her lips, she realized she had fallen on the soft ground with the hard heat of him on top of her. He was wedged between her thighs, and she could feel his hard arousal against her soft core. She gasped as liquid heat coursed through her, making her raise her hips automatically and softly grind against him.

He groaned against her mouth.

"Please," she whispered, wanting that ache inside her gone.

She felt him gripping her hair, and she clung to him as his mouth caught hers in another hard, passionate kiss.

The kiss ended quickly, and he breathed harshly against her lips. "Fuck," he growled.

She didn't understand at first. Her hands clung to his broad shoulders, and she continued to raise her hips, rubbing her core against his hard arousal. But he pulled her hair back until she had to see his face.

"We should stop now," he grated harshly.

"Don't stop," she begged.

"You are not ready."

"I'm on birth control pills," she said, thinking he was referring to protection. She took birth control pills for her irregular periods.

His eyes blazed. "You are still not ready."

She didn't understand his words. "What?" she whispered.

His eyes were still dark and intense. He was watching her possessively. "I want you. But I don't think you are ready for me yet. I don't want you to regret this later."

Shock gripped her as she suddenly realized the circumstances.

He was her client, and she was lying half-naked under him on the estate grounds, begging him to have sex with her. He was the one to stop because he thought she would regret it later. But she didn't regret it. Far from it. She still wanted him. Her body quivered with the need.

Embarrassment hit her hard.

Oh God. What is wrong with me!

Ignoring the ache inside her body, she tried to roll away to run and hide somewhere. But his rock-hard body kept her pinned on the ground.

She sucked in a deep breath. "Mr. Varma," she said in embarrassment. "Would you please mind moving off me."

His eyes blazed while his mouth twisted slightly in amusement at her formal tone.

"Actually, I do mind, Miss Kashyap. I'm quite happy with where I am." His hard arousal lay heavily against her stomach.

Fire shot up in her belly. She blushed. "Mr. Varma, please," she said. "I know what happened just now is not right. I'm sorry to have—"

"Anya, stop," he said, shocking her with the use of her shortened name.

His hand continued to grip her hair while he looked at her with his dark, intense eyes. "I don't give a fuck about what is considered right. We are both adults. I want you. But I want to wait until you want this to happen between us without regrets."

She didn't know what to say. She did want him desperately. She had wanted him from the moment she met him, but she wasn't sure whether she would regret being with him.

"You don't have to answer me right now," he said. "I'll know when you are ready."

The grip on her hair loosened, and he rolled away from her. Immediately, she felt the loss of his warmth and heat. Biting her lip at her confused feelings, she slowly sat up.

She blushed while he watched her and buttoned his shirt that she had nearly ripped apart in passion. With trembling hands, she began adjusting her bra and top. But she noticed that some of the buttons on her top were missing as well. Her cheeks heated more realizing that she hadn't even noticed it until then.

"I have a jacket in the helicopter that you can wear," he said in a slightly amused voice before extending his hand.

"Thank you," she murmured.

As soon as she placed her hand in his, once again, sparks flew. She gasped when he pulled her up until her body hit his hard chest. His eyes blazed into hers as he held her upright.

"I can promise you one thing," he said in a deep tone that fluttered her stomach. "Next time when you beg me to take you, I will. I won't be stopping with a kiss."

With that promise which sounded more like a threat, he released her from his arms.

"Let's go."

Anya's cheeks remained heated while her body hummed with an unfulfilled desire as they headed back.

This is wrong.

He's just a client.

CHAPTER SIXTEEN

The sound of the doorbell and her phone ringing woke up Anya from a deep fog. She opened her eyes and groaned. It was nine o'clock on a Sunday morning.

Rubbing her bleary eyes, she went and answered the door first, only to see her friend standing in the doorway holding a takeout bag and with the phone stuck to her ear.

"What happened!" Trupti demanded. "I thought you were dead or dying! You haven't answered my calls all Friday and yesterday!"

Anya stifled a yawn. "Sorry. I was catching up on my sleep."

Trupti's eyes narrowed. "You slept all day yesterday."

Anya tried to control her blush. "I had an appointment in the morning, but I got back home later and crashed."

"Appointment with whom? I thought you finished transitioning the rest of the projects."

Anya tried to keep a normal expression on her face. "Come in. I'll make some coffee. I need it before I can talk."

They walked into her small kitchen. While she heated water to be poured into her coffee filter, her friend pulled out plates for the takeout breakfast.

Anya's stomach rumbled because she had skipped dinner the previous night. But she waited until the filtered coffee was done before she ate anything. Five minutes later, the aromatic coffee decoction was ready, and she poured it into two mugs along with a generous amount of milk and sugar.

They then sat on the living room couch to have breakfast and coffee. She was only halfway through her cup and had only taken a couple of bites of the delicious breakfast when her friend burst out.

"All right, spill! What happened? And where were you yesterday?"

Anya took another long sip of the coffee. "I went to the estate."

Her friend's eyes narrowed. "Alone?"

Anya tried not to blush. "My client was along with me."

Trupti scoffed. "Your client? You mean Mr. Wicked?"

Anya nodded with a blush.

Suddenly Trupti's eyes widened. "Oh my God!" She leaped up from the opposite couch and came closer. "That's a hickey!"

Anya felt her friend's finger on the side of her neck where the skin was slightly sore and tingling.

Trupti shrieked in excitement. "Good God! You even have whisker burns all over your cheek and neck! Tell me what happened!"

Anya's face was on fire. "Nothing. It must be an insect bite or a thorn while I was at the estate."

Trupti shook her head. "No damn way! I can recognize hickeys anywhere! I bet there are more on your body where mosquitoes or thorns can't reach. The only plausible person who bit you is your hottie hotelier. Tell me!"

Anya felt cornered as she continued blushing hard. "Fine. We kissed again."

"Kissed! You look as though you were involved in more than a kiss. You look as though Bhargav Varma threw you on the ground and ravished you thoroughly!"

Anya's face was on fire at her friend's accurate words.

Trupti was grinning widely. "Ooh. Were you with him last night? Did he finally convince you to fire up the sheets?"

"No!" Anya shook her head. "If anything, he was the one to stop and send me home."

Her friend looked stunned. "What?"

Anya looked at her friend's face and sympathized. Even she was still shocked by the events from the previous day.

"He said he wants me, but he thinks I'm not ready and I need to be sure about this."

Trupti's eyes widened. "My God. And what did you say?"

"Nothing."

"Nothing? You obviously like this guy. And if he was able to stop to give you a choice, he's definitely a keeper!"

Anya sighed. "It's not that simple, Trupti."

"Why not?"

Anya bit her lip uncertainly. After she returned from the estate, her mind had been a mess. She was both embarrassed and restless. She wanted Bhargav Varma. All she had to do was tell him those words, and they could have been together.

But something stopped her.

"I don't know if I can get over him if we spend the night together."

Understanding dawned on Trupti's face.

Anya took a deep breath. "I barely know him yet the way I feel about him... it's just too much. I feel connected to him in a way I never felt before. If we spend a night together, I don't know if I can carry on as though nothing happened."

Trupti held her hand. "What makes you think he would dump you after a night? Maybe he feels that way about you too."

Anya shook her head. "I doubt it. I'm just someone he fancies right now. I don't think he feels anything for me beyond desire."

Her friend frowned. "Then why would he stop and give you a choice when you were willing?" she asked. "He could have had sex and continued a short affair until he was bored. But he didn't."

Anya felt uncertain about that part too. "Maybe I'm a challenge. Maybe he wants me to cling to him and break down at the end of the affair." Even as she said those words, she knew they weren't true.

"I doubt that's the reason," Trupti stated. "He isn't like your ex-husband, Anya. I know that asshole Surya made you feel disillusioned about men. But Bhargav Varma doesn't sound like that at all. Why would he do that when he knows you are the lead architect on his project and he would be risking a lot by breaking your heart?"

Anya nodded, knowing it was the truth. She sighed. "I know I sound like a coward not wanting to trust a man or be with anyone because of my marriage. But I think it's better for me this way."

Trupti didn't look too happy, but she didn't say anything.

Anya smiled and squeezed her friend's hand. "Enough about me. Tell me why are you spending the weekend with me and not with Rishab?"

Her friend slowly smiled at her boyfriend's name. "His parents are visiting him this weekend. He wants to introduce me to them tomorrow for lunch."

Anya laughed in delight. "That's wonderful news!"

Trupti nodded with a shy and sheepish smile. "I guess it is. I can't believe I got to the point of anticipating meeting a guy's parents."

The rest of the morning they spoke about Trupti's boyfriend and their relationship. Anya was truly happy for her friend. Coming from an abusive household, Trupti had flitted from one man to another, using them for her needs but never settling into a relationship. But now, she found a man she could see herself settling down with. Although Anya had never been in love, she did believe in happily-ever-after.

Yes, I believe in love. But Bhargav Varma is just a client.

CHAPTER SEVENTEEN

The following week went by smoothly. But it was frustrating at times.

"Miss Kashyap, I don't think we should be using those childish paintings."

Anya clenched her teeth and forced out a smile. "Mr. Satish, the paintings might appear childish, but these are the originals paintings that the Vardhaman family displayed in their family room. They were painted by that family's children."

The older man waved a dismissive hand. "The Vardhaman mansion is going to be a luxury hotel. I don't think these paintings would appeal to the guests. They would be out of place."

"I don't think so, sir." Anya continued to smile forcibly. "Many families would be visiting the place with their children. This room could be called a family room or a place where children can relax during vacation. It would appeal to their sensibilities."

The older man shook his head. "I don't think so."

Anya was irritated by his dismissive gestures. She had known right away that the older man, who was a well-known and more senior architect, would try to find something or other to undermine her authority as the project's lead architect. This wasn't the first time he had done so in the last two weeks since they had begun working on the project.

Taking a deep breath, she pulled in more patience. "Mr. Satish, unfortunately, our personal tastes shouldn't matter here. This is a restoration project to bring back the mansion to its original form."

"Says who?" he snapped. "I'm sure Mr. Varma would support me in this."

Anya's heart jerked at the mention. She hadn't seen Bhargav Varma all week. After the helicopter had dropped them back on top of the penthouse, he accompanied her to the parking garage where she had hurriedly gotten into her car and driven away.

He hadn't even texted her. Her cheeks heated recalling how she had obsessively checked her text messages every hour to see if there was anything from him.

Maybe, he regrets the moments at the estate.

He must have realized the risks involved in having an affair with his lead architect on an important project. Her heart ached at the thought.

Pushing away her feelings, she focused on the present issue.

"Mr. Satish, whether or not our client would choose those paintings is not relevant at this time. According to the contract we both are bound by the mansion restoration should resemble its original form."

There were murmurs of agreement from other architects.

The older architect fumed but nodded. "Fine."

Anya smiled at the team. "We are going to start visiting the mansion site starting next week onwards. Please free up your time accordingly."

There were excited murmurs which she was happy to hear. She wanted the team to be excited and emotionally invested in the project like she was.

"Thank you all. Have a nice weekend."

Placing her laptop into her bag, she got up to leave when she received a call. It was from Ritu Kapadia, the antique dealer.

Smiling, she answered the call. "Hello, Ritu."

"Anya! Are you free tonight?"

She looked at the time. It was only five. "Yes."

"Oh good. I'll see you at seven thirty tonight. I'll send you the location."

Anya smiled. "Sure."

Ending the call, Anya looked forward to meeting Ritu. Ritu had managed to acquire five more original pieces that once belonged to the mansion. Ritu was also supposed to provide an update on an old craftsman who had agreed to work on the unique furniture at the mansion.

Stepping into the elevator, Anya pressed the button to the underground parking. Ignoring the ache in her chest at not having heard from Bhargav Varma, she left the building.

He's just the client.

***

"Wow, Anya! You look gorgeous."

Anya smiled and hugged Ritu Kapadia. "You look gorgeous too. What's the occasion?" She had received a text from Ritu to dress up for their meeting. Since Anya was feeling a bit low, she went all in and dressed up for the occasion.

Ritu laughed. "It's my birthday."

"Oh wow. Happy birthday!" Anya hugged Ritu again with a smile. "Shouldn't you be celebrating with Keshav tonight?"

"Keshav will be joining us in a while."

Anya smiled. "That's good. Then I'll be quick to show you the latest designs and leave when Keshav arrives."

Ritu shook her head. "Oh no. You don't have to leave. I invited you to join us for the celebration."

Anya felt touched. "Thank you."

The place was quite crowded, but the hostess smiled brightly at Ritu and seated them at a private booth that had a stunning view of the lake and city.

"I haven't been to this place before," Anya commented, admiring the view.

"It's actually new. Keshav opened it only two months ago."

"Oh! I didn't know you owned the place. Congratulations!"

Ritu smiled. "Keshav owns it with his partners. But yes, I guess it's mine too."

They ordered drinks and light appetizers. Anya turned down alcohol. "I have to work tonight. I need to finish up putting in orders for the exterior tiles."

"Come on! It's my birthday!" Ritu insisted. "We can drop you home."

Anya laughed. "I'll have a drink when Keshav joins us. I promise."

Ritu luckily agreed. Soon, Ritu took out her iPad to show the latest acquisitions. Anya recognized them.

"That's the urn Parvathi Vardhaman used to put near the entrance! I used to help her pick flowers to place in it."

Ritu smiled at Anya's excitement. "That's awesome. I recognized it from the pictures you sent. It was purchased by a banker whose family luckily was willing to sell it."

Anya was fiercely glad.

Ritu showed her the rest of the acquisitions, and Anya showed her the updated designs. Anya didn't know how much time had passed when Ritu let out an excited shriek.

"Finally, you are here!"

Anya smiled and turned, expecting to see Ritu's husband, Keshav. But her heart almost leaped out of her chest when her eyes clashed with the darkly, intense gaze of Bhargav Varma.

"What took you two so long?" she heard Ritu demand.

Ritu's husband laughed. "Sorry, sweetheart. Our meeting went longer than expected. We are here now." He sat next to Ritu and kissed her cheek.

Anya's heart continued to race. Bhargav Varma's spicy cologne filled her senses when he sat next to her.

Feeling too flustered, she turned to him. "Hello, Mr. Varma," she greeted.

His eyes flashed at her formal greeting. "Hello, Miss Kashyap."

Anya's cheeks heated, detecting the underlying teasing in his greeting.

Dragging her eyes away from his hypnotic ones, she turned to look at the couple opposite to her. "Hello, Mr. Kapadia," she greeted.

Keshav Kapadia laughed. "Please call me Keshav. We are here as friends to celebrate my wife's birthday."

Anya nodded with a smile even as her heart thudded. She felt extremely aware of the man next to her.

Why was he invited?

Did he know I was going to be there as well?

"Anya, you promised to drink when Keshav joined. Come on, order now!"

Anya didn't mind. She probably needed a drink to get through the rest of the night.

They placed the order for drinks. Luckily, the conversation was driven mostly by Ritu.

"Remember the trip we won at the auction? Keshav and I are planning to go to Paris this December. Hopefully, the mansion would just be starting to come along by that time."

December was only three months away. According to Anya's timelines, the work would be progressing well. "Yes, we would be done with most of the immediate outside landscaping and the mansion's flooring, ceiling and painting should be done too by then."

"That's awesome!" Ritu grinned. "I can't wait to see the place begins to transform."

Anya smiled. "Me too."

Their drinks and food arrived. But Ritu and her husband kept the conversation going. Bhargav Varma was mostly silent through it all. Anya tried and failed not to feel aware of his presence. And it also took a considerable effort not to lean against him the way Ritu was leaning against her husband and laughing.

"It must have been so much fun visiting the Vardhaman Estate during your childhood," Ritu's husband remarked with a smile.

"Yes. It was incredible. I looked forward to my holidays."

Ritu sighed. "I can't believe how it looks right now. Have you visited the estate recently?"

Anya's face immediately heated, and she tried not to blush. "Yes. Last Saturday. Mr. Varma and I... uh... checked the status, and I showed him the estate's rosewood and teak trees."

"Oh yeah!" Ritu remarked. "I was telling Bhargav about your plan to use reclaimed wood from the damaged furniture. Using the wood from the estate trees is an awesome idea! Isn't it, Bhargav!"

"Yes," his deep voice replied. "I was impressed by the idea as well as those trees. The location is all the more interesting."

Anya almost choked on her drink at his comment. Her eyes flew to his face to see if he was referring to their passionate encounter, but he simply returned her stare with his hooded gaze. With her cheeks on fire, she hurriedly looked away from him.

Soon, the dinner was done. Keshav ordered a special cake for his wife which she cut with a birthday song playing in the background. Anya took pictures of the happy couple as they fed each other cake.

It was close to midnight when they went down and waited near the lobby.

Ritu hugged Anya. "Thank you so much, Anya, for coming and making my birthday special. I was telling Keshav how comfortable I feel towards you even though I've only met you recently."

Anya smiled. "I feel the same."

Ritu then turned slightly. "And thanks a lot to you too, Bhargav. I know you flew in just this evening from Singapore. I'm glad you decided to join us for dinner."

"I'm glad too," his voice drawled.

So he hadn't been in the city this week.

That fact shouldn't make a difference, but it did. Anya's heart raced at the fact that he hadn't deliberately avoided her all week. He hadn't been there at his penthouse.

"Babe, we need to drop Anya at her place," Ritu told her husband.

Anya shook her head. "Oh no. I just had one drink. I'm fine. And I was planning to take a cab. Please carry on with your plans."

"It's not a bother at all, Anya. We can drop you."

Bhargav Varma's deep voice cut in. "I will drop her."

Anya looked at him. "I can take a cab, Mr. Varma. It's really not needed."

His eyebrow rose slightly. "It might not be needed, but I want to."

Her cheeks heated at his reply, and she didn't know what to say to that.

"Yes, Anya. We'd feel much better if Bhargav drops you home safely."

Knowing there wasn't a way out without worrying the birthday girl, Anya nodded. "All right. I'll go with Mr. Varma. Happy birthday again and have a wonderful time for the rest of the night."

With final goodbyes, they stepped out where the cars were kept ready by the valets.

Bhargav Varma didn't drive a car. He had a sleek SUV. It suited him somehow.

As soon as she sat in the passenger seat, his spicy cologne once again invaded her senses. Her body tingled in response. Biting her lip, she put on her seat belt and murmured out her address.

She thought he would ask her to repeat, but the SUV began to move.

The ride was quiet. But since the roads were mostly empty due to the late hour, it would only be a twenty-minute drive away.

"I heard Mr. Satish has been causing problems for you," he said.

Anya shook her head. "No. There aren't any problems. Just a few minor disagreements that I can handle."

"I see."

Silence fell again, letting the heavy awareness fill the air inside the car.

She felt slightly relieved when she saw her familiar neighborhood. He drove to her lane, and she asked him to stop right outside the lane since the road was too narrow in front of the house.

"Thank you, Mr. Varma. I'll see you... later." She wasn't sure if she would be meeting him again soon.

"Good night, Anya," he replied.

Her heart jerked listening to her name. "Good night."

She got down from his SUV and walked towards her home. But as she walked away, she felt the strong need to run back to him.

She had missed him all week. She felt confused because even though she had decided not to have an affair with him to protect her heart, she still felt the pain of not being with him.

He made her feel empty when he wasn't around.

"Where the hell have you been all the while?" a man's voice snapped.

Anya was shocked when she heard Surya's voice. She saw her ex-husband standing near the entrance of her house.

"What are you doing here?" she asked. Her heart thudded sickly seeing his angry face.

"Is this why you divorced me and refused to marry me again? So you can live a whore's life?"

Anger shot through her at his hypocrisy. "I told you many times that I divorced you because you cheated on me and because I don't love you. Now leave me alone."

"No. I won't. You humiliated me by flaunting your boyfriend at the auction. You need to be taught a lesson."

Her heart thudded as she prepared to fight him off. But another voice cut through.

"Step away from her," a dark growl warned.

Anya's eyes flew to the side, and she saw Bhargav Varma standing a few feet away from them.

Surya looked at Bhargav. "She is my wife! Get out of here before I beat the crap out of you!"

Anya's heart thudded at the quiet menace he saw on Bhargav Varma's face. He stepped closer until he was only a foot away from Surya and her.

"She *was* your wife," he corrected.

Surya sneered. "I dumped her because she couldn't keep her legs closed. But now I want her back even though she fucked you and many other men. This is between me and her, so get out!"

Anya felt humiliated by Surya's lies. But she couldn't say anything without agitating Surya more.

"You are no longer her husband," Bhargav Varma repeated calmly. "Even if you were, I don't give a fuck because she doesn't want you here. I want you gone right now."

"You cocky bastard!" Surya attacked in rage.

Bhargav Varma easily caught Surya's oncoming fist and twisted the hand at an odd angle. Surya shrieked out and tried to hit using the other hand. But that blow was deflected easily.

Anya was reminded of the time she had seen Bhargav Varma in the boxing ring, fighting with two men at a time. But unlike that trained fight, she saw cold rage on Bhargav Varma's normally calm and reserved face.

Drawing his hand back, he punched her ex-husband in the face several times. Blood spurted out of Surya's nose.

Oh my God.

"Bhargav, stop!" Anya called out frantically. She didn't want Bhargav to be in trouble because of her.

Listening to her frantic voice, Bhargav Varma paused. He looked at her and then at Surya. He then drew his hand back and punched Surya hard in the stomach until Surya yelled and collapsed on the ground.

Bhargav grabbed Surya's arm and pulled him up. "Don't ever come near her or bother her again," he warned. He then shoved Surya away towards a parked car. "Now get out."

With a loud groan, Surya dragged himself into his car. A minute later, he drove away.

Anya felt shaken by the sudden turn of events. She couldn't imagine what would have happened if Bhargav Varma hadn't come to check on her. Surya was angry enough to hurt her.

She stared at him as he came closer. "Are you okay?" he asked her softly.

She nodded. "I'm fine," she said in a slightly shaky voice.

He looked at her face for a moment. "Do you want to call your friend, or should I drop you anywhere else for tonight?"

She shook her head at his question. "No. I'll be okay." Suddenly, chills covered her body.

Her body went into shock.

Bhargav frowned. "Where are your keys, Anya?" he asked.

With trembling hands, she drew them out from her purse. He took them from her and unlocked the door. Placing a steady arm around her waist, he guided her into her house.

The familiar warmth of her home calmed her somewhat.

"Sit down for a while," he ordered. "I'll get you some water."

He made her sit on her living room couch before he went into her kitchen. She wrapped her arms around her body and waited for the chills to disappear.

"Here," he said, handing her a glass. "Have some water."

She took the glass from him and drank the water. She felt slightly better a moment later. Just when he was about to take the empty glass back, she noticed that his knuckles were bruised.

"You got hurt," she said, her stomach sinking with guilt. "Let me bring some ice—"

"No. I'm fine." His mouth twisted into a small smile. "Bruised knuckles are a common enough occurrence for me since childhood."

"Oh." She recalled again that he boxed for exercise.

But what did he mean by since childhood? She wanted to ask him and know more about him. She wanted to know everything possible.

She stared at him, her heart beginning to race in excitement and happiness seeing him properly again after nearly a week. She soaked in his darkly handsome features and his larger-than-life presence while he stood in her small living room.

He caught her staring, and the small smile from his face disappeared, and his eyes hooded in a familiar way. The air around them shifted and buzzed with crackling electricity.

Her heart continued racing, and her stomach began quivering in anticipation. She recalled the last time they were alone together. The passionate memories made her lips tingle and her breasts peak in arousal. She badly wanted to feel his hands and mouth on her body again.

Suddenly, he leaned towards her. She expected him to kiss her, but his warm, slightly calloused fingers caught her chin in a firm grip.

"I want to kiss you again," he rasped out in a rough tone. "But you are too shaken up. I should leave now."

Her breath caught in her throat at the heat blazing in his eyes. A similar inferno raged inside her as well.

"Don't leave," she whispered. "I want you."

His eyes flared at her words. "You are shaken up. What you want is comfort, not this. You'll regret it later."

She shook her head. She had never felt surer about anything. She wanted Bhargav Varma. She had wanted him for a long time. She didn't care if he dumped her later or broke her heart. Being without him made her feel lonely and hurt her deep inside, anyway.

She now wanted to experience the heady passion and need she felt each time she was with him.

She caught his bruised knuckles in her hand. "I won't regret it," she said softly. "I want you."

Desire blazed in his eyes, but he still didn't make a move.

With her heart thudding, she smiled through her trembling lips. "Were you lying, Mr.Varma, when you said that the next time I begged you to take me, you would?"

His nostrils flared at her soft taunting, and his eyes darkened to a molten, predatory look.

A gasp escaped her when his hands suddenly gripped her waist and easily picked her up from the couch. "No," he growled into her face. "I wasn't lying."

His mouth crashed on top of hers.

The moment their lips collided, she felt the tight grip of control and restraint they held between them over the last weeks, explode.

Wrapping her legs around his hips, she gripped his shoulders while his tongue ravaged her mouth. Moaning, she sucked on his tongue, wanting more of the addicting taste of him.

His steps were long and rapid as he carried her effortlessly to her bedroom. Their kiss didn't break even when he dropped her on her bed. His heavy weight lay on top of her while they continued to kiss hungrily.

His hand held her dress and yanked. The tearing noise sounded loud in the quiet room followed by her loud gasp when he cupped her breast roughly. Liquid fire raced through her blood, making her desperate. She tore at his clothes, pushing away his jacket and shirt until she could touch his heated skin. When she finally could, she raked her nails over his toned muscles, making him growl.

She felt his hands gripping her dress and pushing it up her hips. Another hard yank ripped away the delicate material of her panties. Her heartbeat pounded loudly in her ears when he pushed her legs apart, and she felt his rough movements while he adjusted his clothes. She knew he was finally going to take her. Her body screamed with anticipation and need.

But despite her bracing for his entry, a shocked cry escaped her when he drove into her deeply in a single, powerful thrust.

She felt impossibly full, and her body struggled to stretch around him to accommodate his length.

"Fuck," he groaned into her neck when he felt her insides tightening hard around him.

It hurt, but she didn't want him to stop. She was too far gone to stop, and so was he.

"Please," she begged while he gripped her hips and drove into her like a raging storm.

This was what she had wanted and this was what she needed.

She had known this would happen between them. The charged awareness and connection she felt between them was a live wire waiting to catch fire. She had run away from him like a scared little girl and tried hard to keep him at distance. But she finally gave in to the inevitable.

Raw sounds escaped her throat as she clung to him, gasping and crying out his name. Even with the searing pain, pleasure rose quickly like a tidal wave. His rough, harsh guttural groans against her neck drove the pleasure even higher. Soon, the wave crashed inside her, making her scream. He let out a harsh cry at the same time and shuddered hard on top of her, joining her in the explosion.

Her world shattered and was blowing away, and he was the only anchor she could hold on to. She clung to him while they trembled and shook together.

She didn't know how long they clung together. Slowly, the trembling reduced in intensity, and she desperately tried to draw in some much-needed air into her lungs. But when she opened her eyes, her breath was knocked from her chest again when her eyes met with his.

The lights in the room were not turned on, but the street light right outside her bedroom window threw in enough light for her to see his face.

He was breathing heavily and watching her with hooded eyes.

His mouth slowly twisted into a small, familiar smile. "You looked beautiful tonight, Miss Kashyap. I didn't get a chance to tell you that."

Anya blushed, which was ridiculous. Their bodies were still joined together, and the smell of sex was heavy in the air. She also realized they hadn't even gotten rid of their clothes. She was still wearing her dress, and he was wearing his complete suit.

"Thank you," she murmured with heated cheeks.

He pulled out of her and rolled away. Immediately, she felt a huge loss. She missed the hard and heavy press of his body along with his heat. Even with the hot, pleasurable glow of their recent explosive coupling, the burn of disappointment began to creep inside her stomach.

She watched him, knowing he would straighten his clothes and thank her before leaving her house. She didn't know if she would ever be with him again.

Maybe once was enough for him.

Now that the thrill of the chase was gone for him, he lost interest. Her heart sank at the thought.

But instead of buttoning his shirt, he began to shrug it off. She stared at him with her mouth slightly open.

He watched her shocked face with slight amusement. "Did you think I was going to leave?" he asked.

She nodded, feeling uncertain. She hadn't done casual sex before and didn't know the rules. Although the current sexual encounter felt far from casual.

His mouth twisted into a small smile. "I'm not going to leave anytime soon," he said. "I have a promise to keep, Miss Kashyap."

She blushed hard at his deliberate use of her last name. It sounded sexy and hot.

He watched her with hooded eyes and continued to shed his clothes. Soon, his chiseled body was completely bared to her. Her mouth and lips turned dry seeing the raw, masculine beauty of his body, especially the part of him that gave her pain but immense pleasure.

She wet her parched lips with her tongue, staring at him in awe. She wanted to touch him and explore him using her hands and lips. And she was shocked when his arousal began visibly hardening and increasing in length. Her eyes flew up to his.

His eyes blazed. Seeing the predatory look on his face, she unconsciously leaned back with a soft gasp. He took a step towards the bed and leaned over her.

"You can't escape me now, Miss Kashyap," he said with a dark, predatory smile.

Her heart thudded hard, and her body once again heated in desire. "I don't want to escape," she whispered.

"Good." Gripping the hair at the back of her head, he slammed his mouth over hers in a deep, passionate kiss.

For the rest of the night, he fulfilled his promise several more times

CHAPTER EIGHTEEN

Anya woke up to the bright sunlight streaming through her bedroom window.

She tried to turn to her side as always before blinking her eyes open, but unexpected soreness between her legs and pain shot through her body. She gasped out, and her eyes flew open.

Oh my God, I slept with my client!

Although there hadn't much sleeping involved because by the time her eyes shut in exhaustion, the sun was already rising outside her window.

Her heart began to thud as she recalled the events of the night in a flash. The birthday dinner. The ugly confrontation with Surya. And then the explosive encounter with Bhargav Varma after she more or less taunted him to take her.

And he more than obliged.

Her cheeks heated, recalling how she couldn't get enough of him. He had taken her over and over, and she had been with him all along, begging and clutching him greedily.

Oh God!

How am I going to face him again? Especially in project meetings and at the estate!

She was embarrassed by her desperation, but she didn't regret the night she spent with him. She reveled in his passion and would remember the night for the rest of her life.

She stared at the empty spot on the bed beside her.

Did he enjoy the night with her?

Her cheeks heated even more when she recalled the things he had done to her and the words he had spoken during the heat of passion. There was no doubt he desired her and enjoyed their night.

But was it a one-night stand?

She didn't know.

She recalled her best friend's words. Trupti had said that sleeping with a client she was strongly attracted to had made her realize how terribly selfish and narcissistic that person was.

But unfortunately, Anya didn't feel that way about Bhargav Varma. Her body heated recalling that he was far from selfish in bed. And he wasn't a narcissist either. In fact, in the last few weeks of knowing him, he had barely spoken anything about himself.

Anya bit her lip uncertainly.

He probably thinks I'm bad in bed and not as experienced as his previous partners.

She had hardly gotten a chance to explore him the way she wanted. The need and desire had only led to their frantic couplings. There was barely a moment of leisure exploration.

Maybe it was a one-night stand, and she would have to deal with it.

She sucked in a deep breath. *Yes, I'm a mature woman. I can deal with this.*

Even as she said those words inside her mind, her heart ached at the thought of never being able to touch him again.

A masculine curse from the kitchen shocked her out of her thoughts.

"Fuck!" the person cursed out again.

Anya sat up on the bed. *Oh my God. He's still here.*

She could hear more sounds from the kitchen. Ignoring the soreness of her body, she got up from the bed. She then grabbed a wrap from her closet and put it on before hurrying outside the bedroom to the kitchen.

Bhargav Varma was trying to make coffee using her coffee maker. He must have sensed her presence right away because he turned to look at her.

Her heart leaped, seeing his darkly handsome face. And she also couldn't help lowering her eyes to stare at his chiseled body displayed clearly in just his boxer briefs. With her cheeks heating, she dragged her eyes up and kept her gaze on his face.

His mouth twisted into a small smile. "I thought I'd wake you with coffee in bed. But I'm still trying to figure out how to get this thing to work."

"Oh." Pleasure heated her cheeks at his words. "I'll make it."

Unlike the fancy coffee machines he might be used to, she had the basic coffee filter made of stainless-steel jars. She filled up water in a small pan and placed it on the stove to heat it. She then poured ground coffee on the top stainless-steel jar.

While she waited for the water to be heated, she felt his arms enclosing around her waist. Her heart raced inside her chest, and her breaths turned heavier.

"How are you feeling?" his deep, husky voice murmured next to her ear.

She shivered lightly. "I-I'm fine," she whispered. She gasped when his arm moved and his hand slid inside her wrap. He cupped her breast and flicked the hardened bud with his thumb. Her stomach trembled as her body began to come alive again despite the soreness.

"I have a meeting later this morning to finalize the estate sale," he said. "I want you to rest at home and come to my place for dinner tonight."

Her heart thudded.

So, it wasn't just a one-night stand.

Nervous excitement raced through her body at the fact.

"Will you come?" he asked in a deep murmur. The rough stubble around his mouth brushed against her cheek, causing delicious shivers.

With her chest heaving, she nodded. "Yes."

She felt his smile on her cheek. "Pour the water into that jar," he instructed.

She did as he ordered and poured the hot water into the coffee filter. It would take a few minutes for the coffee to be ready.

A gasp escaped her when he whipped her around to face him as soon as her hands were free. Her heart raced seeing the look of hunger on his face.

"You look so fucking beautiful," he rasped. Cupping her cheek, he pulled her into a deep, hungry kiss.

She moaned and wrapped her arms around his neck, kissing him back hungrily.

He pushed away the wrap from her shoulders and picked her up. Without breaking their kiss, he carried her somewhere. But he didn't take her to the bedroom as she expected. He lowered her on her small dining table.

Pulling back from their kiss, he watched her with a predatory look on his face. He looked hungry. Her breaths came out as pants when he gripped her thighs and pulled her closer until her hips were hanging towards the edge of the table.

And then, parting her legs, and keeping their gazes locked, he feasted.

She lost track of how many times she begged and screamed hoarsely. When she finally came to her senses, she realized she was sitting on her couch with her fingers wrapped around a mug filled with steaming, aromatic coffee.

Bhargav Varma was fully dressed in his suit. He watched her with a small smile. "I'll see you tonight at my penthouse. My driver will pick up your car from the restaurant and drop it at your place. He can bring you to my place in the evening."

She stared at him in a daze and nodded. Her mind and body were numbed with pleasure overload.

"Bye, Anya," he said huskily before leaning over and kissing her. The kiss caught fire immediately, but with the deep groan, he pulled away and straightened.

"I better leave," he said. His mouth then twisted into a smile watching her flushed face. "And just so we are clear, I'm not *'just a client'* anymore."

Her heart jerked and she stared at him in shock.

Oh God! How does he know!

"I heard you repeating those words when I saw your lips moving to them."

Her cheeks were on fire as he laughed softly and cupped her cheek again. This time he didn't kiss her. The slightly roughened skin of his thumb brushed over her cheek. "See you tonight," he said huskily.

And then, he stepped away from her and walked out of her small living room.

She continued to sit in a daze, while slowly another thought repeated in a loop inside her mind.

He's not just a client anymore. And I... may be falling in love with him.

CHAPTER NINETEEN

"Congratulations, Mr. Varma. The estate sale is now completed. All five hundred acres now belong to Ventura Holdings."

Bhargav was seated at a guesthouse with a group of men. He went through the final documents and passed them to his lawyers to check if everything was in order.

"But Mr. Varma, you made a powerful enemy because of the disputed fifty acres. Mr. Sampath is very upset."

Bhargav shrugged. "He can be upset all he wants. But this land will always belong to the Vardhaman Estate."

The politician might be powerful, but the older man was easily blackmailed by a compromising video taken of him, while he was with his latest mistress who was half his age.

"The factory will be gone in a few months," Bhargav stated. "When the surrounding land comes up for sale, I want to purchase it."

The agent looked surprised. "You want that land added to the estate as well?"

"No. I want the farmers who sold it to begin cultivating on the land again."

"Oh. That's an excellent idea, Mr. Varma! And also very generous of you."

Bhargav looked at the men. "This is not generosity," he stated. "The area around the estate is to be kept green and sustainable. If any politician or a businessman wants to open a factory in the assigned green area, I need to know."

The men nodded.

Bhargav finished up the meeting. And soon, he flew back to the city.

He sent a brief text to his brothers about the final estate sale.

"Sir, should I tell the Singapore team to move the meeting to later tonight?"

At his PA's question, Bhargav shook his head. "No. I want to be done with it this afternoon. Keep the rest of the weekend free of any appointments."

"Sure, sir."

There were a lot of things going on—he had a pissed-off politician who would want to strike back soon, a shit-ton of things that needed to be addressed in one of his upcoming hotels in Singapore, and things that were moving too rapidly with the plan he and his brothers had made.

But right then, none of those things sat on top in his mind. All he wanted to do was be done with the damn day and get back to the penthouse where the woman who was his obsession would be visiting him soon.

He sat back in the chopper and looked out the window, trying to control himself from saying 'fuck everything' before grabbing a car and driving to Anya's home. He barely had patience to wait until that night.

But clenching his jaw, he controlled himself and let duty take over until that evening. Also, Anya must be too sore for him to maul her again without giving her enough time to heal.

His mouth twisted into a smile as memories of their night and that morning washed over him. Spending the night with Anya was unanticipated. He knew she was going to be at the restaurant because Ritu Kapadia had told him. Ritu had somehow sensed how he felt towards Anya and tried to play Cupid, which he didn't mind.

But what he hadn't expected was to drop Anya at her home. Even though she had asked him to stop his car away from her house, he felt a strong need to speak with her. He had wanted to talk to her using the pretext of getting project updates. He went to her house, expecting her to call out his bullshit but was furious when he saw a man nearly attacking her.

It was Anya's ex-husband.

The bastard was threatening her. It took a considerable amount of control not to break every bone in that bastard's body for daring to threaten Anya and calling her filthy names. So when the fool attacked him in a pathetically amateur way, he had broken the bastard's wrist and kicked him out.

What happened next inside Anya's home was completely unplanned.

She taunted him to take her and told him she wanted him. The tight control he had been keeping on his desire towards her for so long broke loose, and he fell on her like a starving man.

All thought had disappeared except to claim the woman he was obsessed with.

Each time he thought about slowing down, her soft, needy moans and tightening muscles of her wet channel drove him mad. He drove in as deeply as he could inside her, and yet he felt the need to take more. He wanted to possess every inch of her. He did possess her body. He had kissed and tasted every inch until the taste of her was branded into his mind permanently.

Fuck.

He clenched his hands into fists. The helicopter would land soon, and he didn't want to appear with a visible boner. Shaking his head slightly, he tried to calm down.

I need to calm the fuck down. And I need to make it up to her tonight.

He was going to woo her. He was going to wine and dine her, then show her that he was capable of having a normal relationship and not fall on her like a starved animal.

A part of him also knew he was on borrowed time before things would go wrong. He intended to capture every moment of it until she was bound to him in every way.

CHAPTER TWENTY

The doorbell rang at four o'clock in the afternoon.

Anya was at home, trying to distract herself.

She had worked on the updated designs for a while. But each time she shifted slightly, the soreness between her legs and the slight aches in her body made her blush and smile.

She couldn't wait for the evening to arrive. The anticipation nearly drove her crazy.

She felt the need to see Bhargav Varma's darkly handsome face, see the small twist of his masculine lips and hear him speak in his deep voice. And despite the soreness, she also wanted to feel him deep inside her again.

She badly hoped it was just lust.

But although desire dominated her current thoughts, she also felt the strong need to know more about him. She couldn't wait to ask him about his family and childhood. His dreams and desires. And also, his future.

She only hoped she wouldn't scare him away with her eagerness.

Dammit!

She had never dated or felt this way before. She didn't know what the etiquette was when it came to dating someone you desired and were close to falling in love with.

It was frightening, but she couldn't fight her feelings anymore.

She wished she could tell herself what she felt was pure lust and nothing else. But it would be a lie.

Maybe I need to play it cool tonight.

She could try and hide how she felt. But Bhargav Varma had the strange ability to read her mind easily. The man was too wicked and shrewd not to sense her feelings.

She shook her head with a smile. *No. I'm going to let him see everything. If it scares him, then so be it.*

She decided to be her natural self and let things proceed the way she hoped they would. And Bhargav Varma was also not the kind to scare away easily.

The doorbell rang again.

"Coming!" she called out.

She went to the front door and looked through the peephole. There was a man standing with her car keys.

Opening the door, she greeted the man with a smile. "Hello. I'm Anya. Thank you for bringing my car."

"Hello, Miss Kashyap. I am Shankar. I was asked to drive you to Mr. Varma's home this evening."

It was only four, which meant there were at least three or four hours before she could go to the penthouse for dinner. She didn't want to keep the driver waiting that long.

"Thank you, Shankar. But I can drive myself. You can go home."

The man looked uncertain. "Are you sure, madam?"

She smiled. "Yes."

He nodded and handed her the car keys. "All right, Miss."

Thanking the man again, she shut the door.

She somehow knew Bhargav wouldn't be too happy about sending the driver back. Her client turned lover was somewhat of a control freak. She hadn't known him long, but she had observed him closely enough to know he liked being in control and always planned everything perfectly.

But only outside the bed.

She let out a dreamy sigh, recalling how unrestrained and out of control his lovemaking had been the previous night and earlier that morning.

She shivered in anticipation, wondering how his lovemaking would be that night. She felt a strong urge to make him lose control again. She also intended to explore his stunning body, which she couldn't the previous night. She badly wanted to kiss, touch and taste him like he had done to her.

Anya's wicked thoughts were interrupted by the sound of her phone ringing.

Wondering if it was Trupti, she picked up her phone from the couch. It was her mother.

Anya groaned.

She wasn't in the mood to speak with her mother. Surya must have complained to her parents about him being roughened up the previous night at her home. Her parents wouldn't find fault with Surya threatening her. They would latch on to the fact that she didn't stop someone from hurting Surya.

She wasn't the kind of person who condoned violence. But when Bhargav punched Surya, she felt a primitive satisfaction. She had stopped Bhargav eventually because she didn't want him to get into trouble.

She also loved the fact that Bhargav had stood up for her despite Surya's ugly lies.

Taking a deep breath, she answered the phone call to get it over with. She didn't want her mother to keep calling her the rest of the day.

"Hello, Ma."

"Anya, come home urgently!"

Anya frowned at her mother's anxious tone. "What happened, Ma? Is this about Surya?"

"I can't speak to you on the phone. Just come."

Ugh!

"All right, Ma."

Hoping the visit wouldn't last long, Anya began to get ready.

She couldn't spend enough time picking the perfect clothes to wear. She didn't want to wear something too sexy, so she wore a comfortable dress. Luckily, it was easy to remove, and she paired it with sexy lingerie.

Blushing hard, she finished getting ready and stepped out of her house to go to her parents' house.

With her heart thudding in breathless anticipation, she wondered if she would stay the night at Bhargav Varma's penthouse.

Hopefully, yes.

***

Anya saw a few cars parked outside her parents' home.

One of them was the car she had seen parked in front of her home the previous night. It was Surya's. Her father's driver was waiting outside, which meant her father was home too. Considering her father didn't speak to her much, except for demanding that she go back to her ex-husband, she didn't look forward to the conversation.

It would be yet again another confrontation with her parents and Surya trying to get her to agree to remarry him.

She had never loved Surya. She didn't even respect the man. There was no way she would ever agree to marrying him under any circumstances, especially after the previous night.

Taking a deep breath, she parked her car outside her parents' house. Greeting the driver, she went inside. Her mother was waiting for her.

"Oh good, you are here finally. Come quickly! Papa is not well."

"What happened, Ma? Is Papa okay?" It didn't occur to her at all that her father might be sick.

"No, he is not okay."

Anya frowned in worry. "Then why are you not taking him to the hospital? Come, let's go—"

"No. He's not sick. I meant he is not okay because of his business."

Anya recalled her mother mentioning it during the last visit. But her mother hadn't given her any details. Surya mentioned it too and said her father made risky investments.

"What happened?" she asked.

Her mother took a deep breath. "Let Papa tell you."

It sounded ominous. She was reminded of the time when she was barely eighteen. Her father had thrown an ultimatum and more or less emotionally blackmailed her into marrying his business partner's son.

She had foolishly agreed because her college studies depended on her agreeing to the marriage.

There is nothing now that I can't achieve on my own.

She didn't need money or anything else that would force her into an unwanted marriage again.

"They are in the garden room," Anya's mother stated.

Sucking in a determined breath to fight off yet another attempted brainwashing session, Anya followed her mother. She stepped into the familiar room where she often escaped to look at her old photo albums or read a book.

She saw Surya seated along with her father and brother. Thick tension filled the air.

Anya focused on her father. "What happened, Papa?" she asked.

Her father's face was pale. "We lost everything, Anya."

Anya's brother sprang up from the couch. "We might even be sent to jail!"

Anya was shocked. "What do you mean by lost everything? Why jail? What happened?"

"It's this idiot's fault," her father raged. "He gambled and lost his apartment and car and even his inheritance."

Anya's brother looked angry. "You lost our factories and this house. You made risky investments and took loans without even bothering to tell us!"

Anya's head began to throb. "Stop it," she said. "Both of you were at fault. But what do you expect me to do?"

"Marry me again," Surya gritted out.

Anya turned to look at her ex-husband. She nearly gasped seeing his bruised, swollen face. One of his eyes was black and swollen shut completely, and his right arm was in a sling. He glared at her angrily.

Anya knew Surya didn't tell her parents or brother about Bhargav. He was too egoistical to tell anyone that he got beaten up by someone, who was his ex-wife's lover.

"If you marry me, my parents will help your family."

Anya's heart began to thud sickly.

"No," she said in a firm tone. "I will never marry you."

Anya's mother intervened immediately. "How can you say that! Your father and brother might go to jail!"

"For the things they did, Ma. And they did those things knowingly. They were well aware of the consequences when they gambled or made those risky investments. Why is it my responsibility to bail them out?"

"Don't be so selfish!" her mother snapped. "It is your responsibility to sacrifice for your family. And why is it a sacrifice? All you have to do is marry Surya."

Even though Anya was expecting her mother to call her selfish, she was still hurt by her mother's words. "I don't love him, Ma. I don't even like him."

Her mother dismissed her feelings. "You will learn to like him and love him after marriage and when you have children."

Anya sucked in a breath. "I won't ever love him. Because I love someone else."

There were shocked gasps.

"Who the hell is he?" her father demanded. "I'm sure he's some gold-digging loser. I won't allow you to marry him!"

Anya gritted her teeth. She didn't want to marry Bhargav Varma. She didn't know him well enough even though she was falling in love with him. But the fact that her father and the rest of her family thought they could control her life based on their needs hurt and angered her.

"It's not up to you, Papa," she said. "I'm an adult. I'm also independent enough to make my own decisions."

Her father looked angry and didn't say anything. But her mother wasn't quiet.

"Your brother and father will go to jail soon if you don't marry Surya!" her mother shouted.

Anya's heart clenched sickly. "We'll find a way, Ma. I can help a little with the money." She didn't want to tell them about the massive payment she would receive for restoring the Vardhaman Estate. "I... I... know someone who can help stop Papa and Sohan from being arrested. He... he can help us buy more time."

Bhargav Varma was powerful and influential enough to buy an estate that belonged to the government, and he also recently re-acquired the estate land that a powerful politician had seized.

But she didn't know for sure whether he would be willing to help her.

They had only known each other for a few weeks. And somehow, begging for his help would also cheapen what they had between them the previous night. She badly hoped he didn't think she slept with him to ask for his help.

Her heart clenched at the thought of him thinking that their night didn't mean anything to her.

"Who is that man?" her mother demanded. "I don't think your clients will help you."

"He will, Ma." She didn't know that yet.

"Call him," her father said. "Ask him to come here. I will speak to him and see if he can help us."

Anya's heart jerked. "No. I can't call him. He's... busy."

She was supposed to meet him in an hour at his penthouse. So, she knew he was not busy. But she couldn't call him and ask him to come to her parents' place.

"Call him, Anya," her brother insisted. "The police will arrest us anytime."

Anya felt torn.

She hated that she was made to be the sacrificial lamb for the mess her family created. She might even lose the man she was falling in love with because of them.

"Call him here now!" her mother demanded.

Anya took a deep breath. "Okay, fine."

She stepped out of the room and went into the garden area before dialing his number. The phone was answered in two rings.

"Miss Kashyap," Bhargav Varma's deep voice spoke in an amused tone. "I hope you are here downstairs at the parking garage. I can't wait to spank you for sending the driver away. Although I think you might enjoy the spanking."

Her stomach fluttered listening to him. Her heart ached that she would have to cancel their dinner plans and instead beg him for a huge favor.

"I'm sorry I can't make it tonight," she said. "There is a family emergency."

"Are you okay?" he asked immediately.

"Yes, I am. But my family isn't." She took a deep breath to get through the next few moments. "Bhargav... I... I... need your help."

There was a pause. "What help, Anya?" All amusement disappeared from his tone.

Her stomach sank. "Can you please come to my parents' house? I will tell you everything."

There was another pause, a slightly longer one. "All right," he said. "I'll be there in a few minutes."

"Thanks," she whispered. "I'll send you the address."

He didn't say anything. The call ended.

Anya closed her eyes and sat in the garden. *Oh God. Please don't make him hate me.*

She liked him a lot. She was falling in love with him. The thought of him looking at her with disgust, thinking that she was only using him, hurt her deeply. She was determined to convince him that she hadn't known anything about her family crisis when they spent the night together.

***

Anya didn't know how long she sat in the garden lost in her thoughts and staring at the bushes. But soon, she heard the sounds of her brother and Surya shouting.

She frowned. She looked at the time. Only thirty minutes had passed. Bhargav Varma's penthouse was nearly forty-five minutes away from her parents' home. Unless he drove very fast to get there, it wasn't him.

Wondering what triggered the shouting, she headed back into the garden view room.

When she stepped in, her eyes clashed with Bhargav's. Her heart raced with happiness seeing his handsome face after their night together.

She smiled tentatively, feeling shaken and embarrassed by the circumstances. "Bhargav, I—"

Her brother cut her off. "You know Bhargav Varma?" he demanded.

Anya was taken aback. "Yes," she replied.

"How do you know him?" her father demanded.

Anya was confused. Did her father and brother know him too? He had just moved from New York, but she knew he had made contacts very quickly in the few months.

She couldn't tell them about the estate restoration project. "I-I met him through a client," she lied.

"When?" her brother demanded.

"And who is that client who introduced him to you?" her father joined in the questioning.

Something was wrong. And Bhargav's darkly handsome face held no expression while he watched her. The man who had joked about spanking her a while ago was gone.

"I met him a month ago," she replied. She had met him the first time three months ago at the club. "Why are you asking me? How do you know him?"

Anya's brother looked at her with a clenched jaw. "He's the one who I lost my apartment and cars to in the club! He and his friend deliberately pushed me to increase the stakes!"

"I know about him too," her father added angrily. "He is the CEO of Ventura Holdings. Ventura Holdings is the company that is seizing our house and other assets. He bought all of my defaulted loans."

Anya's heart thudded sickly.

She had met Bhargav in the club three months ago. Did he know she was the sister of the man who lost his apartment and cars to him in gambling?

Why would he buy the defaulted loans of her father?

She knew it couldn't be a coincidence that her brother and her father were losing their assets to him. He had come into her life again when he wanted to hire her for the restoration project.

That couldn't have been a coincidence either.

"Who are you?" she whispered. "Why are you doing this to my family?"

His dark eyes remained expressionless as he spoke. "Your brother chose to gamble that night and lost. I happened to win. Your father chose to make risky investments and take out huge loans. I happen to buy those loans which also came with the assets he put up for the mortgage."

Anger rose inside her at his twisting of events that had happened. "What about me?" she asked.

His dark eyes hooded. "Meeting you was purely fate," he replied.

"He's lying!" Surya said angrily. "He trapped you, and he's using you."

Anya's heart jerked.

Using me for what?

She didn't possess anything that a man like Bhargav Varma wanted.

"Get out of my house!" Anya's father shouted.

Bhargav turned to him. "This house and everything you own is mine now."

Her father's face turned red with helpless anger.

Bhargav turned back to her. Keeping his gaze locked on hers, he spoke. "You called me here for help. I'm willing to help."

Anya looked at him disbelievingly.

"She doesn't need your help!" Surya shouted. "She has agreed to marry me, and I will pay back all the loans that her family owes."

Bhargav threw him a cool look. "Last night's warning is still applicable."

Surya's face paled and flushed in anger.

Anya heard her mother gasp. "Did he do this to you, Surya? I thought you said you had a bike accident."

Surya gritted his teeth and fell quiet with embarrassed anger.

Anya stared at Bhargav. "How can you help us? What do you want?"

He watched her with hooded eyes. "Come to my penthouse as planned. We'll talk there."

She wanted to scream out no, but she knew she couldn't. Not when there was so much at stake and when she desperately needed to find out why he was doing all of this. She was in too much shock to respond to him.

"I'll see you later, Anya," he said before turning and walking away.

She kept staring at him until he left the room and disappeared from her sight.

"What does that bastard want from us?" Anya's brother shouted.

"I don't want Anya to meet him," Surya stated in angry bluster.

Strangely, Anya's parents were quiet. It was her mother who shocked her with her words.

"Go and meet him, Anya," she said. "See what Bhargav Varma wants and how he can help us."

CHAPTER TWENTY-ONE

Anya's hands shook as she pressed the button to the elevator that would take her up to the penthouse.

I should go back home.

She was too angry and hurt to have a confrontation right then. Her mind was still unable to process what was happening.

The man she had spent a passionate night with. The man she had been desperately looking forward to meeting again that night. And the man she had been falling in love with—was coldly and systematically destroying the world around her.

He must have slept with me just to hurt my family.

Angry humiliation heated her face, recalling how she had begged him and demanded him to take her the previous night. She must have made it very easy for him by behaving like a desperate fool.

She shut her eyes as tears of hurt and humiliation prickled inside.

No. I won't cry.

She needed to confront him and show him that he did not have the ability to hurt her.

The elevator stopped, and the doors opened. Taking a deep breath, she stepped out and went to the penthouse.

Before she could ring the doorbell, the penthouse door opened and Bhargav Varma stood near the doorway.

Anya's heart automatically leaped looking at his darkly handsome face. She had to fight an internal war not to melt and give in to his brooding charms. She clung to her anger and hurt.

It's all a lie.

He is a lie, and what we had between us is a lie too.

"Come inside," he said and waited.

Anya took another deep breath and stepped into the penthouse.

She recalled the first time she had been to the place. Despite the unnaturally strong attraction she felt towards him, her senses had warned her.

I should have listened to my instincts.

She went to the living room and stood next to the couch.

"Sit down, Anya," he said.

"No, I prefer to stand." She wanted the advantage while demanding answers from him.

He watched her face while she tried not to show her anger or hurt.

"Why are you doing this to my family?" she demanded. "What do you want from us?"

He didn't reply.

Her anger grew. "You targeted my brother and father. You left them with nothing. What is it that you want!"

He watched her with hooded eyes. "You."

She was stunned by his reply. "What?"

"I want you."

She was shaken by his calm, steady tone. Her mind was already a cocktail of emotions, and she couldn't understand his words.

"What do you mean by you want me?" she demanded. "You already had me! We spent a night together."

His eyes swept over her body, leaving a burning trail deep inside her skin. Her stomach fluttered, and her breasts peaked at the memories of his mouth over every inch of her skin.

"I want more. A lot more."

She shook her head at his words while trying to push away the passionate spell he was dragging her into.

"You are mad!" she said angrily. "We already slept together. And if sleeping with me again will make you leave my family and me alone, then take me again!"

She angrily reached behind her and yanked down the zipper of her dress. It loosened and fell around her waist, exposing her bra-clad breasts. She then stepped back and lay on the sofa, widening her legs slightly.

"Come on, take me!" she demanded. "Use me how many ever times you want. But just leave me and my family alone!"

He watched her, his eyes moving over her heaving breasts, her widened legs and then at her angry face. Her breasts rose and fell even more when he slowly came towards her and bent over her on the couch.

His large palm cupped her jaw. And then his rough, calloused thumb rubbed over her bottom lip.

Her stomach quivered and wetness pooled between her legs. Her body recognized his touch and craved more. She held his gaze with an angry flush on her face.

He watched her with a possessive look. "What I want from you isn't just a quick fuck," he stated calmly. "Like I had said before, I want more."

Her heart thudded hard.

He wanted an affair. Or rather, he wanted her to be his mistress. She knew she couldn't refuse.

She would be working for him for another year in the Vardhaman restoration. She couldn't risk sabotaging or leaving the restoration project midway. She loved the estate too much to be giving it up for anything.

At most, an affair would last for a few weeks. He would be bored with her by then and move on to his next victim. She could continue working on her dream project and also convince him not to jail her brother and father.

All she had to do was submit to his baser desires whenever he wanted.

Her life wouldn't change much. She would live her life as usual. The only times she had to be careful was when she met him for sex. She would have to harden her heart and ensure that she wasn't falling in love with him again.

It wasn't that easy. But it wasn't that bad either.

"Fine," she said.

His mouth twisted into a familiar smile, making her heart skip a beat.

"What exactly are you agreeing to?" he asked in a husky and slightly amused tone.

Her cheeks heated in arousal and anger. "You want an affair," she said. "I agree to it. But I want to get some assurances before we begin."

His thumb moved lower from her lips to her chin and then to her throat where her pulse was beating erratically. The simple press of his thumb over her pulse made her skin break out into goosebumps.

"What assurances?" he asked, feeling her throbbing pulse.

Suppressing a shiver and ignoring her body's arousal, she focused on the negotiation.

"I want you to stop the arrest of my father and brother," she said. "I will continue to work for the Vardhaman restoration project. And while we are having an affair, I want you to use protection during sex with me because I don't trust you anymore and you are... free to be with other women as well."

Even though her heart ached at the last part, she added it to protect her heart from further hurt. She hoped that sleeping with other women would make him lose interest in her faster.

His dark, intense eyes flared.

"D-do you agree to those conditions?" she asked, her voice quivering because he began to brush his thumb lightly over her pulse before moving even lower between her breasts. Her heart pounded hard in her chest.

His gaze remained locked on her eyes. "No," he replied.

Her heart jerked at his answer. Taking an angry breath, she pushed away his hands from her body and sat up. "What do you mean by no?" she demanded. "What else do you want from me? And what makes you think I would agree to anything if you don't stop coming after my family!"

He watched her angry face.

"I do want you," he said. "I will stop the arrest of your father and brother. You will also continue to work on the restoration project."

She held her breath as something dark and possessive flashed in his eyes.

"But you need to be mine completely."

She was stunned by his words. "What does that mean?" she asked with her heart beating in panic.

His mouth twisted with a dark smile. "It means we don't fuck anyone else except each other. You will move in with me here in the penthouse. You will sleep next to me each night. We will work and socialize together normally like a couple."

Her mouth opened to speak, but no words came out. She was too shocked.

Taking a deep breath, she forged on. "And if I don't agree to your conditions? If I don't want to live with you here? Or go out with you as a couple?"

He shrugged.

Anger shot through her at his casual dismissal. If she didn't agree to his terms, he would allow her father and brother to be jailed. And he would continue to come after her family.

"You are a monster!" she said. "And I hate you!"

He didn't flinch at her words. "Do you agree to my terms?" he asked calmly.

She felt angry and frustrated. And she also panicked.

I can't live with him.

How can I let him touch me without losing my heart again?

She had known him for only a few weeks, and yet he captured her heart and mind in a way no one ever could. If she lived with him, ate with him, slept with him and let him touch her in ways no one ever could, he would steal her heart along with possessing her body. He would destroy her soul.

No! I won't let it happen that way.

In her mind, he was no longer the brooding, intriguing man who was self-made with a passion for restoring the estate she loved. She now thought of him as a heartless monster who would do anything for his selfish needs.

She wasn't foolish enough to be led by her heart anymore.

What they have would be purely a business negotiation—her body in exchange for the freedom of her father and brother. Nothing else.

I hate him now.

"Fine," she said angrily. "I agree to your terms."

Dark satisfaction flashed in his eyes. "Good. Then let's seal the deal."

Before she could say anything, his hand caught the back of her neck and dragged her close and captured her mouth with his.

Despite her anger, heat exploded inside her.

She opened her mouth to protest, but his tongue thrust into her mouth, filling her senses with his taste and smell. Her body came alive, recognizing the pleasure of his touch from the night before. She moaned and grabbed his shirt to cling to him.

The kiss continued to steal her senses. His large hand cupped her breast possessively, making her gasp at the bolt of pleasure surging through her.

His dark voice whispered against her mouth. "I can't wait to make you mine again," he rasped.

Her eyes fell open in shock when he pushed her on the couch and moved on top of her until his body covered hers.

She stared at the beautiful painting of the river in the Vardhaman Estate while his mouth left a searing trail from her cheek to her neck and then towards the top of her breasts.

Her heart pounded hard. Every cell in her body screamed for his touch and possession. But a small yet significant voice inside her head made her realize what she was doing.

Don't let him possess you. Stop him.

She had already agreed to the deal. But it didn't mean she would let him win so easily. She was determined to fight him in every way she could.

With trembling hands, she gripped his broad shoulders and tried to push him away. But he was too strong and heavy. And he was also in the grip of determination to possess her to seal their deal.

Her body quivered, and wetness continued to pool between her legs when his hot mouth enclosed over her breast. She gasped.

Before she lost her mind completely, she pushed frantically at his shoulders again.

"Stop," she gasped out.

He didn't at first.

Panicking, she struggled underneath him. "Bhargav! Stop!"

This time, he did. He paused. A moment later, he raised his head slightly until his eyes met with hers.

Her stomach quivered seeing the intense heat in his eyes. Pushing away the screaming need of her body, she spoke hurriedly, trying to keep a steady tone even though her body was trembling.

"I'm hungry," she said. "We were supposed to have dinner together. And I-I need to go home and prepare for bringing my things to your penthouse."

He watched her for a few nerve-racking moments. She thought he would ignore her request and take their encounter to its natural conclusion since he had every right to.

But he didn't.

Instead, his mouth twisted into a dark smile. "I see," he said in a tone that shook her stomach.

She held her breath until he got up from her and stood next to the couch. He looked at her with hooded eyes.

"Let's have dinner first," he said. "I'll drive you to your place to pick up your things."

She wanted to protest and tell him that she could go herself. But she needed to pick her battles carefully. She was hanging by a thread as it was and didn't want things to blow up that would risk everything.

She nodded once before slowly sitting up. Her cheeks heated as she straightened her dress with trembling hands, covering the wet spot on her bra where his mouth had been moments ago. Ignoring it, she tried to pull up the zipper behind her dress. But she couldn't reach it.

"Let me," he said.

He reached behind her, and she felt the slightly roughened skin of his fingers brushing over her bare back before smoothly pulling up the zipper. She couldn't stop the shiver due to his touch or the goosebumps that peppered over her skin.

"Thank you," she murmured, stepping away from him.

He watched her with hooded eyes. "Let's go. You must be hungry."

She was barely hungry. After the shocking turn of events, the thought of food made her sick to her stomach. But she nodded and followed him.

She would rather pretend to eat than give in to his desires and lose her mind all over again.

***

They sat at the table. It was beautifully arranged with a crystal vase at the centre which had purple lilies similar to the ones that used to grow at the Vardhaman Estate.

Her heart ached at seeing the set table which was meant for a romantic evening.

The one they had originally planned.

Pushing away the feelings of loss, she focused on her anger and hurt and to keep him at a distance from her.

"Do you want the food heated more?" he asked.

The food was kept warm in beautifully presented crystal dishes.

She shook her head. "This is fine." She wasn't going to eat much anyway.

He opened a bottle of chilled wine and poured it into two glasses. And then picking up his glass, he watched her with hooded eyes. "To our new beginning."

Her heart thudded at his toast. Her fingers gripped the stem of her wine glass, but she didn't toast to their new beginning that was based on lies.

She took a sip of the wine, hoping it would reduce her anger and hurt.

The chilled wine slid smoothly down her throat and caused a flare of heat in her stomach. She took another sip and then another until heat flared in her stomach along with a pleasant buzz.

He was watching her while sipping from his glass.

Despite her feelings, her body continued to respond to his darkly handsome looks. Her eyes fell on his long fingers wrapped around the delicate stem of the wine glass, and then she stared at his lips as he sipped the wine. Her body heated as she recalled the unbelievable pleasure his lips and fingers had given her the previous night. The soreness in her body, especially between her legs, began to throb in a dull pleasurable ache.

His hooded eyes flashed as though he could read her mind.

Ignoring the pleasurable ache, she shook her head, wanting the thick sexual haze between them gone.

"I don't want the project team to know I'm staying at your penthouse," she said.

He watched her with an unreadable look. "Why not?"

Her cheeks heated in anger. "They would think you hired me because I slept with you."

He twirled the stem of the wine glass watching her angry face. "But that isn't the truth," he said calmly. "I hired you because I know only you can do justice to the restoration. You love the mansion and estate."

She sucked in her breath, not knowing whether to believe his words or not.

But considering the scale of the project and the massive budget being put into it, she believed his words. She didn't think sleeping with her was worth that much risk.

"I still prefer to keep it a secret," she said. "Why should everyone know I sleep with my boss?"

His eyes flashed darkly. "You are not my employee. And I don't give a fuck about what others think. Neither should you. What we have between us is no one else's business."

"I care!" she said angrily. She wasn't the kind to care what others thought about her either. But she didn't want anything to interfere with the project.

He didn't say anything.

Soon, they began eating. She served food onto her plate but simply pushed the food around. The dishes prepared were her favorite, but the thought of food made her sick.

"I thought you were hungry," he reminded.

"I'm not hungry anymore," she replied. "I'm thirsty." She took a sip of the wine. It happened to be her favorite too.

It was also her second glass.

There was thick silence as she continued to drink her favorite wine while he ate methodically. The slight buzz in her head turned into a more significant roar. At her third glass, the world began to spin slightly, and the darkly handsome face of her enemy blurred at the edges.

Her mind threw in the images of the time they met at the club.

She had been drawn to him and couldn't forget him. When she met him again, she was drawn more strongly to his brooding charms. Until last night, she thought he was the hero of her love story, but he turned out to be the villain.

"I hate you," she slurred over her wine glass. "You are a wicked lying bastard."

As soon as she finished saying those words, the blurred edges began to spread until everything was blurred, and soon the world turned completely dark.

CHAPTER TWENTY-TWO

Fuck!

Bhargav quickly got out of his chair and held Anya before she crashed face down on the table.

She slumped over his arm. Wine spilled all over her dress, and the glass shattered loudly below them, but his eyes were locked on her face.

Her eyes were closed, and there were wet tears trailing down her cheeks.

Fuck!

He cursed more viciously. He had hurt her and made her cry.

He hadn't intended to, but circumstances had changed in the blink of an eye.

He had planned a romantic evening. He had intended to make her laugh and blush in her sweet, captivating way while sipping her favorite wine and eating her favorite food that was specially prepared for her that night. He had also mentally prepared himself to drive her crazy with slow, passionate lovemaking rather than fuck their brains out like the previous night.

But instead of spending a romantic evening with the woman who utterly captivated him, he was now left with the object of his obsession hating his guts.

He thought he had time, but shit had blown over much earlier than expected. The bastard ex-husband of hers had dug up information on the arrest warrant that would soon be issued on Anya's brother and father. The bastard then tried to use it to coerce her into marrying him again.

When Anya called to ask for help, he knew things wouldn't end well.

He could have easily given an excuse and avoided going to her parents' place, but he wasn't the kind to back away from hard circumstances, especially when Anya had asked for his help. He knew the confrontation would be unavoidable at sometime. So, he met it head on.

Anya's brother and father recognized him and burst out angrily at him. They also knew he was the cause of their ruin.

He saw the shock and anger in Anya's eyes at the revelations. And he knew that if he didn't claim her sooner, he would lose her completely. She would be forced to take up her bastard ex-husband's help and end up marrying him again.

That would never happen as long as he was alive.

She was his to protect. His to cherish. And his to claim.

Meeting her might be purely fate but claiming her was his destiny.

And claim her, he would. Even if she was determined to fight him every step of the way.

Watching her sleeping face, he swung her up in his arms and carried her prone, unconscious body to his bedroom.

CHAPTER TWENTY-THREE

Anya woke up with a groan.

There was a dull throb inside her head, and her mouth felt parched. She shifted to her side and opened her eyes. Instead of her small water bottle she always placed by her bedside, there was a glass next to a crystal jug filled with water.

Shocked, she sat up.

A quick scan of her surroundings revealed a large room with tall wall-to-wall windows and sleek furniture.

I'm in Bhargav Varma's penthouse.

She was supposed to go home the previous night on the pretext of collecting her clothes and things and return later in the morning.

What happened?

Her heart thudded when she felt the sheet covering her brushing against her bare breasts.

Oh my God. I'm naked!

She recalled most of the events of the previous night. The visit to her parents' house. The shocking turn of events when she discovered his betrayal and lies. And then the deal she struck with him at the penthouse when she had agreed to be his live-in mistress in exchange for him stopping her father's and brother's arrests. She also recalled stopping their passionate encounter on the living room couch. She had planned to keep him away from her somehow. But she couldn't recall what had happened after their dinner. She had a lot of wine.

Did I have sex with him again?

Her body was slightly sore, but there wasn't a significant soreness between her legs. The soreness she felt seemed to be from two nights ago.

She bit her lip in uncertainty and raised the blanket. When she saw the delicate, red-colored silk panties she had worn specially for their dinner date, relief passed through her. Her cheeks heated imagining him seeing her in just those panties.

A quick turn to the side revealed he had slept on the bed next to her. The pillow was still dented.

She was confused.

Bhargav Varma was far from considerate. He was a heartless monster who considered her his possession.

Then why did he not have sex with me even though I agreed to the deal?

She even recalled goading him the previous night to take her on the couch and use her however he wanted.

Why didn't he?

It was confusing. Taking a deep breath, she reached for the glass and poured herself some water and drank it greedily. She had just put the glass away when there was a soft click of a door opening.

A moment later, she saw her enemy stepping out from a bathroom wearing just a towel.

Her cheeks blazed, and she pulled her blanket higher over her breasts. He was watching her while he dried his hair using another towel. The smooth movements highlighted his stunning body with well-defined muscles.

Anger and arousal heated her cheeks even more.

"Why did you undress me?" she demanded.

His expression didn't change at her surly tone. "You spilled wine over yourself last night," he said calmly.

She was embarrassed. She recalled drinking a lot of wine. She had been sad and heartbroken with the turn of events. But now, she was just angry and embarrassed.

"Get ready so we can go," he said.

She frowned. "Go where?" It was a Sunday.

"We'll have breakfast and go to your house to pick up your things to bring here."

Her heart jerked at the reminder. "I can go myself," she said.

"I know. But I prefer to take you there."

Anger shot up through her. "Why?" she demanded. "Are you afraid that I will back out and not keep my end of the bargain?"

Her heart began to thud when he watched her while placing the towel over a chair before coming closer to the bed until he stood only a few inches from her. She gripped the blanket tightly to her chest, which was ridiculous since he had seen her body already and touched her in ways no one ever had before.

A gasp escaped her when his hand gripped the back of her neck. He leaned down to her until his warm breaths fell against her lips.

"You won't back out from the deal," he said against her mouth. "Because I won't let you."

His mouth then captured hers, swallowing her words of protest and stealing away her mind.

***

Two hours later, Anya was at her house, packing a suitcase.

Her enemy had driven her there a few minutes ago after their breakfast at the penthouse.

The first thing she did after reaching her place was change out of her wine-stained clothes and take a shower before putting on a comfortable dress. She then began packing her clothes and things she needed during her stay at the penthouse.

She didn't know how long the stay at the penthouse would be.

Maybe a week. Or two. Or at most a month.

By then, her enemy would be bored with her and her resistance. A man like him would be used to women fawning over him and begging him. She had been one of them too.

Her cheeks heated when her eyes fell over her bed where they had torn at each other's clothes and ended with raw, passionate sex all night.

No, don't think of it!

It was hard not to think of passion and sex when it came to Bhargav Varma. He always exuded dark masculinity that brought out the baser instincts in her.

Her lips still tingled from their earlier kiss a while ago. He had initiated the kiss, and she was shocked and angry at first. But eventually, he was the one who ended their kiss and drew away from her while she stared at him with needy eyes.

Her breasts still felt sensitive from the friction caused by rubbing against his hair-roughened, muscled chest while he kissed her.

No! Don't think of it.

She had to fight harder to put up a guard against the sensual spell he put over her.

Taking a deep breath, she reminded herself once again that she had planned to keep him at a distance.

Fake indifference and resist.

She would use that strategy until he was tired and bored of her indifference and would end up chasing after some other woman who would be more than willing.

Ignoring the ache in her heart at the thought of him with another woman, she shut the suitcase. She had packed her clothes and essentials that would last her for a week.

He was waiting in her living room, looking at the lamp that once belonged to the Vardhaman mansion.

"I'm done packing," she said.

He looked at the single suitcase and laptop bag in her hand. When his eyes met with hers, she shivered at the dark, possessive intensity in them.

Just a few more days, and I will be free of his spell.

CHAPTER TWENTY-FOUR

"Anand Kashyap has started an investigation on me."

Bhargav was at his brother's penthouse. He had dropped Anya at his place before heading there.

"Has he linked you to the estate purchase?" Yash asked.

"Not yet. And even if he does, he won't get to the truth."

Yash nodded.

Bhargav saw his younger brother frowning. "Won't Anya tell them now?" Aryan asked. "After the confrontation between you and her family?"

Bhargav's brothers knew about the confrontation at Anand Kashyap's house. Bhargav had told them even before going to the Kashyaps' house.

"She won't." Bhargav knew Anya would continue to follow the conditions in the contract because she wouldn't want to risk the restoration project. "Even if Kashyap finds out that Ventura Holdings has purchased the estate, he will not link it to the truth."

Aryan continued to frown. "I think Anya is a high risk to our plan at this time. She might do the same thing as Narmada and start an investigation on you. She doesn't know about us, but she could somehow find a link between the estate and us."

Bhargav knew that too. "She might find out. But she won't go to her father. She will confront me first."

"Have you spoken to her after the confrontation?" Yash asked.

Bhargav nodded. "Yes. She's at my penthouse. She's going to be staying with me."

Yash's eyebrow rose and even Aryan looked surprised.

"She's not too happy to stay with me, but we struck a deal. She would stay with me in exchange for stopping the arrests of her father and brother."

There was a momentary silence.

"Do you intend to tell her the truth?" Yash asked.

"No. Not yet."

Aryan shook his head. "Anya must be pissed at you even more because of the deal. There's no way she's going to stay calm and pretty at your penthouse and not do anything. She must hate you now."

Bhargav knew that already. "She can hate me all she wants, but she won't risk our plan."

"How are you so sure?" Aryan demanded.

Bhargav looked at his younger brother. "Because her love for the Vardhaman Estate is much greater than her hate towards me."

His brothers fell quiet, knowing it was true. Anya hated him and was angry with him, but she wouldn't ever risk the project.

However, Anya was also a fighter. His beautiful, angry rebel was not going to make it easy for him. She wouldn't let what she thought of as his betrayal be forgotten that easily. She had already come up with a plan to put up defenses against him despite their deal.

But he was going to shatter her defenses.

He had been close to shattering those walls earlier that morning. She had kissed him back and nearly surrendered, but he was the one to step away even as his body and mind willed him to take her.

He stopped because he wanted her to accept him with her mind and not just with her body.

He wanted it all—her body, heart and soul.

CHAPTER TWENTY-FIVE

Anya was working on the designs on her laptop when her phone began to ring.

When she saw who was calling her, she felt a painful bolt inside her chest. She had expected either her mother or brother to call and check on her. The last communication she had with them was when she left her parents' house to meet Bhargav Varma at his penthouse.

She didn't know why, but after all these years, she still expected them to care or worry about her.

"Hello?"

It was a call from her best friend.

"Hey, girlfriend," Trupti's cheerful voice greeted.

Anya took a deep breath. "How was your weekend? Did you meet Rishab's parents again?"

Trupti was happy to talk about her boyfriend. "Yes. I met them this weekend too. They are so nice, Anya. Especially Rishab's father. The man is so jovial and fun-loving. He's opposite to my father."

Anya knew Trupti had to face many hardships during her childhood with an abusive father who often battered his wife and daughter.

"I like Rishab," she told Trupti. "I'm sure his father must be equally nice."

"Yes, they are nice," Trupti replied. "We played board games together with teams. It was so much fun!"

Anya smiled, recalling her childhood memories when she had spent her holidays at the Vardhaman Estate. She had fun playing board games and other outdoor games with the family. Ashok Vardhaman loved children and often involved them in gardening chores by making it a fun event.

There was a loud sigh on the phone.

"Yes, they are nice," said Trupti. "But I don't want to get too attached, Anya. Just in case Rishab decides to break up with me."

Anya frowned. "Why would he break up with you?"

There was a momentary silence. "My past," Trupti replied. "He knows about my father and also has an idea of how many men I had hooked up with over the years."

Anya's heart clenched for her friend. "Why would your past matter now? Rishab already knew about it when he proposed to you."

Her friend was silent once again before letting out another sigh. "Yeah, I guess so. But it's too good to be true. I mean... instead of enjoying the current moment, I keep thinking that something so good must be a sham or would end."

This time Anya was silent. She had always felt Bhargav Varma was too good to be true. The chemistry between them and the night they spent together had even made her believe in love.

But it was a lie.

Trupti laughed. "Enough of my daddy issues and hang-ups. Tell me. What's happening with that yummy hotel tycoon of yours? Have you met Mr. Wicked again and kissed him like I suggested?"

Anya bit her lip recalling the events of the last two nights. But she didn't want her friend to worry. "I've met him. But just for project updates."

Trupti chuckled. "Ooh. I can sense some tension in your voice. I'm sure there were enough sparks during those meetings to burn down the office building."

Anya's cheeks heated. Despite his betrayal and lies, she continued to feel the strong pull and connection towards the man she hated.

Pushing away her thoughts, she focused on the current conversation. "There's nothing between us," she said in a normal tone. "He is... just a client."

She recalled his parting words the previous morning after their night together.

"Just so we are clear, I'm not 'just a client' anymore."

Trupti laughed. "Liar!" her friend said. "But it's okay. I'll pump out more information when I see you soon. I'll drop by your place tomorrow—"

"Let's meet at the office," Anya added hurriedly. "I... might not be home since I'm going out often with the antique dealer I mentioned."

"Oh yeah. She sounds nice and interesting. Hope you guys find more acquisitions from the estate."

"Thanks."

Telling her friend goodbye, Anya ended the call.

She stared at the river painting on the wall once again. But this time, her mind wandered.

Why did he come after my father and brother? What was the need for buying their loans?

Something wasn't adding up.

The previous day had been a complete and devastating shock to her. But now that she somewhat calmed down, she began to think deeply.

There was much more to why Bhargav Varma was targeting her family. She couldn't deny the explosive chemistry between them. But going after her family was beyond the reason of sexual chemistry they had together.

She intended to find out soon.

***

It was evening time, and Anya was still seated in the living room working on her laptop.

The cook was inside the penthouse preparing dinner while the housekeeper who had come in earlier to clean up the place left a while ago. They were both surprised seeing her in the penthouse but did not question her. Even though she was embarrassed, she had introduced herself to them.

She was glad the cook hadn't left yet. She needed as many buffers as she could between her and her enemy.

When the penthouse door keypad made a whirring noise around seven, she expected yet another help, but her heart leaped when she saw Bhargav Varma's tall figure emerge into the living room foyer.

He saw her seated on the living room sofa with her laptop. His eyes hooded when he took in her slightly messy bun and comfortable clothes.

"I'll join you for dinner in a few minutes," he said.

Before she could say anything, he walked away and disappeared towards the master bedroom suite.

Her heart thudded.

She wondered what excuse she could use to avoid sleeping with him that night. Her father and brother were still not safe from arrest, so there's wasn't much she could do to renegotiate.

And Bhargav Varma didn't seem the kind to forgive anyone for breaking a promise.

She shivered slightly.

Fifteen minutes later, her heart leaped once again seeing him. He was dressed in comfortable clothing. It was shocking seeing him in a t-shirt and shorts. His hair was still slightly wet.

"Let's eat," he said.

"I-I'm not hungry. You go ahead."

His eyes swept over her. "Are you sure you are not hungry?" he asked.

She nodded.

"Then maybe we should go to bed early," he suggested.

She sprang up from the sofa. "I am not hungry, but Nina might feel bad if I don't have dinner."

His mouth twisted slightly. "Yeah. I guess she will."

The man was a master manipulator and a mind reader.

With her cheeks heating, she went along with him to the dining room.

The cook had placed the dishes on the table as she did the previous night. Nina smiled at them cheerfully. "Goodnight, Mr. Varma and Anya," she said.

"Good night, Nina," her enemy's deep voice rumbled.

Anya wanted to beg the cook to stay or maybe even join them for dinner. But she forced out a smile. "Good night, Nina."

The older woman left, leaving Anya alone with her enemy in the penthouse.

They sat down to eat. This time, Anya didn't touch the wine. She stuck to water to go along with the delicious food.

Even though her stomach fluttered crazily with nervousness, she was able to enjoy the meal.

Her enemy didn't touch the wine either.

The dinner was mostly silent, and once again she felt thick sexual tension filling the air around them.

"Have you spoken to the concerned people to stop the arrests?" she asked.

His eyes held hers. "Yes. Your father and brother won't be arrested for loan fraud."

Wincing at his choice of words, she looked down into her plate. Her father and brother did deserve to be arrested for loan fraud. But they were being let go because of her.

Her enemy had kept his end of the bargain by stopping the arrests. And she knew he would expect her to keep her side of the bargain.

The rest of the dinner remained silent.

After they were done, she tried to pick up the plates and bowls to put them in the kitchen when he shook his head.

"Leave it. Nina will get to them in the morning."

She nodded while her heart began to pound.

She followed him towards the master bedroom suite while her heart began to pound even harder. Whether it was in anticipation or nervousness, she didn't know. But her body vibrated with the thick sexual tension that crackled like electricity around them.

He pushed opened the bedroom door. She barely took a step inside when his hands gripped her waist and pushed her against the wall next to the door. She gasped out loud, but the sound was caught by his mouth when he captured her lips. His fingers dug into her hair, and his mouth locked on hers in a passionate kiss.

Heat spread like liquid fire through her veins, and her breasts peaked in arousal while wetness pooled between her legs. She wanted to wrap her legs around him and grind herself against his hardness to relieve the throbbing ache of emptiness inside her.

But she controlled herself.

He lied to me, and I hate him.

She had to repeat those words in her mind quite a few times before she could get her body somewhat in control. With great difficulty, she froze and stopped herself from responding to him.

He continued to kiss her passionately for a few more moments until he realized she wasn't responding. He stopped and pulled away to watch her face with heavy breaths.

She held his gaze while her stomach trembled. "I'll keep my end of the deal," she whispered. "But I don't have to respond to your touch. You are welcome to do whatever you want."

His eyes flashed darkly at her words. Her heart pounded as his gaze pierced into hers, almost as if he was looking deep into her soul.

His eyes hooded. "Whatever I want?" he asked. His dark voice shook her stomach.

She swallowed, seeing the predatory look on his face. "Yes," she whispered.

Keeping his eyes locked on hers, he reached for her.

She gasped out loud when his hands held the bottom of her t-shirt and yanked it up forcibly before throwing it away in a single move. He then tugged on her cotton pants until it fell around her feet. With a flick of his fingers, he unclasped her bra and threw it aside.

Her chest heaved, and she stared at him in just her cotton panties. She held her breath when his eyes swept over her. He reached for her again and picked her up by her waist before carrying her to the bed and dropping her on the mattress.

Watching her, he began to shed his clothes in rapid movements. She bit her lip as she watched him.

Her heart pounded as he pulled up his t-shirt and threw it aside and then pushed down his shorts. Her mouth fell open.

He was stark naked. She couldn't help but lower her gaze and move her eyes over his stunning body, including his hard, demanding arousal.

She licked her lips nervously. Her heart raced and breaths came out in pants when he switched off the lamp next to the bed, throwing the room into darkness.

The mattress dipped when he joined her on the bed. She waited for him to roll on top of her. Another gasp escaped from her mouth when his hand wrapped around her stomach and dragged her to him until his hard arousal brushed against her buttocks. His hand then moved higher to cup her breast possessively.

Shocked, her heart pounded crazily. She was sure he could feel her crazy heartbeats under his hand.

Was he trying a new position? Why is he not undressing me fully?

She had no idea.

She waited. But nothing happened. His warm breath fell against her cheek. And it slowly turned deeper and heavier. Much later, she could hear his soft snoring.

She was stunned.

Oh my God. He's asleep. How can he sleep!

His arousal was still rock hard, and the large palm still gripped her breast possessively, but he had fallen asleep.

She waited a little longer, expecting him to do something about his arousal. Her breasts tingled, and her body buzzed with awareness. But nothing happened.

Slowly, her eyes began to droop as tiredness took over.

She then slid into a deep yet strangely disappointing sleep in her enemy's arms.

CHAPTER TWENTY-SIX

Anya woke up alone in her enemy's bed once again.

The blankets were at her feet where she must have kicked them because she felt overly warm from the hard, muscled body pressed up against her the previous night.

Her cheeks heated when she saw that she was wearing only her panties.

She didn't waste any time. She got up immediately from the bed and put on her clothes lying next to the bedroom door. Then quickly grabbing her clothes from the suitcase, she stepped outside the bedroom.

She freshened up in a different bedroom.

While she hurried through the shower, her thoughts wandered.

Why hadn't he taken me? And why didn't he demand that I participate in sex with him?

She was confused by his behavior. According to the deal, he had every right to have sex with her.

The previous night, she was strangely disappointed that he didn't make a move towards her apart from holding her during sleep. But now, in the light of the day, she was glad that her plan was working.

She was able to keep her enemy at a distance despite the deal.

Biting her lip, she hurried through getting ready for the day. She wanted to be done with breakfast and be ready to leave before he returned from his fight training in the gym.

She didn't want to live with him as a couple and spend time together in a leisurely breakfast or other activities.

He is a liar, and I hate him.

She repeated those words in her head.

Stepping out of the guest bathroom, she went to the dining area where the cook was setting breakfast.

"Good morning, Nina," she greeted with a small, trembling smile.

The older woman smiled broadly. "Good morning, Miss Anya. Would you like some coffee before breakfast?"

Anya shook her head. "I'm in a hurry. I'll have a little breakfast."

The woman nodded. "Sure."

Anya quickly ate the delicious breakfast. She only ate a small portion due to the time constraint.

She got up and rushed to the living room. She was putting her laptop back into the bag and grabbing her purse when she saw him. Her enemy had returned earlier than she expected.

Her stomach fluttered seeing him sweaty. His tanned skin glistened and made him look like a men's cover model on an outdoor sports magazine.

He wiped the sweat from his brow with a workout towel as he looked at her. "I'll freshen up and join you for breakfast," he said.

Dragging her eyes away from his body, she looked at his face. Her cheeks heated with angry embarrassment when he caught her staring and there was slight amusement in his eyes.

"I already had breakfast," she said.

His mouth twisted into a dark smile at her challenging tone. "Then join me for coffee."

A strange sense of déjà vu gripped her. She was reminded of the times she joined him for breakfast in his office.

"I'm busy. I have to drive to the estate."

"Give me an update on the project status."

"I-I..." She didn't know what to say to that.

He was still her client. And she had to update him about the project. Her anger and hate couldn't come in between her profession and passion.

She remained silent.

"Fifteen minutes," he said before he walked away.

Taking a deep breath, she dropped her handbag back on the sofa and slowly went back towards the breakfast area.

It's okay. Just don't talk about anything apart from work.

He might no longer be just a client, but she could pretend he was only that.

She was checking her emails and answering messages when a whiff of spicy cologne floated in the air, filling her senses. A moment later, the man she hated sat across her. He was dressed in a three-piece suit.

She stared at him again. This time he looked like a cover model on a business magazine.

She recalled how his bare body looked under the expensive clothes. Standing stark naked with his demanding arousal, he had looked like a

Greek god the previous night. She even recalled how his hard body felt when she slept in his arms the previous night while he held her possessively.

"What time is your appointment at the estate today?" he asked, pushing the tray with her favorite cupcakes towards her.

Dragging her mind away from the wicked thoughts about his body, she fought a blush before she answered him. "The appointment is at one o'clock. I am meeting the sculptor who will repair the base and take the measurements for the west side garden area sculptures."

"Take the helicopter."

She nodded. It would save her time, and she could even speak with some of the landscape architects to reconfirm the designs.

She dragged her eyes away from him. Not wanting to stare at him while he ate breakfast, she poured herself a cup of coffee.

She had skipped having coffee earlier to avoid him. But now that she was forced to join him, she relaxed slightly and enjoyed a cup along with her favorite cupcake.

"An office room has been set up for you downstairs," she heard him say. "You don't have to drive all the way to your other office on the other end of the city unless it's needed."

She frowned.

She wanted to protest, but she knew it made sense. The project restoration team met with her in the conference rooms downstairs. Soul Spaces' offices could not be used because of the confidentiality agreement.

"Okay," she murmured.

He had finished having his high-protein breakfast and joined her in having a cup of coffee.

His hooded eyes watched her while he sipped the steaming hot beverage. "Have you spoken to your family?" he asked.

Her heart jerked. "No. Not yet," she said curtly.

Why does he want to know? Was he planning something else?

She felt hurt that neither her mother nor her brother called to check on her still. She hadn't called them either. She was sure they knew she was forced to negotiate with the man who was out to destroy them.

"Your father must have gotten information about the arrests being stalled."

She nodded.

She knew her father wouldn't bother calling her either, but she was more than disappointed about how she was made the sacrificial scapegoat to save the family once again.

They finished their coffee silently.

He looked at his watch. "I have a meeting starting in fifteen minutes. Ask Ravi to contact the pilot."

She nodded.

She picked up her laptop and purse before they stepped out of the penthouse together. They got into the elevator to go down to the office floor downstairs.

The air felt charged inside the enclosed space as he looked at her. She tried to move away without making it too obvious, but the hooded look with which he looked at her made it obvious he knew.

As soon as the elevator stopped, she felt relief.

She was waiting for the doors to open, so she could step out and escape him. But he pressed a button on the panel that kept the elevator doors shut.

She let out a gasp when he pushed her against the elevator wall and kissed her deeply.

It was a brief kiss, but at the end, they were breathing heavily, looking at each other.

"I'll see you later," he said with a familiar hooded gaze before pressing the button to open the elevator doors.

He stepped out first, and she followed him with her heart continuing to race from their kiss.

The front desk receptionist greeted them both with a smile. "Good morning, Mr. Varma and Miss Kashyap."

Anya somehow managed to smile. "Good morning, Reshma."

"I have seated Miss Kiara Sharma in your office, Mr. Varma," the younger woman said.

Bhargav Varma gave a cool nod. "Thanks. I don't want anyone disturbing me during my meeting. Hold all the calls and divert them to Ravi for the next two hours."

"Sure, Mr. Varma."

Anya was glad he would be in a two-hour meeting. She would leave for the estate by then, and he wouldn't be able to join her. She needed time away from his presence to get her bearings back.

Feeling a bit relieved, she followed him as he led her further into the office area.

He stopped in front of a room that was next to his. "This is your office," he said. "Let the staff know if you need anything."

"Thanks," she murmured.

Looking at her for a moment, he disappeared into his office.

She heard a sultry feminine voice greeting him.

"Good morning, Mr. Varma," the woman said. "I drew up the papers you needed."

Bhargav Varma's deep voice greeted the woman before the door to his office shut with a soft click.

Anya frowned as a bolt of jealousy passed through her.

No! I'm not jealous. How can I be when I hate him?

***

"I was able to finalize the sale of the last two sculptures as well, Anya!"

Anya was on a video call with Ritu, who was excited. Anya felt equally excited.

"I knew you'd be able to convince them," Anya said with a smile.

The west side garden used to have beautiful marble statues of mythological figures. Anya recalled them pretty well because she and her best friend used to play around the statues, spinning stories about each character or simply chasing each other around them.

Ritu laughed. "The credit goes to you because you told me who had those statues."

Anya knew the couple who had purchased the statues at the bank auction. They were acquaintances of her parents, and she had visited their home a few times. She recalled feeling shocked, angry and sad seeing her favorite statues in someone else's home. She had cried and begged her parents to ask the couple to return them to the estate.

Now, those statues would be returning to their rightful place.

Anya smiled into her phone at Ritu. "The sculptor was able to mark the areas of where each of those statues would go. The foundation is still solid. He said only minor touchups are required before installing them. The marble fountain in the front is also in good condition."

Ritu looked happy. "Oh, that's awesome news!"

"Yes."

Ritu shook her head. "Thank God the marble fountain was too heavy to be auctioned off or stolen."

Anya was glad too. A power wash with minor touchups would bring back the massive marble fountain to its original form.

"Anya, are you free tomorrow?" Ritu asked. "If you are, then let's go over the list of items I was able to trace."

"Yes, I am free."

"I'll drop by Soul Spaces then."

Anya's heart jerked, recalling her new office. "No. I'll be in the Ventura Holdings office."

"Oh! That's awesome. Then I can drop by and say hello to Bhargav too!"

"Yes."

Anya tried to keep her face normal. She didn't want Ritu or anyone to know she was living with the owner of the Vardhaman Estate.

"See you tomorrow then, Anya!"

Anya forced out a smile. "Bye, Ritu."

She ended the call and continued to finish her work at the mansion.

A part of the team was present with her, taking notes. She showed them what the priorities were at that point. The paint from the mansion walls would soon be chipped off from the top floor rooms and wood would be collected from the teak and rosewood trees for furniture.

She took the team and workers to the river site and showed them the trees. It was a windy day, but the trees were sturdy and barely moved with the high winds.

"Only chop the trees in the back," she instructed. "Leave the ones surrounding the river and at the front."

Her cheeks heated when her eyes fell on a particular tree. She recalled the events near that tree when she was with Bhargav Varma.

Taking a deep breath, she pushed away those memories.

Had it not been for other older memories and her emotional attachment with the tree with a heart carving, she would have wanted that tree chopped to eliminate the memories with her enemy.

"Also, make sure you only chop the alternate trees. As soon as they are chopped, let me know and I'll have the gardening team plant new ones."

She gave a few more instructions before she headed back towards the mansion. The helicopter was waiting for her and the team members who flew along with her.

"We are expecting a big storm tonight," the pilot said. "Let's leave before the wind picks up even more."

Anya nodded. "Sure. We are done for the day."

It was evening, and the sun was just beginning to set. She and the team got in and the helicopter headed back to the city.

While the helicopter took them away from the estate, she stared outside the window where the storm had just begun.

Her life was caught inside a powerful storm too. Even though she was trying hard to escape the storm, she knew it was a matter of time before she would have no choice but to allow herself to be blown away.

What would happen to her if she fell in love with the man who was determined to destroy her world?

No. I won't fall in love with him. I hate him.

She clung to that fact.

Much later in the evening, the helicopter landed safely.

She asked the team to leave before going to her new office and working there until it got dark outside. By the time she returned to the penthouse, it was close to dinner time.

"Good evening, Miss," the cook greeted her cheerfully. "Where would you like to have your dinner?"

"Good evening, Nina. Anywhere is fine. Give me ten minutes. I'll freshen up and help you set the table."

The older woman shook her head. "Oh no, Miss. I can set up the table. And besides, it's just you for dinner."

Anya's heart jerked. "Oh, is... Bhargav not coming home for dinner?"

Nina looked surprised that she didn't know. "No, Miss. Ravi called to let me know sir would be coming home late."

"I see." Anya forced out a smile. "If it's just me, don't set the table. I'll just get everything from the kitchen."

The older woman frowned slightly. "Oh no, Miss. It's no trouble. I enjoy setting up the table."

Not wanting to offend the older woman, Anya nodded. "All right," she said before going to the bedroom suite to grab clothes and freshen up.

Even as she freshened up, she felt strangely disappointed.

What's wrong with you? You should be happy that you are not being forced to eat or spend time with the man you hate.

Is he with the woman with the sultry voice?

A bolt of jealousy once again hit her at the second thought.

She shook her head, determined not to let anything about her enemy bother her.

She should be glad if some other woman caught his fancy. It would mean that her time at his penthouse would come to an end sooner.

With those thoughts, she went to the dining area and had her dinner.

But even as she stared at the beautiful night view of the city, her stomach sunk with a disappointed feeling. She missed his company. She felt strangely alone even though she was used to having meals by herself at her home.

Taking a deep breath, she finished her dinner quickly. Then clearing up the dishes, she went to the master bedroom.

She hovered over the bed, wondering if she should pick a guest room to sleep in. But she decided against it. Even though she was determined not to respond to him, she didn't want to break the verbal deal they had made.

"It means we don't fuck anyone else except each other. You will move in with me here in the penthouse. You will sleep next to me each night. We will work and socialize together normally like a couple."

A shiver passed through her recalling his words. She lay on the bed, wondering whether the shiver was because of anger or anticipation.

It's definitely anger. I hate him.

Feeling oddly cold and lonely on the huge bed, she curled her body and slipped into yet another uneasy sleep.

***

She woke up briefly from deep sleep when she felt her t-shirt being tugged away, and she was pulled against a warm, muscled body. Once again, her enemy was naked and aroused. She stiffened slightly, expecting him to roll on top of her and demand she fulfill her part of the deal. But he simply held her with his hand cupping her breast possessively.

"Sleep," his deep voice murmured against her forehead.

Her body relaxed slightly. And then slowly, despite her missing t-shirt, the heat of his body surrounded her, and she slipped into a deep, comfortable sleep.

CHAPTER TWENTY-SEVEN

The alarm rang loudly at a distance.

Anya groaned softly and opened her eyes to stop it. But she couldn't move since a muscled arm held her firmly against a hard body.

Her heart began to thud.

It was her third day waking up in Bhargav Varma's bed. She had expected to wake up alone like the first two mornings, but her enemy was still there.

Hoping he would wake up and leave for his early morning exercise routine, she tried to pretend she was asleep by regulating her breathing.

But her pretence didn't last long. Her heart raced and the tip of her breasts pebbled in arousal against his large palm.

"I know you are awake," his deep voice murmured against her ear.

Goosebumps broke all over her skin, but she still tried to pretend she was asleep.

Suddenly, she let out a gasp.

She found herself on her back with him on the top, looking into her face with his intense, hooded eyes. She was wearing her pajama bottoms and bra, but he was completely naked. Naked and aroused.

Her heart beat picked up even more in speed, almost thumping out of her chest. He stared at her, and then he lowered his head to put his mouth over her rapidly fluttering pulse at her throat.

She nearly moaned at the heat and pleasure that radiated from his lips on her skin.

He continued kissing her. His lips left a fiery trail over her throat and neck and then over her shoulders.

Her chest rose and fell rapidly as her breaths turned heavier. She felt his hands moving behind her. With a small flick of his fingers, he unclasped her bra. Cold air fell on her bare breasts. And the next moment, his mouth enclosed over her tingling breast.

She bit her lip hard to stop a moan from escaping her throat.

She stared in shock at his dark head while he began sucking on her sensitive tips. Wetness pooled between her legs and need screamed inside her. With every tug of his mouth, her need grew infinitely.

She dug her fingers into the blankets and grabbed the material into her fists to stop from squirming under him. Forcibly dragging her eyes away from the sight of him suckling on her breast, she looked at the ceiling.

Oh God.

She willed herself to gain strength to resist him. She reminded herself of his lies and deception and what he did to her family. But despite the reminder, she couldn't stop the pleasure from heating her blood.

His mouth left her breasts and moved lower to her stomach. His lips once again left a blazing trail of heat over her sensitive skin. But soon, he paused.

She continued to stare at the ceiling, barely holding on to her control and not respond to him. She could hear his harsh breaths and feel his hard arousal jutting against her leg. Just when she thought he would continue with the mission to drive her crazy before ultimately taking her body, he cursed.

"Fuck," he said in a harsh voice before rolling away from her.

He got out of the bed. She heard him walking away, and a few moments later, she heard the bathroom door banging shut.

She lay on the bed for long moments, still trying to bring her body under control.

But she didn't succeed.

Finally, she forced herself to move, knowing he would return soon as demand they have breakfast together.

She rolled out of bed. With her cheeks heating, she put on her t-shirt thrown next to the bed and hurried into the guest bathroom. Her body was still screaming in arousal. Three nights of being next to him and not giving in to her desires took a toll on her.

She wanted relief from the desire and need.

Biting her lip, she shed her clothes and stepped into the shower cubicle. Over the past three months, she had used his shirt button to find a release. But now, the memories of his touch and kisses nearly pushed her to the edge.

Closing her eyes, she recalled his darkly handsome face watching her with hooded eyes. She also recalled the feel of his hard, muscled naked body on top of hers and his hardness moving deep inside her.

It barely took a minute, and she exploded in a release of pleasure. Even with the shower running, the sound was loud enough to be heard outside. She panted against the cubicle with her cheeks and entire body flushed due to pleasure.

Oh God. I hope this torture will end in a week.

She didn't think she could resist him beyond that.

CHAPTER TWENTY-EIGHT

"I spoke with the lawyer and team. The permission to build homes is on the way."

At Bhargav's announcement, there was a brief silence. He knew how his two brothers felt about the new housing project.

It was an emotional moment for the three of them because it had been their late father's dream.

"Are the plans the same as before?" Yash asked, his voice deeper than usual.

Bhargav nodded. "Almost. Only slight changes to suit smaller families and modern times."

"I see."

The previous plans were made nearly twenty years ago.

Bhargav looked at his younger brother, who had gone unusually silent. Although affordable housing for hundreds of families was their father's dream, that dream had also cost their father's life.

"What do you think, Aryan?" Bhargav asked.

Aryan clenched his jaw. "I guess Ma would be very happy," he said.

"Yes," said Bhargav. "But let's wait to tell Ma until we bring out the truth."

All three of them had agreed to wait. If their mother found out that they had bought the estate to seek the truth of the past, their gentle yet intuitive mother would also find out the path they had chosen as the means to dig up the past.

"It's only going to get harder and harder to hide the truth from Ma," Aryan stated. "Yash's wedding in a few weeks to Mohan's daughter is going to be hard to hide from Ma." Aryan looked at Yash. "That is if he goes ahead with the wedding."

Yash didn't let anything show on his face, but Bhargav knew his older brother was not as unaffected.

"The wedding will go on as planned," Yash stated.

Aryan then looked at Bhargav. "And what about you, dear bro? How are you handling the beautiful architect who is currently your roomie?"

Bhargav didn't react to his younger brother's bait. He didn't want to discuss Anya with anyone, not even with his brothers who were close to him.

"I've stalled the arrests of Anand Kashyap and his son, but his house and properties are going to be seized in three weeks."

Yash nodded. "Good. I'll have Mohan's properties seized around a similar timeframe. We need to ensure they don't communicate with each other."

"They won't."

They continued to discuss the status of the plans targeting to bring down three enemies before forcing out the truth. Bhargav felt uncharacteristically impatient.

He wanted the truth to come out soon. He needed to know what exactly had happened on the day his family suffered a devastating loss and blow.

He wondered if the truth would make any difference in Sukanya Kashyap's hate towards him.

Maybe or maybe not.

The woman was unpredictable. She was sweet and giving to others, but when it came to him, she was stubbornly unforgiving.

Despite the deal they had made, she continued to fight him back fiercely. Over the past two weeks, he was constantly with blue balls around her with no sight of victory.

He wanted to give her time so he could slowly and steadily break down her defenses. He could feel her desire matching his, and yet she stuck to her plan of pretending to be unmoved.

No more. It was time to claim his beautiful rebel.

"Thank you, Miss Kashyap. I'll get back to you with the revised final quote."

Anya shook the hands of the flooring vendor. "I'm going to schedule a follow-up meeting next week. You can bring in more samples."

The man nodded eagerly despite the hard bargain she had just made. She had managed to convince the vendor not to put a premium price on the flooring of the mansion since his company would benefit a lot more from the publicity. Luckily, the man had agreed.

After the man left, Anya picked up her laptop to leave for the day as well. It was close to six in the evening, and she wanted to freshen up before working on the updated designs.

"Bye, Reshma," she greeted the front desk receptionist who was also packing up to leave for the day.

The younger woman smiled. "Bye, Anya. Have a great weekend!"

Anya thanked the woman with a smile before stepping out of the office area.

She got into the private elevator which would take her up to the penthouse. She wondered if people at the office knew she was living with their boss. Her cheeks heated in anger that she was still made to stay in the penthouse.

Why is he not bored of me, yet?

Ten days had passed by since she moved into his penthouse, but the same torturous routine continued with no end in sight.

They ate breakfast together and then left to work in their offices right next to one another. Sometimes, they even had lunch in his office. She couldn't protest because he termed them as lunch meetings where she was to provide him with the project updates. Later in the evenings, they had dinner together. The dinner was mostly silent, but it was filled with heavy sexual tension.

Each night, he took her to his bed and tried to get her to respond to him.

But she resisted. She continued to stare at the ceiling and recall he was her enemy and that she hated him. It ended with him stopping midway and once again dragging her close until she slept in his arms.

He tried arousing her in the mornings as well, but it ended with the same result.

She could feel his dark frustration when she didn't respond. Sometimes, she was ashamed when she wanted him to simply spread her thighs and take her forcibly regardless of her response. She wanted him to put an end to both their torture.

But her enemy had infinite control and patience.

Like a seasoned hunter, he stalked her patiently and got her to a point where she was in agony, both physically and mentally. Her body and mind screamed with unfulfilled desire.

She knew it was a matter of time before she broke.

No! I will hold on.

With that determination, she stepped out of the elevator and went into the penthouse. Surprisingly, Nina wasn't there, and she couldn't smell the usual delicious aromas from the dishes made by the cheerful cook.

Hoping Nina was doing well, she pulled out her phone to call while going to the bedroom. She stood near the bed and was looking up for Nina's phone number when the bathroom door opened, and her eyes met with the sight a wet, muscled and nearly naked man.

She stared. After a long, frustrating ten days, the sight of her enemy's nearly naked body heated her up instantly. He used that gorgeous body each night to arouse her to a fever pitch.

Seeing it now, even as he casually dried himself, made it seem like an elaborate seduction plan.

He watched her with hooded eyes. "Get ready. We are going out for dinner."

Dragging her gaze away from his body, she stared at him. "I have to work."

His expression didn't waver. "You can work tomorrow."

She bit her lip. She wanted to argue, but once again, she was reminded of their deal where she was supposed to accompany him in public as a couple.

"Fine," she murmured.

She also realized that he must have told Nina about their dinner plans.

Where was he taking her? She didn't want to ask. It sounded too much like a couple's conversation. She decided to wear a dress similar to what she had worn for Ritu's birthday.

She was just about to place her phone next to the bed when a text message popped up. It was from Ritu.

Relaxing slightly, she checked the message.

Ritu: Can't wait to see you tonight at the nightclub!

She was surprised by the message. For some reason, she didn't think Bhargav would take her to a nightclub. He looked way too broodingly reserved and serious to be spending time in a dark, noisy place.

But she was excited. And knowing Ritu would be there too, she decided to dress up more than usual. She only had a knee-length red dress that looked a bit too elegant for a nightclub. So she compensated the elegant dress by applying a bit more makeup than usual.

A slightly glittering eye makeup with a smoky look, light foundation and shiny red lipstick completed the look. She wore matching heels with her red dress. Thankfully, she brought a clutch where she could slip in her cell phone for emergencies.

Taking a deep breath, she stepped out of the dressing area and the bedroom to join her enemy while he was waiting to take her out for the first time.

He was standing by the living room's large patio door talking on the phone. He must have sensed her presence or seen her reflection on the glass door because he twisted around slightly until he could see her.

Her stomach fluttered when their gazes met. His eyes immediately hooded as they swept over her, taking in her dress and then returning to her face with makeup. He kept their gazes locked while continuing to talk on the phone.

"No, check the old documents again," he ordered someone. "The old ones too."

She tried to look away, but the pull of him was too strong. Unlike the three-piece suits he usually wore, he was now wearing a black shirt along with jeans. She couldn't help but stare and admire how stunningly magnetic he looked.

He's the devil in a handsome disguise.

She had to tell herself that and remind herself that she hated him.

"I'll talk to you later," he said. "Send me a message when you find something."

Ending the call, he looked at her for a quiet moment before beginning to come towards her.

Her heart thudded faster. "I-I'm ready," she said hurriedly.

She didn't want to risk him touching her. Her self-control seemed too fragile right then.

His mouth twisted with a dark, knowing smile. "Let's go," he said.

***

"This is so much fun!" Ritu shouted over the loud, thumping music as she swayed.

Anya was on the dance floor with Ritu.

Anya laughed. "Yes, it is!" she said, swaying to the music.

They had arrived at the nightclub a couple of hours ago. As soon as Ritu saw her, she had dragged Anya to the dance floor. Ritu's husband remained seated near the private booth with Bhargav.

Anya enjoyed dancing. She and Trupti often went to clubs or events where a lot of dancing was involved. Dancing always made her forget her worries temporarily while she swayed to the music.

"I badly need a drink and some food now," said Ritu.

Anya laughed. "Me too."

She was hungry since she hadn't eaten anything since lunch. Two hours of continuous dancing increased her appetite. But she decided not to drink that night. She was only going to have water and maybe soft drinks. Although she didn't think her enemy would take advantage of her while she was drunk, she did fear losing her inhibitions and giving into him that night if she drank too much.

"Who is that with Bhargav?" Ritu commented as they headed towards the table.

Anya looked, and her heart jerked when she saw a beautiful woman seated right next to Bhargav. The woman was leaning towards him, and his head was bent to listen to her over the loud music. From a distance, the two of them appeared intimate.

A strong bolt of jealousy hit her, shocking her. She wanted to storm to the table and make a scene while claiming Bhargav was with her.

How dare he flirt with another woman when he is with me.

She didn't know whether Bhargav and the woman were flirting with each other or not, but they definitely seemed to be in deep conversation.

Clenching her teeth and trying to appear unaffected, she replied to Ritu. "I don't know who she is. Must be an acquaintance."

As they neared the table, Anya could hear the woman's voice and laughter. Her heart jolted once again as she recognized the sultry voice.

Bhargav had closed-door meetings with that woman in his office.

Ritu's husband greeted them first. "Finally," he told his wife. "I thought you were going to dance away the entire night."

Ritu laughed. "We wanted to, but we are thirsty and starving."

The woman seated next to Bhargav turned. "Oh. Sorry to take up your spot," she said with a sultry smile. "I dropped by to say hello to Mr. Varma and ended up staying longer."

"It's all right," Anya murmured.

The woman turned and smiled once again at Bhargav. "I'll see you next week, Mr. Varma."

Bhargav gave her a short nod.

The woman left right away without introducing herself. She joined a group seated a few tables away.

"How hungry are you ladies?" Ritu's husband asked.

"Starving!" Ritu replied.

There was laughter. Relaxing slightly, Anya joined the laughter.

Luckily, the food and drinks arrived within a few minutes because the orders had been placed beforehand.

She was hungry, but she couldn't enjoy her food much. There was anger simmering deep inside her.

She knew she had no right to feel jealous about Bhargav.

She shouldn't even care about whom he was seeing romantically or flirting with. In fact, she had given him permission to be with other women.

But despite how her rational mind reasoned, she still couldn't stop feeling angry and jealous.

He has no right to flirt with other women when he demanded fidelity from me.

"Anya! Why are you not drinking?" Ritu demanded.

Anya forced out a smile. "I have to catch up with some work tonight."

Ritu laughed and shook her head. "Oh, come. The boss is right here. Bhargav! Tell her she can take it easy with work for tonight. You are working my poor friend way too hard. She's going to break down."

"Indeed," Bhargav's deep voice drawled from next to her.

Anya's cheeks heated, hearing his slightly, amused voice.

She knew he was thinking of her breaking down to his attempts of seduction. The things he did to her, did make her work hard to resist him.

"One drink," she murmured, just so she could put an end to her thoughts.

A lemon margarita soon arrived at their table. It was delicious and quite refreshing. Combined with the delicious food, the alcohol didn't get into her blood stream right away. She was glad because she needed to be alert.

But the drink helped her relax slightly, and she joined the conversation with Ritu when they spoke about the mansion's past.

"Tell me something shocking about the Vardhaman family," Ritu insisted.

Anya smiled. "There was nothing shocking about them," she replied. The family was too loving and perfect. "But I was almost engaged to their oldest son."

Ritu's eyes widened in shock. "What!"

Anya laughed. "Our fathers were childhood friends. So, they verbally decided to get me and the oldest son married in the future."

Ritu was excited. "Oh my God! Imagine if that had happened! You would now be living in the mansion instead of working to restore it!"

Ritu looked at Bhargav. "And you wouldn't have had a chance to purchase the estate!"

"I can be quite convincing when I want something," he said as a reply.

Anya's heart jerked. But she turned to him with a raised eyebrow. "If Vardhaman Estate belonged to me, I wouldn't let you or anyone buy even an inch of land, Mr. Varma."

His eyes flashed at her challenge. "Like I said, I can be quite convincing, Miss Kashyap," he said.

Her cheeks heated at his hooded look that spoke of something else. Dragging her eyes away from his hypnotic ones, she took another sip of her drink.

"Were you happy with that verbal marriage promise?" Ritu asked.

Anya shook her head. "No," she murmured.

Ritu looked shocked. "Why not? I thought you said their family was sweet and affectionate."

Anya smiled. "They were. But I didn't love him. He was more like a brother to me."

"Oh." Ritu smiled. "I'm sure feelings would have changed over the years. Close friends can easily become lovers and life partners. In fact, they make the best life partners."

Ritu and her husband exchanged a sweet look. Anya knew that they were college friends turned couple.

Anya smiled.

The rest of the dinner continued in a lighthearted vein.

Much later, when it was well past midnight, they got up to leave. That's when the woman who had been speaking with Bhargav stopped him as they passed by her table.

"Mr. Varma," she said in her sultrily voice. "Why don't you join me and my friends for some time?"

Anya didn't hear Bhargav's deep response. She continued to walk behind Ritu and her husband.

Anger began to simmer inside her once again.

He's welcome to join her and maybe take her to his penthouse too.

Meanwhile, she could take a cab and go to Trupti's house for the night since her house keys were in the penthouse. Even if Trupti wasn't there, she could find an alternate place to stay the night.

She inhaled a deep breath to control herself.

The effect of the single margarita she had was long gone along with her relaxed mood. She was now wound up tight with simmering anger once again.

"Where is Bhargav?" Ritu's husband asked when they stopped near the entrance of the nightclub.

Anya was about to tell them that he wouldn't be joining them when she saw him arrive.

"Thanks for inviting us," he said, shaking Ritu's husband's hand.

"We enjoy yours and Anya's company," Keshav Kapadia said with a smile.

Meanwhile Ritu hugged Anya. "I had a lot of fun tonight. We should go dancing more often."

Anya nodded with a smile. She had enjoyed dancing and Ritu's and her husband's company too.

Soon, the vehicles arrived in front of the club and Anya got into the sleek SUV.

The ride back to the penthouse was tense and silent. The anger continued to brew inside her. But even as her anger simmered, she knew the cause of it. Jealousy.

CHAPTER THIRTY

Anya stepped into the penthouse and went straight to the kitchen area.

She was thirsty, and she also didn't want to go into the bedroom with Bhargav Varma right then.

But her enemy followed her into the kitchen.

While she sipped cool water from the fridge, he watched her with hooded eyes. Her stomach fluttered, and her breasts peaked behind her dress, pissing her off at her body's reaction.

She hated being drawn to him. She was sick of fighting not only an attraction but also a strong connection with the man she should be hating.

"How long?" she demanded.

"How long what?" he asked calmly.

"How long will this contract last? When will I be allowed to leave this penthouse for good?"

"You are free to leave anytime," he said.

Her cheeks heated in anger. "And risk the arrest of my father and brother?"

His expression didn't change. He quietly observed her angry face. It made her all the more angrier and drove her crazy. She wanted him to get angry and riled up and jealous like her.

"Maybe I will leave," she said in a deliberately determined tone. "I have another option."

There was a dark warning flash in his eyes.

She didn't heed it. In fact, she was satisfied that she got a reaction.

With her eyes shining victoriously, she goaded him further. "Surya's family can help my parents."

"No, they can't. No one can."

"They will help," she insisted stubbornly. "All I have to do is marry Surya again."

Raw anger radiated from his face and the stiffened posture of his body. Her heart raced as he slowly stalked towards her. When he stopped and loomed above her, she stood her ground and raised her chin to look at him.

"If he ever comes near you again," he growled out the words. "I will not top with punching his face or breaking his wrist. I will break every damn bone in his body."

The angry, possessive look on his face made her heart race in victory. Bhargav Varma was always so cool and collected.

"You can't do anything if I decide to marry him," she goaded him further. She didn't know why she was egging him on, considering she would never marry her disgusting ex-husband.

She just wanted her enemy as angry and jealous as she was.

He watched her silently for a moment. "If you break our deal, I will fire you from the project," he said in a deceptively calm tone.

She gasped in shock. "You can't," she whispered.

"I can. It's written in your contract that I can rearrange the team anytime, which includes you."

Her heart thudded sickly. She was sure he knew how much she loved the Vardhaman Estate.

He was ruthless. Despite their stormy relationship, she felt betrayed by him that he used the estate as a threat to bend her to his will.

Fury burned through her. "You are a heartless monster!" she shouted.

She was so pissed that she attacked him. She wanted to hurt the man who was able to hurt her because he easily captured her heart using lies and deceptive means.

She raised her knee to hit him between his legs, but he easily caught her thigh with one of his large hands. Gripping her leg, he dragged her closer until she was more or less riding his legs.

Heat and sexual tension exploded as they stood in such close proximity. Even as fury emitted from her, she was unable to draw her eyes away from him.

His mouth twisted into a dark smile as their gazes locked together. "I like this violent streak of yours," he said in a rough tone. "You should know that I thrive on fighting. But with you, I'd prefer if the violence is channeled in a way we'd both enjoy."

She shuddered at the dark wickedness oozing from his words. She hated him right then, but her body reacted to his words, wanting and craving the images he put into her mind.

Pushing away her body's reaction, she clung to her anger. "Fuck you!" she spat.

Dark heat flashed in his hooded eyes. "With pleasure."

His fingers gripped the back of her hair and his mouth slammed on top of hers. Heat sizzled in her nerves, making her body catch fire.

She moaned out loud as his tongue slid deep into her mouth and filled her senses with his taste. Before he stole her other senses completely, she wanted him to feel her anger first.

She bit his tongue hard enough to hurt. But he didn't jerk back. He groaned harshly and dragged her even closer until she was molded to him.

She tore at his shirt then, wanting to feel him even closer and to mark him in other ways. The dark, primitive possessiveness she felt towards him was unstoppable. He seemed to feel the same.

With a rough growl, he held her waist and picked her up bodily before carrying her to the kitchen island. Placing her on the top of the granite counter, he attacked her dress.

She heard the loud sound of her favorite dress ripping, but she didn't care. She yanked apart his shirt until buttons flew all over the kitchen. They tore savagely at each other's clothes while continuing to kiss passionately.

His kisses always stole her mind. He didn't just kiss. He possessed and laid claim. He kissed like he was never letting her go.

Day and night, his mouth drove her insane while she tried to resist him.

No more.

She was letting go.

She let out a cry when a hard yank ripped her panties apart. Her legs were spread wide, while he tore at his jeans. She waited desperately, wanting the empty ache deep inside her to be appeased.

Keeping his gaze locked on hers, he held her thighs and pushed them even wider apart before he thrust into her in one deep stroke.

She gasped out loud at the sudden fullness and pressure. But he didn't let her catch her breath. He slammed into her repeatedly with a shocking intensity. His savage urgency increased the need scorching through her body.

Raw sounds escaped her throat while she tried to grip the cold and hard granite countertop beneath her. But she didn't feel the cold hardness of the stone because the heat of the man on top of her lit her body on fire.

The material of her dress was slippery, but the sheer power with which he slammed into her body kept her pinned firmly against the countertop.

"You are mine," he grated in a tone that sent a bolt of pleasure running through her body.

She wanted to rebel. She wanted to hate. But instead, she put her hands on his shoulders and dug her nails deep into his skin before leaning and biting him on his chest. He let out a harsh cry.

As soon as she marked him, she exploded.

He groaned harshly again, throwing his head back as he joined her in a powerful release.

His hot seed spurted deep inside her, making her feel as though he had marked her too. But he marked her with something other than anger and possessiveness. He marked her with their connection.

The strong connection she always felt with him turned even stronger than before.

Fear shot through her. Her eyes met with his as he continued to connect them irrevocably by something other than just their bodies.

"I can't," she gasped.

He was already inside her in every possible way. Inside her body and around her heart, smashing through the barriers she held against him.

His eyes flashed, knowing what she meant. It only seemed to make him more determined. "You can and you will," he said, pushing into harder, shaking her inside out.

She gasped, clutching him and fighting the bond and need.

But he didn't let her escape. He watched her panic-ridden face and kissed her savagely until once again, need arose. She gave in to it. Clinging to him, she got lost while they surrendered to the need that gripped her like a fierce storm.

She didn't know when or how she ended up on the bed. But before she slipped into sleep in his arms, she tried to convince herself that whatever happened didn't mean much.

This is just lust.

***

Bright sunlight woke Anya.

She groaned as she shifted and tried to open her eyes. Just like the last time she had sex, everything, including her hair was sore.

I slept with him. Again.

This time, she didn't regret it. She finally felt free and alive to be able to give in to her desires.

Yes, she still hated him. And he was still her enemy. But the constant pull she felt towards him was too hard to deny.

Now that I gave in, maybe he'll lose interest.

A dull ache throbbed inside her chest at the thought.

Pushing away all her aches, she sat up slowly on the bed. She was just about to step down, when the bedroom door opened. It was him. Her enemy lover.

"Coffee," he said in a deep, husky voice while pushing a cart towards her.

Her cheeks heated once again at seeing him in the light of the day. He was only in his boxer shorts, and his body displayed the light scratches from her nails and the dark bruise on his shoulder where she had bitten him during passion.

Oh God. I can't believe I did that to him.

She had been uninhibited the previous night. All she wanted was to slake her desire towards him.

She had let him do what he wanted, and in return, she had clung to him hard and tried to push him away when things felt too intense.

But he didn't let her go at anytime. Like his kisses, Bhargav Varma's lovemaking felt as though he was laying claim to her forever.

No. It was another lie.

He didn't want her forever. There was no reason for him to feel that way.

Dragging her eyes away from him, she looked at the floor. Then suddenly, she recalled something embarrassing and sprang up with the sheet around her.

"Where are you going?" he asked, seeing her reddened face.

"Our clothes are on the kitchen floor!" she said.

Nina and the housekeeper would soon see the torn clothes lying on the kitchen floor along with the scattered shirt buttons. With five bedrooms in the penthouse, they still chose to have sex like animals in the kitchen—on the kitchen counter and on the kitchen floor.

Her cheeks heated in embarrassment, imagining what the cook and the housekeeper must have thought seeing the mess left in the kitchen.

"Nina and the housekeeper haven't arrived yet," he said. There was a hint of amusement in his voice. "I asked them not to this morning."

"Oh."

Her cheeks heated because she was sure the older women must have guessed the reason. But since there wasn't anything she could do, she sat back on the bed.

"Each time we are together, buttons go missing," he said. "Maybe I should switch to t-shirts around you."

Her face was on fire at his teasing. He did lose a shirt button during their first meeting, and then she had ripped his shirt buttons when they kissed and made out near the river on the estate. And last night too when she ripped his shirt apart in angry passion.

Oh God.

Trying not to blush more, she pulled up the sheets until they covered her decently. She then sat with her back against the wide headboard.

The coffee aroma tingled her nose and mouth, and she badly needed a cup to stop the nervousness and trembling she felt deep inside her.

He poured hot coffee into a cup and handed it to her.

"Thank you," she murmured.

Taking a sip, she felt a little better. Pouring himself a cup as well, he drank along with her.

While they sipped their coffees together, awareness and familiarity made her body tingle once again.

"Do you want to have breakfast or lunch?" he asked after a while. He placed his empty cup on the cart and took hers as well since she was done.

"What time is it?" she asked, having no idea.

"It's noon."

She stared at him in shock. "Noon?" she asked dumbly.

Once again, there was amusement in his tone. "Yes."

She had never slept until noon before.

How long were they at it? It must have been all night.

No wonder my body feels sore.

With her cheeks flushing, she replied. "I'll have lunch directly, but I'm not that hungry."

His eyes hooded as he watched her. "Good. Neither am I," he said. "Maybe later, we can order a light take out meal from one of the restaurants downstairs."

Her heart thudded at the plan. It was sounding way too cozy and familiar—almost like how a couple would spend a lazy weekend together.

"This is just sex," she blurted.

He raised an eyebrow at her sudden declaration.

She felt nervous, shaken and also embarrassed, but she forged on.

"I... I was keeping my end of the deal. There's nothing more to what happened between us last night."

There was a familiar dark, challenging flash in his eyes that increased her nervousness. Her heart thudded as he walked towards her.

Her breaths turned faster as he neared. She gasped when he gripped the back of her neck and dragged her closer to his face.

"Good," he spoke against her lips. "Then let's not waste time and continue with our deal."

He sealed her mouth with his, while cutting off whatever words she would have spoken.

CHAPTER THIRTY-ONE

"Congratulations, Mr. Varma. The housing project has been approved."

Bhargav flipped through the pages as he looked at the documents.

"Mr. Varma, I still feel you are wasting a golden opportunity by not building high-end villas in your estate. I don't understand how building lower-income homes would help with the profits for your venture."

Bhargav looked at the puzzled men in front of him. "Tax breaks," he stated.

Some of the men frowned wondering how building lower-income homes would help a billion-dollar company with tax breaks. But Bhargav didn't owe them or anyone an explanation.

However, the lawyers that Bhargav had hired came up with an explanation.

"Mr. Varma plans to use the people living in the lower-income housing to work in the mansion as well as at the estate."

Bhargav had no such plans, although the people would be welcome to work in the mansion as well as the estate if they wanted. But building the lower-income homes was his late father's dream. Bhargav and his brothers were determined to achieve that dream.

He looked at the men in front of him. "We'll start the construction of those houses in parallel with the restoration effort. I want the announcement made to the nearby villages first in the coming months."

"Sure, Mr. Varma."

Bhargav nodded at the men before getting up and leaving the meeting. He was going to fly back to the penthouse.

Over the past week, it was the first time he had been away from Anya for more than a couple of hours. He already missed hearing her voice and touching her.

A smile twisted on his face wondering if she was hatching another plan to keep him from her. He wouldn't mind. Because breaking down those plans would make claiming her all the more sweet.

She surrendered her body, but he knew she was continuing to put up defenses to keep her mind and heart detached from him. He didn't allow her to because claiming her body had never been the only thing he wanted. He wanted it all.

And very soon, no matter whatever hurdles came their way, he was going to completely claim Sukanya Kashyap.

CHAPTER THIRTY-TWO

"Whoa! Anya Kashyap, that's quite a bit of glow on your face. What have you been up to since we last met!"

Anya blushed at Trupti's teasing while her best friend stepped inside her house.

Anya had dropped by her home a few minutes ago to pick up additional clothes. Since her only party dress was ripped in the kitchen the previous week, she needed a few more dresses as backup.

She had called Trupti since she missed her best friend. And she also wanted to meet Trupti because it was the only few unexpected hours she had without the confusing, demanding and passionate man occupying her mind.

All Bhargav Varma had to do was be in the same room as her, and her body and mind craved him. Sometimes, he didn't even need to be present, and she still wanted him.

Taking a deep breath, she pushed away the thoughts of her enemy.

"Nothing," she murmured. "I have just been busy with work."

Trupti smirked. "I want to meet Mr. Work. I'm pretty sure you have been doing your work very hard these days."

Anya blushed at her friend's outrageous yet close-to-truth remark. "Stop it."

Trupti grinned. "It's obvious that the glow on your face isn't just because of your passion for the Vardhaman project. What's going on?"

"I slept with Bhargav Varma."

Although there was hardly any sleeping involved when her enemy was around. The man was insatiable and made her the same way. She simply couldn't get enough of him.

Her cheeks heated as she recalled their passion-filled moments. Nearly every square foot of the huge penthouse was used to satiate their desire for each other. And yet, she still craved to be near him again.

"Oh my God!" Trupti was shocked. "Really? I expected you to tell me that you kissed him again or maybe made out with him at the estate. But this is huge!"

Anya still didn't want to tell her friend about moving into the penthouse and the deal she struck with her enemy.

"It's just a temporary affair," she murmured.

"Hmm..."

"What?" Anya questioned her friend, who was looking at her speculatively.

Trupti shook her head. "I don't know if you are really the kind to have a temporary affair."

Anya frowned. "Why not?"

"I've known you for a long time," said Trupti. "I know you are a dreamer. Even though you had a bitter experience with your asshole ex-husband, you still believe in love and happily-ever-after. I don't know if you can ever detach emotionally during sex."

Trupti was right. Anya did believe in love and happily-ever-after. She was passionate about her work because she wanted a family to create happy, loving memories in the house she designed.

But that didn't mean she was going to dream of a future with Bhargav just because of their temporary affair. She was fighting her feelings against him, but at no point did she think she would have a future with her enemy.

He would break her heart and destroy her soul.

"He... sees other women too."

Trupti looked shocked. "What the hell? He's cheating on you already, and you are okay with it?"

Anya shook her head. "No. He's not cheating on me because we are not together. And yes, I'm okay with it because I told him he could see other women."

"Hmm..."

Anya squirmed at her friend's speculative look. "What?"

"Sorry to break it to you, but Mr. Wicked hardly sounds like he would do a half-assed job in pleasing a woman. I think if he were with someone, he would give it his all. Looking at the glow on your face, it's obvious he succeeded."

Anya's heart jerked at her friend's analysis. "How do you know? You haven't even met him properly."

Trupti grinned. "Oh, please. I maybe have only met him once, but you spoke so much about the man that I feel as though I know him well."

Anya blushed, knowing it was somewhat true. "It's only an affair," she insisted.

"If you say so." Trupti's eyes sparkled with clear disbelief.

Anya knew her friend wouldn't be convinced until Bhargav Varma ended the deal.

I hope it's soon.

It was only a temporary affair.

***

It was late in the evening when Anya returned to the penthouse with a small suitcase.

Right away, she could sense her enemy lover's presence in the bedroom even though she couldn't see him. It was scary how strangely connected she felt to the man she thought of as her enemy.

Just as she began unpacking the suitcase, the bathroom door opened, and he stepped into the large walk-in closet. His mouth twisted slightly when she saw what she was doing.

"You should bring a bigger suitcase," he suggested. "Or there would be more suitcases in this closet than your clothes."

Her cheeks heated at his deliberate teasing. Despite her anger with him, his lighter side with dry humor appealed to her.

"I won't need more clothes," she murmured.

His eyes hooded, and he came closer. "True," he said huskily. "I prefer you with no clothes."

Her cheeks heated all the more. Before she could say something, his towel dropped, baring his stunning body. Her lips tingled, and her mouth watered at the sight.

She preferred him without his clothes as well.

He came closer, and slowly placed his mouth on her throat where her pulse was beating frantically. When he carried her to the nearby bed, along with no clothes, there were no more words.

An hour later, she lay naked and content beside him on the bed.

She realized how much she started to get used to his presence in her life. It wasn't just the sex. She simply even loved falling asleep with his tanned, muscular arm wrapped around her waist and their bodies pressed close together.

She also loved waking up to see his darkly handsome face when he was still asleep.

His harsh features softened slightly and appeared relaxed. She wanted to kiss his face until he woke up and looked at her with hooded eyes. She also wanted to see heat, passion, slight amusement and something else that was always present in his eyes when he looked at her.

She didn't want to know what it was or acknowledge it, but she wanted it to be there always.

Am I supposed to feel this way during a temporary affair?

CHAPTER THIRTY-THREE

"Mr. Varma, would you like chairs placed near the river for you and Miss Kashyap? Maybe a table too?"

Anya was at the Vardhaman Estate with Bhargav. They had just finished checking on the status of the ongoing restoration work. She had expected them to leave after a couple of hours, but her enemy lover wanted to stay longer.

He had planned a picnic lunch.

"That's not required, Mr. Raichand," his deep voice replied to the newly hired estate manager. "We'll be back in a couple of hours."

The manager nodded before going back to his work.

Bhargav looked at her while holding a big picnic box. "I hope you don't mind sitting on the ground for our lunch, Miss Kashyap."

She fought a blush at his deliberate use of her last name.

"I'm used to having impromptu picnics, Mr. Varma," she retorted.

His eyebrow rose slightly. "Really? Your family doesn't strike me as the type to have picnics."

He was right. Her parents weren't the kind to take her or her brother out on picnics. Her mother would be horrified sitting on the ground and eating in the open.

"I went on a lot of picnics until I was ten," she said. "In fact, I know the best picnic spots on this estate."

His eyes flashed, and his mouth twisted at her bragging. "In that case, pick a spot for us to enjoy our lunch together."

Her heart jerked at his suggestion. He sounded darkly charming. Once again, she felt as though she was going to be caught in a web she would be unable to escape.

The last two weeks with Bhargav Varma were filled with hot passion.

But now, he was slowly revealing the charming side of him, which seemed more dangerous. She was determined to harden her heart.

"The company matters more than just a beautiful spot," she said.

He didn't seem fazed by her rude remark. He looked at her with slightly amused eyes. "I agree," he said. "The company matters more than a comfortable spot."

Her cheeks heated at his deliberate teasing. She was reminded of all the unusual and some uncomfortable spots where they had spontaneous sex in the penthouse.

"I was talking about the picnic," she said primly.

He looked at her with a small smile. "And I am simply making an obvious statement."

Dragging her eyes away from his handsome face, she looked ahead while they continued walking towards the river. The path to the river had been cleared, making the journey much shorter. The walk was silent yet enjoyable.

A part of the garden area had been beautifully restored. New flowering bushes with seasonal lilies were planted, which had already begun blooming.

They reached the narrow river where some of the trees had been chopped to be used to build furniture inside the mansion. But the trees chopped were not visible from the river. Only the logs were neatly stacked up at a distance.

He chose the spot right next to the tree that had a heart carving. It was also the tree where they had kissed the last time they were there together. Despite her constant reminder not to be affected by him, her heart still raced in anticipation.

He didn't touch her and only watched her with a hooded look as he set up a thin blanket on the ground before unpacking the large picnic box.

It was a simple lunch with salad and wraps packed in individual boxes to avoid using additional plates. Nina had also packed small dessert bowls. Anya knew it was Nina who had packed their picnic lunch because the dessert was her favorite as was the cold and creamy thick milkshake that accompanied their meal.

When had he asked Nina to pack a lunch? The cheerful cook hadn't mentioned anything during breakfast, which meant it was a surprise.

Her heart jerked at the thought.

"Tell me more about your near engagement to the oldest Vardhaman son," he asked, taking a bite of his wrap.

The good food made her relaxed. "I wasn't supposed to know it. But I overheard the conversation when my parents discussed it with the

Vardhaman family."

His mouth twisted. "You must have been quite adventurous if you managed to hide and listen in on a conversation."

She blushed. "It wasn't me. It was my friend who insisted we listen in."

There was an amused look in his eyes. "Were you close to all the children?"

"Yes, but I was the closest to the one who was the same age as me."

"I see."

It felt odd to be having a simple, relaxed lunch. Normally, if they ever found themselves alone for more than a few minutes, they would be shedding their clothes and attacking each other in passion. The man was insatiable and even shameless. He had even made her that way.

She blushed, recalling their last encounter in his office when she was lying under him on his office sofa with his hand covering her mouth to muffle her passionate cries.

"What about your family?" she asked, quickly pushing away her thoughts.

There was no change in his expression. "My mother lives in New York."

She knew that already when she had snooped on him. She also knew he had a brother. Was he not close to his brother?

She didn't ask. Instead, she focused on his mother. "Did your mother visit you here?" she asked.

He watched her closely. "Not yet. But she might soon."

She wanted to ask him more, but she didn't want to come off as eager to know about him. Her idea was to show a lack of interest in him, so *he* would lose interest in her eventually.

"Which one is your favorite room in the mansion?" he asked.

"The room that overlooks this river. It has a tree next to the window, which my friend and I often used to slip away during the nights."

He smiled. "I see. You are welcome to restore it as you wish."

Her heart jerked. The current design suited a child, but if he gave her the freedom to redesign it, she would match it to suit a couple.

Does that mean he would let her stay there when she wished?

Her heart jerked again at the thought.

"Would you like some more dessert?" he asked.

"No, I'm full. I ate everything. Nina is one of the best cooks."

He nodded with a small smile. "Yes, she is. She likes you, so she made your favorites."

"What about you? What are your favorites?"

As soon as she asked him that, she cursed herself.

Dammit! I'm supposed to be indifferent.

But the pleasant atmosphere at her favorite spot near the river lowered her defenses. It almost felt like they were a normal couple relaxing and enjoying a romantic picnic.

"I don't have favorites. I am used to eating whatever is available."

She frowned. "But I noticed that you like seafood better than red meat or poultry. You also hate potatoes. You never touch any dish with potatoes in it." And she happened to like potatoes a lot.

His mouth quirked at her observations. "You are right. I prefer seafood and dislike potatoes. I'm glad you noticed."

Her cheeks heated.

What is wrong with you! Pretend indifference!

But she somehow couldn't. Not right then.

They finished eating and repacked the reusable containers. When he put aside the picnic box, her heart began thudding in anticipation.

Her body heated, knowing what was to come, especially when her gaze locked with his hooded eyes.

"Are you ready?" he asked.

"Yes," she replied breathlessly.

"Then let's go."

She was stunned. *He wants to go?*

She expected him to kiss her and for them to have passionate sex near the riverbed.

But he didn't make any move.

He only brought me here for a picnic and pleasant conversation?

Just like a normal couple?

The thought should make her panic, but strangely she was touched.

They headed back to the mansion, where the helicopter was waiting for them. But they didn't get in right away.

"Give me a few minutes," he said. "I need to check on something inside the mansion. I'll be right back."

She nodded.

Not wanting to wait inside the helicopter, she explored the freshly planted garden area outside. A few workers were still working even though it was close to evening time. She vaguely recognized an old man.

She knew he was the head gardener, but she somehow never got a chance to meet him or introduce herself to him. Smiling, she went to the old man.

"You have done a wonderful job with the lilies and the rest of the garden," she said.

The old man turned towards her. When he saw her, he smiled. "Thanks, Miss Anya," he said.

She was surprised he knew her name. Maybe he heard one of the other workers mentioning to him that she was the lead architect for the restoration effort. But once again, she felt a nagging feeling the old man was familiar.

"I'm sorry I didn't get a chance to meet you before," she said. "I am the lead architect of the Vardhaman mansion restoration."

His smile got wider. "Oh, that's great. I'm glad that the little girl who loved this place is leading the restoration effort."

She was shocked by his words. This time, she looked at the old man closely. Looking past the heavy wrinkles, she finally recognized him.

"Mr. Rao!" she said in delight. "I'm so sorry, I didn't recognize you before!"

Mr. Rao had worked as the Vardhamans' driver for many decades. He used to often assist Ashok Vardhaman in gardening as well.

Mr. Rao's wrinkled smile widened. "I'm much older now. And so are you. You are no longer little Miss Anya."

Anya smiled. "Yes. But please call me just Anya now."

"I don't think I can. I'm used to thinking of you as Miss Anya who was always with Master Bobby up to some mischief."

Anya laughed again. "Yes."

"I'm hoping the restoration of the estate finishes soon. Then Mr. Varma and his family, with hopefully a lot of children, can live here."

Her heart jerked at the thought of Bhargav and his future family.

"Mr. Varma is restoring the mansion to use it as a... hotel."

Anya expected to see disappointment. But Mr. Rao's eyes twinkled.

"I see," he said.

Anya was glad Mr. Rao didn't care about the mansion and estate being used as a hotel as long as it was brought back to its former glory.

"How is your granddaughter, Mr. Rao?" she asked.

Anya recalled he had a granddaughter who was her age. But Anya's mother wouldn't allow her to play with the driver's granddaughter or other help's children. Anya had hated it, but she had no choice because her mother threatened they wouldn't visit the estate again if she didn't listen to her orders.

The old man's face lit up. "Oh, my Maddie now owns her own company in the city. She visits me often in the village."

Anya was happy for him and his granddaughter. "That's so great to hear."

The old man smiled. "When Maddie comes to the village the next time, I'll surely bring her to the estate. She would love to meet you."

"Yes. I would love to meet her too." Anya definitely wanted to meet the girl who grew up at the estate. Anya vaguely recalled a pretty girl who mostly spent time in the library with the Vardhamans' oldest son.

Mr. Rao had a wistful look. "Hopefully, most of the mansion restoration is completed before the housing project begins in the estate."

Anya was confused. "What housing project?"

Mr. Rao looked at her. "Mr. Varma didn't tell you?"

She had no idea. As far as she knew, only the mansion was going to be restored. There were nearly a dozen living quarters for the help within the mansion premises. Was he referring to that?

"They are going to build hundreds of homes on the estate," he said.

Anya was stunned. "Houses at the Vardhaman Estate?" she asked, thinking that the old man might be confused with some other project.

"Yes, Miss Anya. I heard Mr. Varma telling the engineers to check the places where they can begin building. And not fancy houses, but actual homes where people like me from villages can afford to buy."

Anya didn't know what to say or feel.

Bhargav Varma was a businessman. A hotelier. Why would he care about building homes for the lower-income groups?

It was shockingly odd and generous.

A familiar deep voice broke through her confusion.

"Hello, Mr. Rao," Bhargav greeted as he joined next to her. "How are you doing?"

The old man smiled. "I'm doing great, Mr. Varma. I was speaking to Miss Anya. I knew her when she was a little tyke playing in the estate."

"I see."

The sound of the helicopter being readied filled the air.

"We'll see you later, Mr. Rao," he said. He then looked at her with an unreadable expression. "We have to go back."

Nodding, she smiled at the old man. "I'll catch up with you next time, Mr. Rao."

The old man waved at them before they turned to head towards the helicopter.

The chopper noise was too loud for conversation, so she decided to wait until they got back to the penthouse before she could converse.

When the chopper took off, for the first time, instead of feeling the loss of flying away from the estate she loved, she was waiting in anticipation to reach the penthouse.

***

It was late evening when they landed on top of the building.

They took the elevator down and went into the penthouse. As soon as the door shut, Anya began the conversation.

"When is the housing project—" She broke off with a gasp when he pushed her against the wall and covered her mouth.

All thoughts disappeared when his lips met with hers. She had been anticipating their kiss all day, especially during their picnic.

Wrapping her hands around his neck, she kissed him back.

He pushed her up against the wall, and she wrapped her legs around his hips. And then, pulling away from the wall, he carried her to the bedroom.

Their tongues tangled while they continued to kiss frantically. This time, they didn't even get to removing all their clothes.

As soon as he dropped her on the bed, he only slightly adjusted their clothes and then he drove into her. She clung to him as intense pleasure exploded. Her hands gripped his hair as he grunted harshly against her neck, driving into her with a force that shook her soul.

When release came, it was equally shattering.

Even as her world shook, she wondered if it was too late. Despite fighting hard and trying to hate him—had she fallen in love with the villain?

***

"Tell me about the housing project," Anya demanded.

They were seated at the penthouse balcony having an intimate dinner together.

Bhargav took a sip of his drink. "What do you want to know?"

"Is it at the estate?" she asked.

"Yes."

"How many homes?"

"Two hundred in the first phase and five hundred more in the remaining phases."

It was a shockingly large undertaking.

"Why?" she asked. "Won't that negatively impact your high-end hotel?"

"I need people to work at the estate."

Anya knew having hundreds of families wasn't just to help find workers. Her enemy lover actually wanted to help the villages nearby.

That fact touched her heart. And it also made her feel more conflicted because she couldn't hold on to a spec of hate against him.

"Why didn't you tell me?" she asked softly.

He didn't have to necessarily tell her. She was only hired to take care of the mansion restoration. But after having spent most of their moments together over the last few weeks, she expected him to share something as big as this.

"The approval was recent," he said. "The woman you saw talking to me at the club, she is the lawyer who is helping with the approvals."

Shit.

Yet again, she had jumped the gun, thinking he was two-timing like her ex-husband.

"I see," she murmured. "I thought she was someone you were seeing along with me."

His eyes flashed. "I already told you we were going to be exclusive. And besides, I quite liked what happened that night when we returned from the club."

Her cheeks heated, recalling her tantrum driven by anger and jealousy. It had led to angry yet passionate sex. It completely shattered her strategy to pretend indifference and keep him at a distance.

"Why didn't you tell me about her?" she demanded, feeling embarrassed.

"You didn't ask."

She didn't believe even for a moment he hadn't known how she felt.

"You are a master manipulator!" she accused.

His small smile grew as he watched her with hooded eyes. "I can't deny that. But so were you initially when you played your little game to pretend indifference to my touch."

Her face was on fire, knowing it was the truth. She could barely keep herself from responding to his touch. She had to use every bit of her self-control. The man emitted a magnetic pull large enough to fit a stadium. All he had to do was be in the same office building or house, and she was hyperaware and drawn to him.

And now, she knew that under all the wicked lies and his ruthless villain persona, he was actually a generous-hearted man who wanted to help the underprivileged. She hadn't meant to fall in love with him, but she couldn't deny that he stole her heart.

She loved him.

CHAPTER THIRTY-FOUR

Bhargav knew something had changed in the way Anya thought of him.

He could no longer see uncertainty in her eyes. She looked at him with desire and something else that made him want to carry her somewhere and never let go.

"Are you done?" he asked, wanting to get the dinner over with, so he could have her in his arms again.

He wanted to see her eyes from close when he was deep inside her.

Would she still look at him with desire and uncertainty? Or would he see the new emotion along with her desire?

At his not-so-subtle heated look, her cheeks reddened slightly as she nodded. "Yes, I'm done."

Despite telling her it wasn't required, she stacked up the dinner dishes neatly for the cook to clear up the next morning. And then blushing slightly, she placed her small hand in his and followed him.

But he stopped in the living room.

"Let's dance," he said.

There was surprise in her eyes followed by excited pleasure.

Wanting to capture more of the sweet, excited pleasure in her eyes, he turned on the music. Thumping pop music came from the speakers in the ceiling. It was music Anya often listened to when she was alone in the penthouse.

He pulled her into his arms until her soft breasts pressed against his chest, and her head was tucked under his chin.

She smiled at him warmly as they moved to the music.

"I didn't know you enjoyed dancing," she said.

He didn't. He wasn't much of a dancer, but he enjoyed holding her in his arms and watching her beautiful face while they moved to the music.

"There are a lot of things about me that would surprise you, Miss Kashyap," he said before dipping her dramatically over his arm and then pulling her close and twirling her around in the room.

She laughed in pleasure.

Listening to her laugh and seeing the sparkle in her eyes, he smiled.

She once again looked at him with a soft look in her eyes. "Yes, there are a lot of things I'm discovering about you, Mr. Varma," she said.

They danced for some time. Anya continued to laugh and giggle. Towards the end of one song, he picked her up high in the air and twirled her around.

But soon, laughter gave away to heat and awareness. He sensed when she began to get affected by his touch. Her breaths turned faster, and different kind of sparkle filled her eyes.

Soon the songs ended.

"Do you want to dance more?" he asked huskily.

She shook her head as her cheeks reddened. "No."

Holding her small hand once again into his larger one, he pulled her towards their bedroom.

He began to undress them both rapidly. Their breaths came out faster and he could sense her need as he carried her to the bed.

She clung to him, and watched him with the same soft look of desire and something else that made him want to give her the world.

He laid her on the mattress, and joined next to her on the bed. Then rolling on top of her, he kissed her throat at the rapidly fluttering pulse. Her skin was slightly damp and tasted salty due to their dancing. He loved the taste and he couldn't get enough. He licked her skin.

He was just about to move lower to suck the sweet aroused buds of her breasts into his mouth when she stopped him.

"Bhargav, wait," she gasped, pushing at his shoulders.

He frowned.

He recalled the last time she had stopped him similarly right after their deal.

Was she planning to put on pretence of indifference once again? Had he imagined the soft look in her eyes a while ago?

No. He had sensed something different in her eyes. It wasn't his imagination.

Raising his head, he looked at her.

She looked at him with uncertainty. "I-I... want to touch you," she said. "I have never—" she broke off with a blush.

The storm inside his head reduced. He understood what she was saying.

The sex between them had always been urgent and passionate, and he drove it because of his need for her. Even now, his body screamed to be inside her. But he held back.

Watching her face, he lay back on the bed next to her.

Slowly, she sat up and looked at him. Her eyes swept over him with a slightly awestruck look on her face. He knew she was fascinated by the various scars on his chest and arms from his fighting days. They didn't disgust her. He often found her watching them curiously, but she never asked him about them. He knew she tried to distance her heart from their relationship.

Her eyes then moved lower, and he could see her cheeks reddening when she saw his hard and demanding arousal. She had touched him at times during sex, but he hadn't given her the time to touch or taste him intimately like he did with her.

Her eyes rose to his face again, and he could see that she wanted to explore him.

He continued to lie still, simply watching her.

She touched his chest first. She traced the scars gently with her fingers, and then using her soft, lips, she kissed them as though trying to remove the hurt from when he received them.

His breaths grew heavier at her simple touch, and he felt an ache deep inside his chest.

She continued to explore him using her hands and mouth. When she reached his arousal, his body jerked to see what she would do.

With her cheeks reddening again, and with the soft look in her eyes, she watched his face as she put her mouth on him intimately.

Fuck!

Seeing the sight of her pink lips surrounding his hardness, he almost blew his load right then.

She drove him crazy. What she lacked in skill, she more than made up with her curiosity and excitement.

"Enough!" he growled, unable to take it after a while. He wanted and needed to be inside her.

She let out a startled yelp when he pulled her by her waist. He was about to push her next to him on the bed to roll on top of her, when she pushed his hands away and sat on top of him.

Their breaths came out harsher as they gazes clashed. Keeping her eyes on him, she slowly took him inside her.

His eyes almost rolled back with intense pleasure, but he kept them open to watch the beautiful sight in front of him.

Continuing to watch him with a soft look in her eyes, she moved slowly on top of him, taking him in and out of her body.

It took every ounce of his self-control not to flip her over the bed, and take her in hard and fast thrusts like he usually did. But keeping his control on leash, he only touched her. He cupped her beautiful, heavy breasts in his palms and worked the hardened rosy nipples.

Her breaths splintered and her eyes glazed. She bit her bottom lip as her movements turned faster and deeper.

Unable to stop, he raised his hips and began thrusting, pushing deeper into her and joining them together. She cried out, and her movements grew even faster and frantic. Barely a few moments later, they exploded together.

His release was hard and powerful. With a rough animal noise, he held the back of her neck and dragged her head close until his mouth caught hers while he shot his seed deep into her. She cried out against his mouth and held him tightly while she trembled and shook on top of him.

As they climaxed together, he barely held back from calling her by the name he wanted to.

Annie.

CHAPTER THIRTY-FIVE

Anya woke up to her phone ringing.

Groaning slightly and hoping it would be a brief call, either from work or maybe from Trupti, she opened her eyes.

She blushed and smiled when she saw that her enemy lover was not next to her on the bed. Hoping he would return soon, she answered the call.

"Anya!" her mother's voice greeted.

Anya almost groaned again. "Good morning, Ma."

It was only seven in the morning. Usually, her parents and brother didn't wake up this early. It must be a crisis of some sort for her mother not only to be awake but also to call her daughter who she hadn't bothered calling in the last few weeks.

"They are going to be here, Anya! You must stop them!"

Anya frowned. "Who? What are you talking about, Ma?"

"The bank goons that your lover hired are going to seize our home today in a few hours."

Anya's heart jerked.

Did Bhargav know that the bank would be seizing the house this morning?

No. He probably didn't know. Or he would have said something.

But what if he did know?

She heart thudded with uncertainty. She was yet to know why he decided to purchase all the loans her father made with the banks. Yes, it wasn't Bhargav's fault that her father took loans that couldn't be easily repaid.

Her mother continued to speak. "Are you going to ask your lover to stop his goons from coming inside today?"

"I don't know if Bhargav sent them or if he can stop them."

"It was him! Tell him to stop!" her mother demanded.

Anya knew her mother was panicking. "I will try, Ma. Let me talk to him."

The call ended, but Anya stayed frozen while her heart began to thud sickly.

She was back to square one when she had made a deal with Bhargav. Her body in exchange to letting her family go.

But over the weeks, she broke her own deal and fell in love with him.

Taking a shuddering breath, she was about to get out of the bed when the door opened. It was Bhargav.

He was holding a breakfast tray. "Good morning," he said.

Her heart skipped a beat seeing his charming smile. She had never seen him so relaxed. She felt terrible to bring up the conversation after their special night together.

"Bhargav, c-can I ask you a favor?" She felt a sense of déjà vu. She recalled making a similar phone call to him asking him to come to her parents' home for help. And after he arrived, all hell broke loose.

She knew things would once again go terribly wrong.

"Sure," he said, pouring coffee into a cup before adding cream and sugar the way she liked. He threw her a glance with a small smile. "Tell me, Miss Kashyap. How may I serve you today?"

Her heart ached at his teasing.

"Stop the banks from seizing my parents' house."

At her softly uttered statement, his hands paused mid-stirring. And then, he went completely still.

With her heart continuing to thud sickly, she forged on. "O-our deal was that if I slept with you, you'd stop the arrests of my brother and father. I will continue to be with you. But stop the foreclosure of my parents' home as well."

He turned towards her and watched her. His eyes slowly swept over her, taking in the way she clutched the bedsheet to her chest, her naked shoulders and then her face.

"Done," he said quietly.

He handed her the coffee cup.

She took it with trembling hands and frantically thought of what she could possibly say right then to break the tense atmosphere.

"Let's get ready for work," he said. His voice was still eerily quiet.

He walked away from her and went into the closet area before entering the bathroom suite and shutting the door.

She continued to sit on the bed staring blankly.

She had more or less told the man she fell in love with to treat her as an expensive whore in exchange for her parents' home. He probably even thought that she had driven their lovemaking the previous night to ask for the favor.

Oh God.

She knew it was a matter of time before it would be over between them soon. She was going to lose the man she loved.

***

"I think Rishab's family is a bunch of serial killers. What do you think?"

Anya nodded absently. "Yes."

Trupti laughed. "You are not even listening!"

Anya was meeting her best friend for lunch. She needed the break to have her feelings sorted. The sick feeling she felt when she made a new deal with Bhargav earlier that morning wouldn't leave her. She felt as though she had cheapened their relationship.

The ease and sweet closeness that had developed recently between her and Bhargav was now gone. He was back to the reserved mode.

That morning, when he stepped out of the bathroom and saw her on the bed still, he had come to her. They had sex. It was hard, frantic and passionate. He drove her wild, and her body responded eagerly to their frantic sex. But she could sense his dark anger. When they found their shattering releases, he pulled away from her soon after and asked her to get ready.

She felt hurt, and she knew she had hurt him too.

Oh God. I hope I can fix this. I don't want to lose him.

Taking a deep breath, she looked at her friend with a trembling smile. "I'm sorry. Something came up at work. I was thinking about it."

Trupti smiled. "How is your Mr. Work doing these days?" she asked.

Anya was just about to reply when her phone rang. She looked at the number, and her heart jerked excitedly. It was Bhargav.

Was he looking for me during lunch?

She hadn't told him she was stepping out to meet Trupti. He had left the penthouse, and he wasn't working in the office building that morning. He had gone somewhere else.

Hoping that he was calling to check on her to make plans for later, she answered the call quickly.

"Hello," she said, also hoping her voice didn't sound too hesitant or shaken.

"Where are you, Anya?" his voice was still eerily quiet.

Her heart began thumping when he called her by her name. He usually did only during passionate moments. In the office or during work, he addressed her formally.

"I-I came to have lunch with Trupti," she said.

There was a momentary silence before he spoke again.

"After your lunch, go to your place. I'm having someone drop your things off at your home."

Her heart stopped.

He was breaking up with her.

She knew it would happen. Initially, she had hoped it would happen soon after their first deal. And now, when it was happening, she felt numb with shock and pain.

Her voice got stuck in her throat with the hurt, but she somehow managed to reply.

"Okay," she whispered.

"Take care, Anya," he said quietly and ended the call.

Anya held the phone to her ear for a few more moments, hoping she could still hear him speak or make sense of what was happening.

Slowly, knowing the call was cut and she wouldn't hear from him, she lowered her phone.

She looked in front of her. Trupti was watching her with a worried look.

"My God, Anya. Are you okay? You look like you are about to faint. What happened?" her friend asked.

Anya stared at her friend blankly for a few more moments before replying.

"I fell in love. And now, I lost him."

With those words, she burst out crying.

CHAPTER THIRTY-SIX

"Is everything fine?"

Bhargav put his phone aside and looked at his older brother seated across from him on their private jet. They were flying to New York to meet their mother.

Bhargav gave Yash a nod. "Everything's fine."

"You look upset and pissed, bro," Aryan remarked from next to him.

"I'm fine," he said.

Aryan shook his head. "Then why is your jaw clenched, and you look like you want to beat the shit out of someone?"

Bhargav did want to hit someone. After thinking that Anya was finally falling in love with him, his dreams got smashed once again by the harsh reality. Anya's useless piece of shit father who was pimping his daughter yet again to save his ass. The old man made his wife call Anya to stop the rightful foreclosure of their house. The man and his son had already evaded arrest, but instead of feeling grateful, the old bastard got greedy.

Not for too long.

Bhargav also felt a fuckload of anger and hurt towards Anya when she made her so-called second deal. He knew she was doing it for her useless family, but it still made him angry that she would bargain with him after what they felt for each other.

"Cheer up, bro," Aryan continued. "We are meeting Ma after a long time. And it's going to be a happy occasion for big bro's wedding next week. A lot to do."

There was slight sarcasm in Aryan's voice. Bhargav knew Aryan wasn't happy with Yash breaking their plan and marrying the wrong woman. Instead of marrying their enemy's daughter as planned, Yash was marrying the enemy's widowed daughter-in-law.

Bhargav noticed that Yash didn't seem too elated by his upcoming wedding either. It was odd because Yash was obsessed with the woman he was marrying.

Just like me.

Bhargav was obsessed with Anya. But he couldn't allow his obsession to ruin the plans they put together. He had gone easy on Anya's father in the first place. And now, it was time to make some fucking amendments.

But when things go downhill soon, would he ever be able to let Anya go?

CHAPTER 37

"Anya, you have to eat. You haven't eaten well for two weeks! I'm worried about you."

Anya was staring at her computer screen while changing the color palette slightly in the mansion's music room 3-D design. Trupti had dragged her outside to sit in the small garden area and work. But nothing cheered her—not the birds chirping in the trees or the beautiful sunny day.

She felt nothing. She had been numb for the past two weeks.

"You skipped dinner last night, and it is afternoon now," Trupti continued. "Come! Eat something."

Anya shook her head. "I'm not hungry. I'll eat later. You go ahead."

"It's Saturday! You can take a break in the afternoon. You have literally been staying in your office for twelve straight hours from Monday to Friday."

Anya knew Trupti was right. She had gone to the office each morning by seven. She stayed there until seven in the evening, hoping she could catch a glimpse of the man she loved.

But Bhargav didn't come to the office for two straight weeks.

She didn't know if he was travelling or simply avoiding her. She recalled the conversation she had with his personal assistant during the first week.

"Mr. Varma is away on business, Miss Kashyap."

"Oh. Thanks, Ravi. C-can you tell me when he is back in the office?"

The man looked surprised. "Of course, Miss Kashyap."

It had been humiliating asking someone else to let her know, considering that in the last two months, she and Bhargav had spent most of their time together.

Five days ago, Ravi came to her himself with an update.

"Mr. Varma is back, Miss Kashyap. But he has asked me to inform you that he is not to be disturbed. All restoration inquiries are to be handled by you."

Anya's heart broke right then.

She knew it was truly over between her and Bhargav. She knew he would eventually meet her for the sake of the restoration project, but it would only be in the official capacity.

"Call him and talk to him, Anya," Trupti insisted.

Anya shook her head. "I can't."

"Why not?" her friend demanded.

"He ended our deal."

Trupti frowned. "What deal?"

Anya looked at her friend. "Me sleeping with him in exchange for him stopping my father and brother's arrests for financial fraud and lack of loan repayment."

Trupti looked stunned.

Anya stared in the distance blankly. "It was supposed to be a simple deal. But he demanded more. He said he wanted us to be like a couple. I fought him and my feelings. I tried hard not to fall in love with him, but I lost."

Trupti looked outraged. "He broke up with you because you fell in love with him?"

Anya shook her head. "No. He broke up with me because I asked him to stop my parents' home foreclosure."

Trupti frowned. "He didn't want to stop the foreclosure?" she asked.

"He stopped it."

Trupti looked confused. "Then why did he break up?"

Anya felt ashamed. "I made a deal saying I would continue sleeping with him only if he stopped the foreclosure."

"Shit." Trupti shook her head. "That was a shitty deal, Anya. It was obvious that he liked you right from the beginning. You making the deal was a slap in the face, letting him know he meant nothing."

Anya's heart clenched. "I know."

She recalled his coldness and anger when she made that deal. She had hurt him.

Before their breakup sex, each time they were together, he had always looked at her as though she were someone he wanted beyond anything. He looked into her eyes until she felt the bond and connection between them. It wasn't just desire. It had always been more than that.

But the last time they were together, there was just passion driven by cold anger.

"Why aren't you talking to him, Anya? Tell him how you feel?"

Anya looked at her friend. "I tried, but he's avoiding me."

Trupti looked confused. "You aren't the kind to back away from a problem, Anya. You always faced them head-on. Hell, you dumped that cheating ass of your ex even though you were barely twenty-one. You dealt and solved so many problems for our company. I don't understand why you are backing away from something as important as this."

Anya knew her friend was right.

Maybe it was because she had been expecting a heartbreak right from the moment she met Bhargav. She had known he was capable of stealing and breaking her heart.

And yet, she let herself fall in love with him.

No. I didn't just fall. He made me fall in love with him using his wicked lies.

She still didn't know why he was targeting her family. The coincidences were too many. Although it initially appeared that he went after them because of her, she knew it was beyond that.

I have to find out.

She put aside her laptop and stood up from the chair. "I'm going," she said.

Trupti smiled. "To him?"

"Yes, he owes me answers. A lot of them."

Their relationship began with wicked lies. But it was time to find out the truth.

***

Anya's heart raced in nervousness and anticipation as she went up the private elevator.

Luckily, the codes hadn't been changed. Her cheeks heated, imagining what she would have done in case he had changed the elevator code to keep her out. Or even called the security to have her escorted out.

He can still do it.

No. He won't be able to keep me away.

He owes me answers.

She was going to find out the truth.

The elevator stopped on the penthouse floor. Her nervous anticipation hit the roof as she stepped out and went to the penthouse to ring the doorbell.

She couldn't wait to see his darkly handsome face again. Or feel his hooded gaze on her even if it was in anger. She had missed him badly.

She was about to press the doorbell again when it was answered. It was Nina.

Anya smiled at the cook. "Hello, Nina. How are you?"

The cook smiled back cheerfully. "I'm fine, Miss Anya."

"Is... Bhargav home?"

"Sir is not home right now."

Disappointment hit her hard.

But Nina continued speaking. "But madam is here. Would you like to meet her?"

Anya was shocked, and her heart twisted painfully.

Has he replaced me already?

Was the bonding and connection between them just a lie? Yet another wicked lie?

Before Anya could say no and leave, a woman's voice could be heard from the living room.

"Who is it, Nina?" the woman asked.

The woman sounded sweet and kind. Anya raised her eyes and looked behind Nina while a beautiful woman dressed simply approached the door. The woman had liberal grey hair near the temples, making Anya realize the woman might be older than she imagined.

It was only when the woman stopped near the door and Anya could see her face clearly, that shock ripped across Anya's heart.

The woman smiled. "Please come inside. Bhargav is not home yet, but he should be back soon."

When Anya kept staring at her, the woman frowned slightly. "I'm Bhargav's mother. You seem a little familiar, my dear. Have we met before in New York?"

"I'm Anya," she whispered. "Sukanya Kashyap."

At the words, there was shock on the older woman's face as well.

"Anya, you have to eat. You haven't eaten well for two weeks! I'm worried about you."

Anya was staring at her computer screen while changing the color palette slightly in the mansion's music room 3-D design. Trupti had dragged her outside to sit in the small garden area and work. But nothing cheered her—not the birds chirping in the trees or the beautiful sunny day.

She felt nothing. She had been numb for the past two weeks.

"You skipped dinner last night, and it is afternoon now," Trupti continued. "Come! Eat something."

Anya shook her head. "I'm not hungry. I'll eat later. You go ahead."

"It's Saturday! You can take a break in the afternoon. You have literally been staying in your office for twelve straight hours from Monday to Friday."

Anya knew Trupti was right. She had gone to the office each morning by seven. She stayed there until seven in the evening, hoping she could catch a glimpse of the man she loved.

But Bhargav didn't come to the office for two straight weeks.

She didn't know if he was travelling or simply avoiding her. She recalled the conversation she had with his personal assistant during the first week.

"Mr. Varma is away on business, Miss Kashyap."

"Oh. Thanks, Ravi. C-can you tell me when he is back in the office?"

The man looked surprised. "Of course, Miss Kashyap."

It had been humiliating asking someone else to let her know, considering that in the last two months, she and Bhargav had spent most of their time together.

Five days ago, Ravi came to her himself with an update.

"Mr. Varma is back, Miss Kashyap. But he has asked me to inform you that he is not to be disturbed. All restoration inquiries are to be handled by you."

Anya's heart broke right then.

She knew it was truly over between her and Bhargav. She knew he would eventually meet her for the sake of the restoration project, but it would only be in the official capacity.

"Call him and talk to him, Anya," Trupti insisted.

Anya shook her head. "I can't."

"Why not?" her friend demanded.

"He ended our deal."

Trupti frowned. "What deal?"

Anya looked at her friend. "Me sleeping with him in exchange for him stopping my father and brother's arrests for financial fraud and lack of loan repayment."

Trupti looked stunned.

Anya stared in the distance blankly. "It was supposed to be a simple deal. But he demanded more. He said he wanted us to be like a couple. I fought him and my feelings. I tried hard not to fall in love with him, but I lost."

Trupti looked outraged. "He broke up with you because you fell in love with him?"

Anya shook her head. "No. He broke up with me because I asked him to stop my parents' home foreclosure."

Trupti frowned. "He didn't want to stop the foreclosure?" she asked.

"He stopped it."

Trupti looked confused. "Then why did he break up?"

Anya felt ashamed. "I made a deal saying I would continue sleeping with him only if he stopped the foreclosure."

"Shit." Trupti shook her head. "That was a shitty deal, Anya. It was obvious that he liked you right from the beginning. You making the deal was a slap in the face, letting him know he meant nothing."

Anya's heart clenched. "I know."

She recalled his coldness and anger when she made that deal. She had hurt him.

Before their breakup sex, each time they were together, he had always looked at her as though she were someone he wanted beyond anything. He looked into her eyes until she felt the bond and connection between them. It wasn't just desire. It had always been more than that.

But the last time they were together, there was just passion driven by cold anger.

"Why aren't you talking to him, Anya? Tell him how you feel?"

Anya looked at her friend. "I tried, but he's avoiding me."

Trupti looked confused. "You aren't the kind to back away from a problem, Anya. You always faced them head-on. Hell, you dumped that cheating ass of your ex even though you were barely twenty-one. You dealt and solved so many problems for our company. I don't understand why you are backing away from something as important as this."

Anya knew her friend was right.

Maybe it was because she had been expecting a heartbreak right from the moment she met Bhargav. She had known he was capable of stealing and breaking her heart.

And yet, she let herself fall in love with him.

No. I didn't just fall. He made me fall in love with him using his wicked lies.

She still didn't know why he was targeting her family. The coincidences were too many. Although it initially appeared that he went after them because of her, she knew it was beyond that.

I have to find out.

She put aside her laptop and stood up from the chair. "I'm going," she said.

Trupti smiled. "To him?"

"Yes, he owes me answers. A lot of them."

Their relationship began with wicked lies. But it was time to find out the truth.

***

Anya's heart raced in nervousness and anticipation as she went up the private elevator.

Luckily, the codes hadn't been changed. Her cheeks heated, imagining what she would have done in case he had changed the elevator code to keep her out. Or even called the security to have her escorted out.

He can still do it.

No. He won't be able to keep me away.

He owes me answers.

She was going to find out the truth.

The elevator stopped on the penthouse floor. Her nervous anticipation hit the roof as she stepped out and went to the penthouse to ring the doorbell.

She couldn't wait to see his darkly handsome face again. Or feel his hooded gaze on her even if it was in anger. She had missed him badly.

She was about to press the doorbell again when it was answered. It was Nina.

Anya smiled at the cook. "Hello, Nina. How are you?"

The cook smiled back cheerfully. "I'm fine, Miss Anya."

"Is... Bhargav home?"

"Sir is not home right now."

Disappointment hit her hard.

But Nina continued speaking. "But madam is here. Would you like to meet her?"

Anya was shocked, and her heart twisted painfully.

Has he replaced me already?

Was the bonding and connection between them just a lie? Yet another wicked lie?

Before Anya could say no and leave, a woman's voice could be heard from the living room.

"Who is it, Nina?" the woman asked.

The woman sounded sweet and kind. Anya raised her eyes and looked behind Nina while a beautiful woman dressed simply approached the door. The woman had liberal grey hair near the temples, making Anya realize the woman might be older than she imagined.

It was only when the woman stopped near the door and Anya could see her face clearly, that shock ripped across Anya's heart.

The woman smiled. "Please come inside. Bhargav is not home yet, but he should be back soon."

When Anya kept staring at her, the woman frowned slightly. "I'm Bhargav's mother. You seem a little familiar, my dear. Have we met before in New York?"

"I'm Anya," she whispered. "Sukanya Kashyap."

At the words, there was shock on the older woman's face as well.

CHAPTER THIRTY-EIGHT

Sweat rolled down the forehead as Bhargav hit the punching bag repeatedly.

The way he felt, he didn't want to fight with the trainers. Instead of restrained fighting, he hit the punching bag with everything he had.

Despite fully concentrating on the punches, his mind wandered to the same place.

Anya.

He knew she must be hurting the way he was hurting from the inside. But there wasn't a damn thing he could do right then to stop her hurt.

He and his brothers wanted revenge for the past. They felt justified and entitled to it because of the devastating loss and grief they suffered. They lost their father. Their beautiful, kind mother cruelly lost the love of her life—all because of a few bastards' greed.

He and his brothers wanted retribution. They wanted to make the people responsible pay over a hundred times. He wanted to break those men in every way.

But in the process of breaking his enemy, he knew he might break the woman he loved.

Anya was his enemy's daughter.

If he destroyed her father and drove the old man to suicide, would Anya look at him with love in her eyes again?

It was fucking impossible.

And that's why he had to stay away. Anya would hate him and fear him soon.

Despite the reasoning, the longing he felt for Anya and the hurt of being away from her couldn't be appeased.

Fuck!

Grunting harshly, he pounded the punching bag even harder.

But even as he tried to let out anger and pain through aggression, he felt the presence of something sweet. He froze and caught the punching bag still.

The sweet smell of a familiar perfume drifted to him even through the smell of bleach and chemicals used in the gym. He wondered if he was dreaming or imagining her presence again like he did over the last two weeks.

Slowly, he turned. It was Anya.

She looked incredibly beautiful. His body roared to life, and his heart and mind urged him to go to her and grab her into his arms. But he waited.

She stared at him as though she had seen a ghost. Her next words confirmed it.

"Bobby," she whispered.

CHAPTER THIRTY-NINE

"There's no way I'm going to marry Yash!" Nine-year-old Anya placed her hands on her waist as she declared that after eavesdropping on her parents' conversation with the Vardhamans.

Nine-year-old Bobby nodded. "Of course not. Because you will be my wife. We both decided that a long time ago."

Anya smirked. "You will have to kiss me when I become your wife."

Bobby looked horrified. "I don't kiss girls! Especially not my best friend!"

Anya laughed. "We have to, silly! How else will we have children? I heard God puts a baby into a woman's stomach when she kisses her husband."

Bobby looked skeptical. "I heard something else."

Anya frowned. "What?"

Bobby looked victorious. "If we carve a heart and our initials on a tree, God will make sure we will marry and have children."

Anya recalled seeing hearts along with initials carved on many trees. "Oh. That makes so much sense. It sounds much better than yucky kissing!"

Bobby nodded in agreement.

"Come on!" Anya held Bobby's hand and dragged him out. "Let's go find a favorite tree and carve our initials."

One year after Anya and Bobby carved their initials and heart on a tree, her best friend died in a tragic fire accident along with his entire family.

Or so she thought.

Anya stared at the man in front of her. "Why?" she asked in a whisper.

Her eyes moved over the darkly handsome features desperately trying to find the boy he used to be. Despite the overtly masculine face, she could see the small traces of her best friend—the slight upturn of his lips, the shape of his eyes and the high cheekbones that were prominent among the Vardhaman men.

He was her Bobby. Seeing his mother a while ago more than confirmed it.

"How did you find out?" he asked calmly.

"Your mother," she replied. "I went to the penthouse to meet you when I saw her there."

He didn't say anything.

"Why?" she asked again. "Why did you all pretend to die? Why did you return? And why did you pretend to be someone else! And why did you make me fall in—" Her voice broke.

She was unable to ask him why he had made her fall in love with him.

Once again, she wondered if anything about what they had between them was true.

Had it all been a lie?

He stepped closer and gripped her jaw. "What we had between us during the last two months is real." His tone was fierce.

Tears leaked out of her eyes. She was incredibly shocked, happy, angry and hurt at the same time. "You were my best friend," she whispered as though she expected him to remember how close they were more than a decade ago when they were small children.

"I'm still that boy who adored you," he said quietly. "When I left, I grieved your loss along with my father's. I could never forget you."

That broke her. She threw her arms around his neck and burst out crying against his chest.

"Oh God, Bobby. I missed you so much."

He stroked her hair gently at the back of her head. "I missed you too, Annie."

Her heart leaped in joy when he referred to her in the name he used to call when they were children.

"I-I was told y-you and your brothers along with your mother d-died in the fire on the night of your father's funeral. I s-screamed and cried and told my mother she was lying. I didn't believe her because she had been telling me not to play with you or speak with you because y-your family was going to be poor. I-I didn't believe her and threw tantrums until they took me to the mansion and showed me the burned family wing." She shuddered, recalling how shocked she was and had gone into terrible grief barely eating for days.

"W-why?" she demanded again. "Why did you and your family fake your deaths and leave?"

He was silent.

She pushed away from his hard chest and looked at his face. "Tell me, Bobby!"

His face went cold. There was dark rage in his eyes, which she knew wasn't directed at her. But still, her heart thudded because she knew something terrible would be revealed.

"Because the people who murdered my father wanted to kill the rest of his family too." He looked deeper into her eyes. "One of the men responsible is your father."

***

Anya stared at the man she loved. "My father had your father killed?"

He looked back at her. "He is one among them."

Anya wanted to deny it, but she knew there could be truth to it. Her father could be incredibly jealous and selfish. She had, at times, heard him speaking derogatory things about Ashok Vardhaman. Her father had been jealous that his friend was rich and influential while he wasn't.

Ashok Vardhaman was kind and generous hearted too. The only reason he included her father in his business venture was because they were childhood friends.

"I-I know my father was jealous, but I don't know if he is capable of k-killing his friend."

Bhargav's jaw clenched. "We are still investigating to know what happened the night of my father's murder."

"S-so you came back to take revenge on my father? And I-I am a... pawn in your plan?"

She felt incredibly hurt by that fact. She looked down to hide the tears of hurt that were filling her eyes.

He gripped her chin and turned her face up. "No. I wasn't lying when I said meeting you again was purely fate. I didn't plan to meet you at the club on the night your brother lost to me while gambling."

Her heart jerked. She recalled feeling an incredibly strong connection and pull towards him right from their first meeting. Now she knew why. A part of her deep inside recognized he was the boy who had been her best friend and soul mate.

"What's going to happen now?" she asked quietly.

She knew he was going to destroy her father as revenge. Her heart ached at the fact. Even though she wasn't close to her father and didn't like how he was as a person, he was still her father and she loved him.

"I don't know yet," he said grimly. "Let's go up. I think my mother must be anxious to know what happened."

She nodded.

210

He dropped his hand from her face and wrapped it around her waist. Despite the grim situation, her heart raced with joy at his touch. Now that she knew his real identity, she didn't fight her feelings.

He was Bobby. Her best friend and soul mate.

But he's also the man who will destroy your father.

***

Parvathi Vardhaman was waiting anxiously inside the penthouse. When she saw Anya and her son, the older woman came to Anya right away.

"What happened? Are you all right?"

Anya nodded.

Bhargav's mother looked at her son. "Did you hurt Anya and her family?" she asked in an anxious tone.

Bhargav didn't let anything show on his face, but he replied honestly. "Yes."

His mother looked devastated. She shook her head. "First Yash and now you. I didn't tell you the truth about your father's death so you could destroy the men responsible and their innocent loved ones."

Bhargav was quiet.

Anya was the one to come to his defense. "I'm fine, Parvathi aunty. Bhargav... I mean Bobby didn't hurt me."

There was disbelief in the older woman's eyes. "He really didn't hurt you?"

He had hurt her initially by hiding the truth. But now, she understood why. "No."

The older woman tentatively smiled. "I'm glad. You have always been like a daughter to me, Anya. I can't let anyone hurt you, not even my son in an attempt to seek justice for a past wrong."

Anya's heart clenched at the incredibly generous-hearted woman in front of her.

Anya grew up with parents who were indifferent to each other. But Parvathi Vardhaman and her husband loved each other a lot. It could be seen in the sweet smiles they exchanged and how much they enjoyed each other's company.

To lose a loving husband cruelly like that was a devastating loss, especially when someone deliberately harmed the loved one. It took an incredible amount of forgiveness to let go of such a betrayal.

Anya hugged the older woman. "Thank you."

Parvathi Vardhaman hugged her back and then pulled away slightly with a smile. "We have a lot of catching up to do," she said.

Anya nodded with a smile. "Yes."

"Ma, are you going to Yash's place right now? Aryan is on his way."

At her son's reminder, Parvathi Vardhaman's eyes widened slightly. "Oh! I forgot. I have to go. Or that stubborn brother of yours will elope and marry Narmada."

Yash must be Yashwanth. Just like Bharat Vardhaman became Bhargav Varma. And Aryan must be the youngest Vardhaman brother, Arjun.

She was still shocked by the revelation.

She wanted to know so much more, but she would have to wait until later when she and Bhargav were alone.

As though on cue, a tall, handsome man who slightly resembled Bhargav entered the penthouse.

"Stop hacking into Yash's and my security systems," Bhargav said in a dry tone.

The man was grinning. "What's the fun in ringing the doorbell," he replied. "Hello, Ma," he greeted Parvathi Vardhaman.

But the man's smile died when he saw Anya. He looked at Bhargav accusingly. "I thought you broke up with her. How the hell can we strike if you keep romancing his daughter!"

Anya's heart twisted. She understood what Aryan was saying.

There was a look of shock on Parvathi Vardhaman's face. "You both are together?" she asked Anya.

Just when Anya was about to reply saying no, Bhargav answered. "Yes, Ma. Anya and I love each other."

The older woman looked shocked before a smile broke on her face. "This is excellent news! Oh my God. Maybe I'll have another wedding planned soon. I can't wait for you and Narmada to be my family again."

Anya blushed even as she knew things would not end happily between her and Bhargav.

"How can you say that, Ma!" Aryan said angrily. "At least Narmada's family is innocent, and her grandfather helped us. But Anya's father killed Papa! How can you think of having a murderer's daughter as a part of our family!"

Anya's heart clenched, knowing it was the truth.

"That's enough," Parvathi Vardhaman told her son. "How can you place blame on Anya for something her father did. I taught you boys better."

Aryan looked angry, but he remained silent. Bhargav was silent too.

Parvathi Vardhaman shook her head. "I want the three of you to resolve everything soon. Stop this retribution. Ashok also taught you boys that revenge is never the solution."

Anya knew it wasn't as simple. Not when she could see incredible grief and loss in Parvathi Vardhaman's eyes when she spoke of her late husband.

Taking a deep breath, the older woman continued. "Let's focus on the happy occasion of Yash and Narmada's wedding." She looked at Anya. "We'll talk again soon, Anya. I can't wait to hear more from you."

Anya nodded with a trembling smile. "Me too."

The older woman hugged Anya and Bhargav before dragging her younger son away.

As soon as they left the penthouse, Bhargav looked at her.

"I need to shower. Come join me."

Despite the grim situation, Anya's cheeks heated, and she nodded. She followed him and they came across Nina who was still in the penthouse.

"Nina, you can leave for the day."

At Bhargav's instructions, Anya's face heated even more.

Nina nodded. "Sure, Mr. Varma." She then smiled at Anya. "I'm so glad you are back, Miss Anya."

Anya's heart twisted listening to that. "Thank you, Nina." She had missed the cheerful woman too.

As soon as Nina left, she and Bhargav were completely alone. Her heart thudded in anticipation as she followed him into the master bedroom suite.

She didn't know how long they could be together.

It all depended on what Bhargav chose to do to her father. She knew it wasn't easy for him or his brothers or anyone, for that matter, not to take revenge for a murder of a loved one.

She was on borrowed time with him. And she wanted to make it memorable and lasting.

As soon as they stepped into the bedroom, he pulled her close and captured her mouth.

Tears prickled her eyes even as intense desire coursed through her body. She missed him so much. And now, knowing he was the boy who had always held her heart, she even missed him for the lost years.

She kissed him back frantically. He held her hips and picked her up. Continuing to kiss, he carried her to the bathroom where he lowered her on the cool marble floor.

He pulled away slightly. Then looking at her, he shed his clothes and hers. His eyes blazed seeing her bare body. She had lost a little weight over the last two weeks, but seeing the intense desire in his eyes, she felt beautiful.

Dragging her inside the shower cubicle, he pressed a button.

His eyes locked with hers while warm water sprayed on them from all directions.

Hunger and something more flashed in his eyes. With a harsh growl, his mouth crashed on top of hers once again. Moaning, she threw her arms around his neck and kissed him back.

He pushed her against the shower wall and lifted her high. Then gripping the back of her thighs, he drove inside her. It was raw and with no preliminaries. It was just the way she wanted it to be. She gripped his hair and dragged his mouth to hers and let the taste of him fill her senses.

He kissed her desperately while he took her body in a way that pleasure dominated everything else. No other thought remained in her mind.

His mouth left hers, and he looked into her face as he thrust deep inside her. "I missed you," he said harshly, pulsing inside her. "There were so many damn times when I thought about meeting you these last years. I dreamed of several ways. So when I finally saw you at the club, I knew I couldn't let you go or forget about you. I've always loved you. And after meeting you and being with you these last few months, I know I will continue loving you until my last breath."

Tears prickled in her eyes. "I love you too," she choked out.

His mouth locked on hers in a deep kiss, capturing her words while he continued to take her in a harsh intensity that spoke of his longing, desire and love.

Release ripped through her like a tidal wave. It was shockingly intense, and he joined her in it. She clung to him as they trembled together.

Much later, when her legs began to strain, she opened her eyes slowly to the sound of running water. He lowered her gently. He washed them both using soap and water before turning off the shower. He then dried her body briefly before picking her up and carrying her into his bedroom.

He placed her on the bed and lay next to her. She put her arm across his chest and clung to him once again. Her body was sated, but the fear and pain of losing him was still inside her heart and soul.

Pushing away those feelings, she clung to the present moment.

"Tell me what happened," she asked softly.

His deep voice rumbled inside his chest while he spoke. "My brothers and I always thought that our father died by suicide. But five months ago, my mother finally revealed to us that my father wouldn't have killed himself, and that it was my father's close friends and acquaintances who were involved in his death."

Her heart ached as she recalled the handsome and kindhearted smiling face of Ashok Vardhaman. She remained quiet and listened as he spoke.

"Your father and Rajesh Mohan made my father invest a lot of money on a housing project my father was interested in."

She recalled Rajesh Mohan and his family. They used to socialize sometimes with her family, but after the Vardhamans' alleged deaths, her family lost touch with the Mohans.

Maybe it was her father's guilt.

"The project was to provide affordable housing to thousands of poor people living in the city."

Her heart jerked again as she realized that the project he began on the estate to build lower-income homes was similar to his father's dream.

"Instead of using the money for the project, my father's friends reused the money in their own investments. They even collected money from the poor people as advances before the houses were built. My father had initially planned to invest what he had, but his two friends convinced him to borrow huge amounts in loans from the bank."

A sick feeling sat heavily inside Anya's stomach. She could imagine the shock and helplessness of Ashok Vardhaman when he realized his two friends' betrayal.

"My father was shocked and disappointed. But he was finding a way to repay the banks and do justice for the people who were swindled by his two friends and partners. The day before he was supposed to file a lawsuit for fraud, he was found hanging from the ceiling, making it seem like a suicide."

Guilt and heavy loss sat inside her chest for what her father had done to a generous-hearted and trusting man.

No one would forgive what her father had done. How can she expect Bhargav to let go of the betrayal that led to the devastating loss of his father?

Bhargav was taking revenge by doing the same to her greedy father. He somehow made her father invest in risky ventures by taking huge loans that he was unable to pay.

"But why did your family leave?" she asked in a whisper.

Bhargav was silent for a moment. "There was information about our lives being in danger as well. My father's murderers didn't want my mother or us children to take up the legal case. Two hours after my father's funeral, Mr. Rao drove us to the airport, and we flew to New York. Mr. Rao then set fire to the family wing in the mansion and staged our deaths. "

Oh God.

She knew her father had always been greedy and selfish, but she never imagined he was capable of plotting the murder of his friend and his family that included children.

She felt devastated knowing that.

And she could only imagine the painful and terrible experience Bhargav and his family had to go through after the loss and to leave their home to save their lives.

She could understand Bhargav's rage, not just on behalf of his father, but also for what his mother and brothers had gone through because of the betrayal.

He looked at her. "My brothers and I decided to avenge our father's death. We also wanted to bring our mother back to her rightful home."

Anya's heart jerked. "The mansion restoration..."

His eyes flashed. "It was never meant to be used as a hotel. It would continue to be a home to my family."

Anya was fiercely glad of the fact.

Her eyes filled with tears realizing what a homecoming it would be for his mother. Parvathi Vardhaman would miss the man she loved, but she would be back to the place where she spent most of her happy and loving memories with her husband.

He cupped her face. "You weren't meant to be a part of my plan," he said softly. "I was shocked seeing you in the club. I didn't recognize you at first in the long jacket. And then, when I saw the determined look in your eyes, even when you were out of your comfort zone in that gambling club, I knew you were my stubborn Annie."

Anya's heart flipped. "How did you recognize me? I have changed a lot since I was ten."

There was a flash of longing in his eyes. "I had looked you up many times over the years. I knew what you looked like and that you got married to someone and then got divorced. I knew you were an architect and started your own firm. I was proud and fascinated by what you have become over the fifteen years since I last saw you."

She was proud of him too. She had also been fascinated and drawn to the person he was even when she didn't know his true identity.

"I was supposed to stay away from you and follow the plan I put together."

She held her breath as the burning desire and longing intensified in his eyes. "I tried damn fucking hard to stay away. I was only supposed to watch you from far as I executed my plan to trap your brother and father. But I wanted you. I hired you because I could once again get close to you and because I knew you were the only one who would restore the mansion with both passion and love. I was right in sensing that you still loved the place and held the memories close to you."

He was right. She did love the estate and the memories of their past. She closed her eyes briefly as love, longing and loss swirled through her. She opened them again and looked at him.

"What will happen to us now?" she asked softly.

She could see similar conflict and longing in his eyes. "I want you more than anything in my life," he said. "But I also want to see justice prevail for what was done to my father. My brothers and I can't give up what we started."

Her throat tightened, and she nodded in understanding.

They loved each other before as innocent children. And when they met as adults, they fell in love again. But love alone wasn't enough for them to be together forever.

Yes, she could still choose to be with him, even if he destroyed her father and drove her father to suicide. But she knew she couldn't.

He would not be able to bear to see his father's murderer as his children's grandfather, just like she couldn't bear the thought that her children's father was responsible for their grandfather's death.

Her heart twisted painfully, wishing things were simpler between them just like their sweet childhood.

She raised her head and kissed him softly. "Leave me with more memories," she whispered against his lips.

He held the back of her head and kissed her back fiercely. He held her and kissed her as though he would never let her go. He rolled on top of her and pushed into her body, joining them together once again. She clung to him and loved him back equally hard.

They joined their bodies, hearts and souls together, knowing that when it ended, all they would be left with were more memories.

CHAPTER FORTY

"Wow. The wedding dais looks so stunningly beautiful, Anya. I can't wait for Narmada and Yash to be married here in a few hours."

Anya smiled at Parvathi Vardhaman. "Thank you. Most of it was your idea. My team and I just helped put it all together."

The older woman laughed. "There was no way I would have thought of fusing modern sensibilities with traditional ones the way you did here. It's really superb."

Anya was happy that Parvathi Vardhaman liked it. She hoped the bride would like the décor as well. Narmada was quite sweet and friendly. Anya had met her a couple of times in the last two weeks. But at that time, Narmada was worried sick since Yash was still healing from a gunshot wound.

"By the way, is Bhargav ready?" Parvathi Vardhaman asked. "Is he wearing the traditional suit we picked and not a business suit? I can't believe that even at this age, I have to keep reminding my sons to follow tradition."

Anya smiled. "Yes, he's wearing a traditional suit."

The older woman laughed. "Oh, good. That second son of mine can be quite as stubborn as a mule. You will have work cut out for you in the future to convince him for the smallest of things."

Anya's heart ached. She badly wanted to be a part of the sweet woman's life. Parvathi Vardhaman was sweet and nurturing. During the last two weeks, they became closer while they planned the wedding of her oldest son.

"Oh. Looks like the guests are arriving early."

Anya turned to see that a few people had arrived. Since it was a small wedding, she knew they must be close friends or relatives.

Anya smiled. "I'll take care of the arrangements. Please go and receive the guests."

"Oh. Thank you!" Parvathi Vardhaman hugged her before hurrying to receive the guests.

While Bhargav's mother took care of the guests, Anya continued with the last-minute preparations until the wedding. With barely twenty guests in attendance, it was a small, intimate wedding and easier to handle.

The wedding ceremony began on time. The groom arrived along with his brothers.

Anya's heart skipped a beat when she saw Bhargav. All three brothers looked handsome, but it was Bhargav who caught her eye. He looked in her direction as though sensing her gaze.

Her stomach fluttered as their gazes clashed, and then his hooded eyes slowly swept over her, taking in the long, heavily embroidered dress she wore for the wedding.

Over the last two weeks, they had spent every moment possible with each other.

Knowing their time was running out made them all the more frantic and desperate to create memories together. They went on intimate dinners, spent time at the penthouse and at the estate. They spent hours talking together while trying to catch up on the last fifteen years of their lives.

Bhargav told her about his rough childhood in New York when he dropped out of school to begin earning along with his older brother. He even told her about the secret fighting where people paid money to watch him get hurt or him hurting someone. Her heart ached for the little boy who had been her naughty yet sweet best friend. His innocence was cruelly snatched away, and his comfortable life was thrown into grueling hardships.

But despite the hardships faced, he and his brothers came out winning. She was proud of the man he had become.

They spoke about everything except for her father. She didn't ask what Bhargav planned to do, and neither did he speak to her about it. But she knew the retribution was coming soon.

Even though her parents didn't bother to remain in touch, she knew things were about to get worse for them again.

"Miss Kashyap, where should we set up the return gifts?"

Dragging her eyes away from Bhargav, she looked at the woman who was part of the team to organize the wedding.

"I've placed them in the music room," Anya told the young woman. "Either I or someone can bring them out once the lunch begins."

"Oh, sure."

The wedding began, and the bride joined the groom on the dais as well. Anya was busy with preparations and didn't get to watch all of the ceremony. But whatever glimpses she did catch, and also from meeting Narmada and Yash a few times before, she knew they made a great couple. The love and passion were evident in their eyes as they looked at each other during the ongoing ceremony.

Pushing away the ache inside her chest, she continued with the preparations.

Soon, the ceremony was over and lunch was about to begin. She went into the mansion which was only partially restored. The formal living room area was made beautiful for the wedding even though the artifacts and furniture were yet to be placed.

She walked past the living room and went into the music room. She was about to assess the packages with the return gifts when the door shut behind her.

Before she could turn, she was pushed against the large piano and a hard body pressed against her.

"I missed you," Bhargav growled against her ear.

Her heart thudded in excitement. "It's been barely six hours since we left the penthouse," she pointed out with a short, breathless laugh.

"That's too damn long."

It was, especially when they spent every moment together during the last two weeks.

His hands curled around her waist and cupped her breasts. Even with layers of clothing in between, her breasts responded to his presence and touch. Her breaths grew heavier as well.

"Bhargav, we are at a wedding!" she said breathlessly.

"I want you," he rasped against her ear. "I need to be inside you."

Oh God.

Her body was coming alive. And his hot breaths and hard arousal that she felt from behind didn't help.

"Someone might come looking for you or me," she reasoned in a whisper.

"I locked the door."

"But—" Before she could complete her sentence, he whipped her around to face him.

She gasped softly looking at the fierce hunger and longing in his eyes. She knew she couldn't refuse him. She didn't want to. She needed him too right then.

"You look so beautiful," he said in a deep, harsh tone. "Like a dream. My dream."

He looked stunning as well. She was about to tell him that, but his lips caught hers in a passionate kiss. All thought flew away, and she moaned softly throwing her arms around his neck.

He held her hips and picked her up before placing her on top of the piano. The surface was slippery because of her heavy silk dress, but he kept her pinned with his body. He pushed her dress up while he adjusted his suit. And then, a moment later he entered her in a single thrust.

She cried out at the harsh yet incredible sensation.

"All day, I have been thinking of this moment," he rasped, pulling out and thrusting deep into her again. "I've always known I can't be without you. Without seeing your beautiful face or hearing your sweet voice or touching you."

She was shocked by his words.

His harsh thrusts continued. "I love you, Annie. I want you in my life. I want us to marry. I want us to have children. I want us to get old together. And I want to die in your arms."

Her heart swelled, and her throat seized up with emotion because she wanted all those things more than anything.

"I am willing to give up anything for you and our love," he said before he drove into her like a wild storm.

She shattered hard.

With her body and her heart.

His words broke the walls of fear and uncertainty around her heart—the fear of losing him.

Instead, her heart was now filled only with his love.

"I love you so much," she cried out as she clung to him.

He broke as well and shuddered in her arms as his powerful release filled her body. They held each other while their words of love echoed inside her head.

Slowly, he pulled away and straightened. She wanted to cling to him for some more time as she usually did after the post-release.

"Someone is here," he said softly.

She blinked her eyes and focused before she heard someone calling out Bhargav's name.

She began to panic. "Oh God! They probably want to take pictures for the wedding, and you went missing."

She tried to push him away, but the outrageous man simply twisted his mouth into a small smile. "Relax. It's okay."

"No. It's not! Your hair looks wild as though—" she broke off blushing.

"As though someone pulled it during hot sex against a piano?" he asked. "You should see how you look."

Oh my God!

She had left her hair loose, so it wouldn't be that much of a mess. But her beautiful silk dress was mercilessly crumpled where he had shoved it above her hips.

"Bobby!" she said as she panicked. "Everyone will know!"

He grinned. "It's fine. Someone is looking for me. I'll go out first, and then you can straighten up and join in a few minutes."

He moved away from her and straightened himself in barely a few seconds while she desperately tried to pull at her gown so the wrinkles weren't obvious.

"Go!" she said when he stood watching her once again with a hooded look.

He smiled. And then, grabbing her chin, he kissed her hard before raising his head again. "We'll talk after the wedding. I'll tell you what I have decided."

She nodded, knowing that he had decided to stop destroying her father.

Kissing her again, this time softly, he walked away and slipped out of the music room.

She stayed with a post glow heating her face and body while she straightened her hair and dress. She was just about to step out when her phone rang. Thinking it was someone from the wedding organizing team, she answered.

"Anya," her brother's voice said in a panic. "I-I'm in trouble. I need your help urgently."

Anya felt a sense of déjà vu. She was reminded of the call when her brother had called from the gambling club asking for her help.

"What happened?" she asked, hoping he hadn't gambled again or done something equally worse. She was in no mood or mindset to rescue him again. She had done enough for her family at the cost of her own happiness.

"Anjali is pregnant," her brother replied.

Anya was surprised. Anjali was her brother's on-and-off girlfriend whom he refused to commit because she was from a humble background.

"It's okay that she is pregnant, Sohan. She loves you and you love her too."

Once again, there was victory in Surya's eyes. "Good. Now come and sit next to me for the ceremony and sign the documents."

"I want to change my clothes first," she said. "I'm sure you have clothes and jewellery prepared."

The flash in his eyes confirmed that everything was pre-planned.

"No need to change," he snapped. "This is fine. You will come up with an excuse to reject me, so you can be with your lover again."

Anya leaned towards him and spoke softly so only he could hear. "I need to change because I was with him a while ago. Do you want me to marry you in the same clothes that I had sex with him in?" she asked.

Rage flashed in Surya's eyes. Anya knew she was taking a huge risk with the crazy man. But she had to buy time.

His eyes swept over her dress, and he noticed the wrinkles. He must have seen other tell-tale signs as well because he was convinced she wasn't lying.

"Go wash that bastard away from your body and sit next to me in new clothes," he seethed.

He dragged her towards a room and pushed her inside.

"If you try to do anything, I will shoot your mother," he warned before leaving.

Anya shut the room door and leaned against it. She saw that the room was decorated with flowers, especially the bed. It was a room meant for a newlywed couple to spend their first night.

Oh God.

She couldn't believe what was happening. Everything felt so surreal. Despite her recent stance of not going to her parents' rescue, she was once again in the same situation.

But the threat was real. She couldn't risk her parents or brother being shot dead in cold blood by a madman.

What the hell do I do?

With trembling fingers, she began changing her clothes, knowing Surya would demand her to come out soon.

Her mind raced at the implications.

She would have to marry Surya again. She wasn't worried about the legalities of the marriage. It was just on a paper that could be easily cancelled anytime when she applied for a divorce again. She would hopefully even have Surya arrested very soon for threatening to shoot her family and forcibly marrying her.

She was more worried of the current situation.

Surya was forcing her to marry because he felt entitled to her body. By refusing to have sex with him during their short span of marriage, she had hurt his ego.

He wasn't going to wait this time. He would take what he felt was owed to him by force, especially when he had the legalities of a wedding certificate. He was planning to consummate the wedding soon after the ceremony.

She shuddered, unable to bear the thought of him touching her.

She badly wished she had the phone to call for help. And even if she did have the phone, she couldn't call Bhargav because she wouldn't risk his life with a gun-holding mad man.

She would have to contact the police somehow. She badly hoped her brother or her parents would somehow call the police for help.

How did such a happy day end in such a terrible way?

She knew there was no way out right then. She wore the sari and jewellery that were placed on the bed. It was obvious that her mother had chosen them.

Was Surya just pretending to threaten her parents? Are they a part of it too?

She didn't know for sure, but she couldn't risk taking chances.

She looked at herself briefly in the mirror. She winced when she saw the dark bruises on her upper arm where Surya held her painfully. She knew those wouldn't be the only bruises he would leave on her body once the ceremony was over.

With her heart thudding sickly, she sat on the bed and waited as thoughts flew through her mind.

How would Bhargav react to her marriage and forceful consummation?

She knew he was going to want to destroy Surya. And he was not going to spare her parents or brother either. He had decided to spare them for the sake or her and their love. But now, knowing that they were responsible for her forceful marriage and violation, he was going to destroy them no matter what.

Oh God, please help me.

She didn't know how long she sat on the bed, feeling angry and helpless when she heard sounds coming from outside the room.

She could hear Surya's shouting. At first, she thought it was Surya shouting and threatening her parents or brother. She hurriedly went and opened the door to see what was happening, but the sight in front of her shocked her.

Surya was on the floor at a distance with one of his hands at an odd angle. There was blood splattered on Surya's face, and he was screaming in pain while Bhargav was beating him viciously. Surya's men stood back because Aryan was standing guard for his brother.

The pilot must have told Bhargav where he had dropped her. And if Bhargav was following her father closely, he must have known about the guesthouse.

"Bhargav!" she shouted, running towards him.

She had to placate the man she loved. She couldn't risk him killing someone because of her. And the way Bhargav was hitting, Surya was definitely going to die.

"Bhargav! Stop!"

Bhargav didn't stop. He continued punching repeatedly. Surya's face was a bloody mess, and he barely even fought back.

The rage and bloodlust she saw in Bhargav's face made it clear he wasn't thinking of sparing Surya.

"Bobby, please stop!" she begged.

Listening to his pet name, he paused. And then, he slowly turned towards her.

"Don't kill him," she said desperately. "He's not worth it. And I'm okay!"

Letting go of Surya's collar, Bhargav stood up and came to her. He looked at her face for signs of abuse. And when his eyes fell on her arm with the bruise, his eyes once again flashed in rage.

She immediately placed her palm on his jaw. "I'm fine," she repeated. "Please, let's just get out of here. I want to go home."

Rage slowly left from his eyes. "All right," he said.

He held her waist and took her away from Surya. He stopped in front of his younger brother. "Aryan will take you and my mother home."

Anya shook her head and held his hand. "No, you can't stay here, Bhargav. Please come with us."

"I need to speak with your father first." His dark, stony expression made it obvious that the conversation wouldn't end well.

"Then talk to my father while I'm here," she said. "I already told him about—"

She broke off when there was a loud gasp from her mother.

She turned to see both her parents with pale, shocked faces. And they were looking at Parvathi Vardhaman who had just walked into the guesthouse.

"My God," her father whispered. "You are alive."

Parvathi Vardhaman held her dignity even as she faced her husband's murderer. "Yes, I am alive. So are my sons."

Anya's father's face whipped towards Bhargav and Aryan. His face paled even more as he realized who Bhargav was and why he was ruining him.

Her father broke down. "I'm sorry," he said, sobbing with tears in his eyes. "I know that I betrayed my best friend."

Aryan went towards him threateningly. "You didn't just betray my father. You murdered him!"

Her father shook his head and looked at Parvathi Vardhaman. "No. I swear, I wasn't the one to kill him."

Parvathi Vardhaman looked devastated. "Then who killed Ashok?" she asked. "And why? What did he or his family do to anyone? All he tried to do was help his friends and the less fortunate people."

Anya's heart went out to the older woman. She wanted to hug her and comfort her.

Anya's father looked guilty and ashamed. "I know," he said. "I was jealous because I was the poor friend who lived on his charitable scraps. I betrayed him, but I didn't kill him. I only knew they were planning to kill him soon."

"Who?" Aryan demanded. "Who was planning to kill my father?"

"Rajesh and Girish with the help of some hired outsider. I told them not to kill Ashok, and to just have him arrested for fraud. But they didn't listen."

There was rage on Aryan's face.

Anya turned to Bhargav who looked equally cold and furious. She held his hand and squeezed it in assurance.

Anya heard her father sobbing uncontrollably. "I swear, I didn't want Ashok hurt or killed. He was my best friend."

There was disgust on Aryan's face. "With friends like you, my father didn't need any enemies."

Anya knew Aryan was right. Friendship with her father and others cost Ashok Vardhaman his life. Her father might not have been the one to plan his friend's murder, but he didn't stop it on time or get help either.

"Bhargav!" Parvathi Vardhaman shouted in panic. "Look behind you!"

Anya turned and her heart almost stopped. Barely standing due to a broken leg, and with a broken arm and bloodied face, Surya was pointing a gun towards Bhargav and her. Anya knew Surya's target was her since his swollen eyes were looking at her.

"I'm going to kill you, you bitch. Don't think you won and can live happily with your lover."

Anya's heart thudded.

"Surya!" Anya's mother called out in panic. "What are you doing! Put down the gun!"

Surya looked at her and shot a bullet. Anya's mother screamed, and Anya could see her mother's leg bleeding.

"We are not going to press charges," Bhargav's calm voice spoke to Surya. "I already hit you, and we have it settled man to man. Just put down the gun and leave."

Surya shook his head. "No! The bitch has humiliated me many times and played me for a fool. If I can't have her, no one else should. I'm going to kill her!"

Anya knew Surya was going to shoot her. He was crazy enough to think killing her would be worth it, and that his rich father would somehow get him out of jail after a while.She didn't want to die.

"I love you, Annie. I want you in my life. I want us to marry. I want us to have children. I want us to get old together. And I want to die in your arms."

Her eyes filled with tears because she wanted to live her life to experience all those things with the man she loved.

She looked at Bhargav. "I love you," she whispered. "I'm glad I spent my happiest days with you."

Bhargav's jaw clenched, and his hand squeezed hers, hanging on to her.

Surya's voice cut through. "You deserve to die, you bitch."

Ignoring his rant, Anya closed her eyes, recalling her happiest days—she and Bobby running and playing inside the Vardhaman mansion, the two of them often sneaking out together to play near the river, them promising each other they would be together always. And then, the memories of meeting a darkly handsome stranger whom she was instantly drawn to and felt a connection with. Meeting him again and falling in love with him with each of their meetings. She recalled the last time together when he declared that he chose her above anything else.

She was lucky she loved a man like Bhargav and would die holding his hand.

A loud shot rang in the air, and she felt Bhargav pushing her down on the ground. Her heart thudded in fear, but there was no pain. She wasn't shot. Bhargav had got to Surya before he could shoot again.

But there were screams in the air and they were from Parvathi Vardhaman. She was calling out her son's name. "Bhargav! Oh my God."

Anya opened her eyes and saw that Bhargav was on top of Surya, tackling him.

The gun was shoved aside, which relieved her. She got up and was about to grab it when Aryan came to her. "Get him to the hospital right now!" he shouted. "Go with my mother."

Anya was taken aback. Why did Aryan care about Surya?

That's when she saw it. They weren't talking about Surya. They were talking about Bhargav.

Blood was leaking down from Bhargav's shoulder. He had been shot. He had taken the bullet aimed at her.

This time, it was Anya's screams that filled the air.

Epilogue

Two weeks later...

"I don't know if I should be happy that my sons are willing to take a bullet for the women they love... or be terrified that my sons get married only soon after they are shot."

At Parvathi Vardhaman's statement, there were bursts of laughter and chuckles in the bridal dressing room. The older woman smiled and held Anya's face.

"You look so beautiful, my dear. And I'm so happy that my son loves you so much."

Anya was dressed as a bride. She smiled at the woman who was soon to be her mother-in-law. "Thank you, I love him too," she said.

She loved Bhargav Varma with everything she had. Two weeks ago, she almost broke apart, thinking she was going to lose him. She had been in shock and nearly fainted in the guesthouse, but she had to gather courage to take him to a hospital.

The doctors had told them it was only a flesh wound, but the amount of blood she had seen made her nearly panic. Bhargav had to constantly reassure her that he was fine.

Ritu's voice cut through the dark thoughts. "You look radiant, Anya. This dress suits you so well. I can't believe it is nearly a hundred years old."

Anya smiled at her friend. "Thank you."

It was Bhargav's grandmother's dress. It had been with Parvathi Vardhaman before the mansion was seized and the items were taken or sold. Anya's mother had taken some of the expensive clothing and heirloom jewellery, which she had returned a few days ago.

Anya's heart still ached, thinking about what had happened in the guesthouse. Her parents and her brother's greed nearly cost Bhargav's life.

Her parents and brother had apologized several times over the last two weeks, but Anya wasn't ready to forgive them. She wanted to take time as it might heal the hurt slowly. But until then, her family was asked to stay away from her.

"I agree that the dress and jewellery look beautiful on you, Anya," said Narmada with a smile while adjusting the flowers in Anya's hair.

The flowers were from the plants nurtured outside the mansion by Narmada's grandfather. Narmada and Yash returned from their honeymoon a week ago. But when the newlyweds found out what happened, Yash was upset. Bhargav hadn't wanted anyone to call or tell Yash about his bullet would while Yash was away. Luckily, Parvathi Vardhaman was able to convince Yash that his younger brother was doing well.

"I can't wait to see Bhargav's face," Narmada added. "Yash texted me a few minutes ago saying they are starting earlier than expected because the groom is impatient. Must be the two-day long gap of not seeing each other."

Anya blushed. According to tradition, Bhargav was made to stay away from her for the last two days. As if the maddening man would listen. He had snuck into her office and her house during that time. She had tried to stop him, but he was unstoppable.

Anya blushed as inappropriate images and thoughts of what he did filled her mind while she was surrounded by family and friends.

"As far as I know," Trupti said with amusement. "Mr. Varma had come into our office to whisk Anya away."

Anya blushed even harder at her best friend's teasing.

Everyone laughed.

There was a knock on the door. It was Aryan.

Aryan grinned. "The priest is wondering if the groom has any female relatives to receive him." He looked around the room. "I can see you all ganged up with Anya."

His mother laughed. "Yes, we were helping her get ready. Tell the priest we are on our way."

He shook his head and left to convey the message.

Narmada laughed. "Maybe there will be another wedding in the mansion in the next two weeks or a month. Aryan's."

Anya smiled. "Without the gunshot wound."

Narmada nodded. "Now that Aryan has seen Yash and Bhargav getting shot, Aryan will be more careful," she said.

Parvathi Vardhaman shook her head. "I doubt it. My youngest son has always been a hot head. In fact, I'll be happy and shocked if the woman Aryan falls in love with doesn't shoot him first."

Everyone laughed.

Anya agreed that Aryan was a hot head. Although at first, Aryan had hated Bhargav being with her, but he slowly began to warm up to her, especially when she called him Arjun, his childhood name. He now thought of her as Anya, his childhood friend rather than his enemy's daughter.

Parvathi Vardhaman hugged her. "We'll see you on the ceremony dais, Anya."

She and Narmada left to receive the groom. Ritu and Trupti stayed back.

"Can't believe I'm saying this," said Trupti with a wide smile. "But you make me want to be a bride soon too."

Anya hugged her friend. "I know you will make a beautiful, happy bride for Rishab."

Ritu smiled at her. "I always knew you and Bhargav would end up together," she said. "I could sense something strong and meaningful between the two of you."

Anya smiled. "Thank you."

Apart from Narmada and her grandfather, no one else knew the true identity of Bhargav and his family. Anya's parents and brother knew as well, but they promised not to reveal until the truth about Ashok Vardhaman was out. Surya was another person who had heard everything. But her ex-husband was in jail. Not even his rich and influential parents could get him out. And a guard was set up to watch him.

Anya shuddered, recalling the events of that evening again. Pushing away those dark events from her mind, she focused on the happy occasion. The trumpets turned louder indicating that the bride was to arrive.

Trupti smiled at her. "Let's go before Mr. Wicked comes looking for you."

Laughing and blushing, and knowing it was quite possible, Anya went out to join the wedding ceremony.

***

"Why can't I remove the blindfold and see?" Anya asked her husband as he led her somewhere.

Based on the fact that they were at the estate and were walking in a direction familiar to her, she knew they were heading towards the river.

There was a deep chuckle. "Patience, my love. Weren't you the one asking me to be patient during the last two weeks?"

She blushed. "That's because you were shot by a bullet and recovering! And later we weren't supposed to meet according to tradition."

Not that any of those things stopped him.

"I hear the river," she said, feeling curious.

She knew the mansion and estate quite well, especially the river with their favorite spot. So why was she blindfolded?

Finally, they came to a stop. And then, he removed the blindfold.

Anya gasped out loud in surprise and pleasure. Their favorite spot looked magical during the night with the beautiful subtle lighting added to the trees nearby. It looked like a fantasy land.

There was a tent right in front of the tree with their carved initials.

"It's beautiful," she whispered, feeling choked up and overwhelmed with emotion.

"I knew you would like it." Suddenly, he bent down and swept her into his arms.

Laughing, she threw her arms around his shoulder. "This is the best honeymoon spot in the world!"

His mouth twisted in a familiar smile as he looked at her. "Our world," he said.

It was truly their world. The world which the two of them had dreamed of during their childhood.

As soon as he placed her on the soft, plush bedding inside the tent, they kissed each other. It was a sweet kiss at first, which spoke of the childhood friendship and sweet promises they had made to each other.

And then, the kiss caught fire. Desire grew and burned brightly. Clothes disappeared and heated bodies moved together, joining frantically until the final explosion. This time, when he kissed her again, it was a promise of a future together.

"I love you," he said, looking into her eyes.

She smiled and cupped his face. "I've always loved you," she replied.

He was her best friend. Her villain. Her hero. And her forever.

THE END

Author's Note

Thank you for choosing *Wicked Lies*. I hope you are enjoying the Wicked series so far.

The second Varma brother's love story began from a sweet and innocent childhood friendship and turned into a strong, undeniable love. Ruthless and brooding yet charming and protective, Bhargav is my favorite type of antihero! I hope you enjoyed reading Bhargav and Anya's passionate love story and were able to escape into their happily-ever-after.

Do check out the other Varma brothers Yash and Aryan's passionate love stories.

Thank you and stay safe.

MV Kasi

Email: manyavkasi@gmail.com

FB/Instagram: @mvkasi

Twitter: @author_mvkasi

M.v. Kasi's Book List

WICKED TRAP
WICKED LIES
WICKED DECEPTION
WILD IN LOVE
CRASH IN LOVE
DEVIL'S LOVE
DEVIL'S DESIRE
DEVIL'S KISS
UNTIL YOU
ACCIDENTAL HUSBAND
THE PROMISE
THAT SAME OLD LOVE
THE HOLIDAY AFFAIR
MISSION SUPERSTAR
UNTIL FOREVER
BOUND BY HATRED
THE CAPTIVE
SOULLESS
RUTHLESS
BREATHLESS

Short Stories (20-Minute Reads)
HIS CAPTIVE BRIDE
RECKLESS LOVE
THE ROYAL WEDDING
THE PROPOSAL
BOUND BY FOREVER
BILLIONAIRE ESCORT